READER, I MURDERED HIM

BETSY CORNWELL

CLARION BOOKS
AN *IMPRINT* OF HARPERCOLLINSPUBLISHERS

Clarion Books is an imprint of HarperCollins Publishers.

READER, I MURDERED HIM

Library of Congress Control Number: 2023933837
ISBN 978-0-35-869723-7

Typography by Erin Fitzsimmons
23 24 25 26 27 LBC 5 4 3 2 1

First paperback edition, 2023

for all the attic girls

You have not quite forgotten little Adèle, have you, reader?

—Charlotte Brontë, *Jane Eyre*

PROLOGUE

ALL I COULD SEE was red darkness.

The stain his blood made might only have been a shadow—a shadow like the one that concealed me, still standing where we'd stood when he fell.

When I pushed him.

I couldn't make myself see the blood I knew was there. The moonlit night, the lamplit street, were dark enough that the gory lines curling and feathering as they scrawled their way across his body, across the cobblestones, could have been nothing but ink: India ink, the kind the mistresses gave us for practicing penmanship at school. I was forever scrubbing smudges off my fingers after class.

I clutched at my skirts as if they could clean my hands of what I'd done. Of him. Of the fact that he'd ever touched me or my friend, that I'd ever had to touch him.

He'd touch no one anymore, not ever.

I had turned him into a shadow.

Looking down at him from above like that, I wished I could feel like an avenging angel, my friend's heroic rescuer. I longed to feel myself cloaked in golden light or hellfire. But no divine or damning light surrounded me: just darkness, darkness like the backstage shadows at my mother's shows, curtains and ropes strung around the edges of the pools of light like cobwebs.

Someone gasped behind me.

My heart lurched.

I unfisted my hands from my skirts and dragged my gaze away from the bloody darkness below.

I was no angel or demon. I was as human as the man whose life I'd ended.

I was Adèle Varens, and I was a murderess.

I raised my chin and turned to face my judgment.

PART ONE
THORNFIELD

Can't you see there's no other man above you?

What a wicked way to treat the girl that loves you

—Beyoncé Knowles-Carter, *Lemonade*

ONE

MY MOTHER ALWAYS SAID every married woman is a ruined garden.

I remember her saying so as she stroked pencil under her eyes, out toward the edges and up, to make them look dark and wide. I remember the sounds of the other dancing girls, most of them younger than Maman by the time I was old enough to hold on to memories, their giggling and snapping and elbowing each other out of the best spots at the crowded dressing-room mirrors. The air around their painted faces was thick with smoke. The floral stench of their mixed-up perfumes, the smell of women's sweat underneath. Tulle skirts like falling petals.

He will lock up his garden, and the flowers will go to seed, and the fruit he does not eat will drop to the ground and rot. Why do you think, when women tell the stories of their lives, they end with marriage? It's not a happily ever after, cherie, only the end of happiness.

She had been married once, briefly. All she ever told me about it was that she had been very young, and her husband had not died quickly enough.

She wore a gold ring on her little finger that she often twisted as she spoke, and until the day she gave it to me, it never left her, no matter what costume she wore for the stage or for her customers. She would finger it often as she spoke about gardens and men and rotting fruit, looking into her own eyes in the mirror. She spoke as much for the other girls as she did for me.

None of them fought Maman for her place, even though she had the best seat of all. Some people are good at letting you know, without ever acting on it, that they could hurt you if they wanted to. That was Maman with the girls at Le Moulin. She was kind to the younger dancers, helped them, taught them, would never hurt them . . . but if she wanted to, she could.

They knew it, and they let her be.

(To think I used to tell myself she and Papa had nothing in common.)

The dancers let me be too, which left a worst taste in my mouth than the stale-smoke, stale-perfume air in that place. I wanted to play with the girls. I thought their work was play back then, so young a child I was. I wanted to be like them. Blossom like them. I wanted to prove to Maman that she was not ruined after all, that she had grown again in a new season, and I could flower for her, my mother's heart blooming again in my young body. That she could live her youth again through me.

So young a child I was.

I did keep a part of Maman's dark, wide heart, though, when I left her. I planted it deep in my own like a seed. I swallowed it, like the evil queen in Snow White's story, when I kissed her lips for the last time.

She grew cooler even as I touched her, and I felt the heavy warmth of her heart slide down my throat.

I carried it to England when he took me.

I first saw Papa from backstage, during one of Maman's shows. I noticed him long before I knew who he was.

I was allowed to stand at the edge of the velvet curtain so long as I kept myself draped carefully in shadow, not letting one prick of light touch my hands or my shoes or my eager eyes. I'd had to prove myself many times over to be a careful, responsible child before the surly ex-sailor stagehands would allow me so close to the limelight's edge.

I don't know, now, if my affinity for vanishing into shadows was born from my longing to watch the shows or if the ability came first and brought the longing with it. I know many people who long for impossible things, but I've never been like that.

I want what I know I can have.

He gleamed. I remember that well.

He wore no silk suit jacket, no shiny monocle; no slick, oiled moustache drooped over his lips. He wasn't holding opera glasses to his eyes, like so many men did even though Le Moulin wasn't half big enough to warrant it, in hopes of seeing more than the dancers wanted to show.

Perhaps his eyes glittered, now and then, with reflected light as he sat in the darkness of the seats, as my own eyes might have done at the edge of the stage if I were a little less care-ful. He was not a handsome man, as he would readily tell you himself; his features would not have drawn much notice in their own right.

Perhaps the end of his cigar glowed ember red, as the other men's did, like cats' eyes in the dark. The smoke in the theatre smelled different than the smoke backstage; these rich men could afford American tobacco and Cuban cigars. After shows, the girls rolled up the spent ends of cigarettes left on the floor, crushed tobacco fronds still damp with male saliva, and mixed it with the cheap, dusty stuff that was all they could afford themselves. They wrapped their smokes in La Croix if they had it, in tissue paper from old bouquets if not. They never left ends big enough to smoke again.

But then, I cannot recall ever seeing Papa smoke before we came to England.

The truth is he gleamed darkly—it was the darkness in him that gleamed. He was *there,* manifest, a heavy, looming presence in the center of his row. As if he had his own gravity, so that everything and everyone else in the theatre would soon begin to orbit around him.

I had no notion of gravity then, much less of the habits of planets. Two things, out of many, that I would eventually learn from my dear governess—from Miss Jane Eyre's teachings.

There but for the grace of God.

So she taught me, as well, to say.

I'd seen Papa in the audience for several nights before his and Maman's reunion. He drew me toward him like a moon or a comet—some heavenly body—until I came near enough to force his notice.

I used to sell little posies outside the music hall for the men to place in their boutonnières in case their wives were still awake when they got home, to cover up guiltier smells. I'd wear a dress I'd torn to make it look ragged, and I'd smudge a bit of Maman's eye pencil on my nose to look like soot. My blond hair, however, I made sure was always combed and bright, and I knew how to flutter my lashes and widen my dark eyes so they sparkled under the lamps.

It was there, in the sputtering gaslight, that I first met Papa.

I'd waited, watching the theatre doors intently and quite possibly missing more than one ready customer, so determined was I to see the unhandsome man who gleamed so darkly.

Et finalement, he came. He walked onto the glistening Montmartre street that rainy night like a man pursued, his broad shoulders tense beneath his cape, glancing from side to side as if preparing for someone to leap out of the shadows and strike him.

I spoke very incorrect English then (although I knew far more of the language than I let on, since Maman had rightly taught me that you should never let a man know just how much you understand him), and his French was rough. I still know what we both said at that meeting though, from the many times he retold the story since. He had such a sharp mind and such a sure way of speaking that no one ever thought to question his retelling.

"She tripped toward me out of the shadows like a little elf," he always said, "that yellow hair glowing like fairy gold. I knew, of course, what she was. An imp, a sprite, maybe a very lovely little girl demon—but nothing mortal."

And the men to whom he told the tale would smile.

It always seemed strange to me when he said that because there was never a time in my childhood when I felt more human, more sure that my body was my natural home, than when I lived with Maman, spent my days at the showgirls' boarding house and my nights in Le Moulin. I had an easy relationship with my limbs then, more than I ever did at Papa's Thornfield, where my childhood reached its eventual end. An ease I have only recaptured in fleeting moments—dancing or riding horses or in certain people's arms—ever since. Not a cell of myself was separate from my person then.

But if Papa said I was no person, it must have been true—or he made it true. As he told and retold the story of my capture, I began to remember myself and my early years in Paris as if I viewed them from outside: a golden little spark like a bog light, flitting around my dark mother—for in Papa's stories she was always dark, although I must have gotten my blond hair somewhere, and it was not from him.

Of course, he always said I might not be his daughter after all.

"As if something so fair could have sprung from my—" he'd begin, then cut himself off.

From his loins, of course. I would have known how to end that sentence even as a child; no child of my mother's, no child of Le Moulin, could not.

12

But then, I took his word for everything, and even my own story, my own life, was colored by his telling of it. I began to think I ought to be ashamed of all the things I understood.

I sold monsieur a posy. He put it in his lapel, smiling, careful that his big hands wouldn't crush the petals. Unlike most of the men who bought from me though, he did not scurry away into the shadows. Instead he peered down at me thoughtfully, despite the baleful gaze of the huge guards paid to make sure no one stayed around Le Moulin after hours to make trouble.

(The men who wanted trouble, *bien sur,* knew to go to the boarding house, where Mother told me she and the girls sold posies of their own. It was better for me to do so out front, she said, where I'd have no competition from the grown-ups—and where, I realize now, the bright lights and glaring guard would keep me safe.)

Monsieur slipped the guard a coin, and he let us be.

"You look familiar, little pet," he said. "Like someone I once knew."

We regarded each other.

"The difference in our heights so great," Papa would always add, "that we looked like the balcony scene in *Romeo and Juliet,* although an uglier Juliet than myself one could never hope to see."

We were still looking when Maman came to fetch me. She'd wrapped herself in drab, modest street clothes, her greasepaint scrubbed off almost entirely.

She always missed a streak by her jaw. I remember that so clearly. And when I do, I sometimes manage to recall that her hair was fair too, although redder than mine.

It is so hard to lift Papa's vision away.

"Edward?" Maman said. She walked forward a little faster and grasped my shoulder, her fingers digging into my collarbone.

"And then I looked up, into the face of a woman near my own height, and I saw that the little French imp was a kind of mirror, for her reflection stood above her—only marred, of course, by an old and darkened glass."

And the men, at least, would laugh.

Papa liked to think of himself as so reclusive, but oh, he had a gift for turning his own life into theatre.

Jane Eyre, to her credit, never laughed at that line.

"Celine," said monsieur. He looked from my mother's face to mine and back again. "Of course. I thought I recognized this girl; she is so much like you." His voice was deep and rough, a rumble you could feel down in your belly.

Maman held me tighter, smoothing my hair. "And like her father. She will be nine years old on All Souls' Day, Monsieur Rochester."

Papa never mentioned flinching, but I think he must have. After all, he'd just learned that he might (and only might, he always said, for who knew how many men might have shared some time that month with Maman) have a daughter. I flinched a little myself; Maman rarely mentioned my age because it revealed something about her own and about how long she'd been living and working at Le Moulin. Youth and innocence made money, she said, and she was not old yet.

Papa's and Maman's eyes met above my head, and I knew I'd spend that night outside our room.

It wasn't so bad; the boarding house where we lived had a room that was special for the children to sleep in while their mothers had men with them. I could usually find at least one friend there. It was a narrow, empty space with a damp floor and mold working its way hungrily across the walls; no one would ever pay to stay there, so it was ours.

And if you were young enough, you could imagine it into a castle or an enchanted wood.

The night Maman and Papa reunited, the only other child there was a boy called Jean, not yet two. He was still scared of staying there without his mother, a fifteen-year-old named Anouk. But Jean knew me, and he let me rock him to sleep on one of the thin, musty mattresses on the floor. I didn't get much sleep myself that night, but it was a comfort to have someone else to care for. I rested my cheek against his, and I let his sweaty hands cling to my fingers and my dress. Quietly, dreamily, I sang a few mismatched bars of the songs I'd learned from Maman and the girls.

In the darkness, in the place where songs bring you, we both rested, even if only one of us slept. The baby's hands drifted in sleep across mine, and he fiddled with the ring on my finger, a gift from Maman, who had in turn been gifted it from one of her patrons. A signet ring, the top was carved with lily of the valley, and beneath that, a small compartment held poison. Real gold, Maman said, and if I was ever in a spot of trouble when she wasn't near, I could use it to get myself out.

But she was always near, Maman. I never doubted that then.

I did like that little room, narrow and damp as it was. It was covered in dark red wallpaper that blossomed and curled with some old floral print that had almost, by my time, faded away. But the fade made it appear more natural, as if the redness had grown up out of the earth itself, like some deep, fiery forest. If I kept one of my own posies close to my nose, to cover the smell of years of bed-wetters, the room became quite pleasant.

Anouk, a baby sling hanging on her still-slender hip like a holster, came back at daybreak.

Maman didn't.

I begged a misshapen roll from the boulangerie across the street and stuffed it down, then steeled myself to knock on Maman's door. I was never supposed to do that when she was with a man, but then, she never kept them with her after dawn.

There was a girl who had died a few years before, and no one had known for days because the man who killed her had left and no one had checked on her. All the working girls carried the shame of that neglect; they always tried to look out for each other.

So I'd filled myself with fright by the time I knocked on her door: fright both that I'd be scolded for interrupting her and that I'd be too late to save her. My imagination ran deep enough that both ideas caused me real pain.

"Her mother was already consumptive by then, of course," Papa always said. "Blood smeared on her handkerchiefs, blood dried on the edges of her rouge pots. She had only weeks to live. She begged me to take her daughter to England, out of that mire, and to raise her into something worthwhile. God knows what she would have become if she were left to the tender mercies of the other dancing girls."

Dark and bloody edged. That's how I see my mother now.

I don't remember her consumption, although she could have hidden it from me; indeed it would have been like her to do so. She hid anything that might make it seem as if she were aging or going to die someday. It was her stock-in-trade, hers and all the girls': the kind of youth that makes them seem immortal, that makes the men who watch and touch them feel like gods. (I knew enough, even as a child, to see the value in Papa's perception of my youth and beauty—my inhumanity.)

I have a strange, flickering half memory of my parents' discussion about taking me back to England, about whether I was Papa's daughter. I think they were still arguing over it when Maman opened the door. She was still speaking to him even while her eyes met mine, full of anger or fear, and she gestured with a firm wave that I should go back to the children's room and wait. "Come back in an hour, *ma fille*," she told me, her voice both soft and hard.

At least I'd seen that she was still alive.

I went.

There were a few books hidden under a loose floorboard in the red room, and now that the sun had risen, I could see to read. There was a one-eyed doll under the boards too—we often left little things there to amuse ourselves with, while our mothers made their money and kept us fed—but I had recently decided that I was too old for dolls. That day, while Maman and Papa finished their talk, I paged through an illustrated book about birds. Half the pictures were torn out, and the ripped ends of the pages looked like wings. I traced their fibrous softness with my fingers, closed my eyes, and imagined myself flying.

Papa opened the door when I returned. Unlike the other men who spent time with Maman, he did not flush at the temples to see me waiting there, and he did not scurry away.

"How would you like to see England, little elf?" he asked.

When he let me back into her room, Maman did indeed look sick. "We have made a pact, *ma chère*," she said.

Three days later we were gone, and she was dead.

Maman had told me I must always call him Papa. "He'll like that," she'd said, "even if he isn't your real papa. Especially then."

I said it the same way I'd heard Maman and the other dancing girls say it to so many men, nestling onto the men's laps, sliding their strong, soft arms around the men's necks like snakes. "Ooh, Papa, you're too good to me," with a pout in the lips, a sweet little moue in the voice.

I know now that they were grown women mimicking little girls. But then, I thought I was mimicking grown women. I thought Mr. Rochester, perhaps my papa, wanted to have a sophisticated French daughter of whom he could be proud. A little souvenir of Le Moulin.

He had once loved my maman, I thought; he must have if he came back to her a decade after they'd first known each other and if he agreed to her wish for me to go to England.

I thought if I could be enough like her, he'd love me too.

But perhaps I do not remember it so clearly: the corridor, the muffled noises, the red wallpaper. Miss Eyre told me a story later of a red room from her own childhood, a kind of memory mixed with nightmare, and I suppose I might have gotten it jumbled with my own. Papa was always very rigorous with us, the women of his house, that we should keep memories and figments of imagination separate. If we thought we remembered something differently than he did, he was sure to set us straight right away.

So when he asked me what I remembered of meeting him, of our passage to England—he did this whenever he had guests who needed entertainment, trotting me out as a novelty—I parroted his own memories, as docile as one of the caged, bright birds that he ordered all the way from Jamaica, for my first English Christmas.

And maybe, after all, the red-papered room I remember is the same as Jane's red room. Like the one I remember, hers was secret and dark, a place where she waited for ghosts while her life changed around her.

Perhaps all little girls have the same red room inside them.

TWO

I LOST MY last milk tooth on the passage to England. I'd been tonguing it loose for weeks, but it was stubborn, and there was something about mashing the root back and forth in my tender gum that I nearly liked, despite the pain, the same way I liked breathing the sooty air around the big, smoke-heaving chimney of the ship we rode. I used to bite my lips, as a kind of nervous habit, until Maman chided me out of it—the gnawing left the skin there unattractively scabbed. I started biting the insides of my lips instead, which I was careful to make sure she never knew. I had bands of ridged scarring on the inside of my mouth, but the only hint of it to the outside world was the way it pushed my lips out, plumped them; since that only made me prettier, Maman stopped worrying. She didn't know my mouth always tasted of blood.

But whenever I lost a tooth, I briefly also lost interest in biting my lips, in favor of tonguing the raw new space inside me, and my mouth had a chance to heal.

I asked her before we left—in truth I begged her—to come with us. She refused. "Your papa's riches are for you, cherie, not me," she said. "I bought them for you when we made you all those years ago. He will leave you a good inheritance in your own right and not for any future husband; I have made him promise that. But there is not enough wealth in all of England to persuade me to leave my bones in English soil, and I must choose their place before long. They shall stay in Paris, and I will go to my rest easier knowing in what luxury you're kept across the sea."

I cried, holding on to the starboard-side railing and looking down into the cold, white-churning water. Tears slipped into my mouth and stung my healing lips, and they tasted like the salt water we crossed.

I wiped my face and put my fingers in my mouth. I pulled the tooth before I could think of pain, and by the time I flinched, the act was done. The rounded chip lay in my palm, red at one end.

No bones in English soil.

I dropped the tooth into the waves.

I made myself a promise then: however long I lived in England, when I died, I would be buried in Paris, with Maman.

The channel crossing was supposed to take only a day, and Papa told me I'd have the freedom of the deck for all that time, but as night approached, rough seas forced every passenger indoors. Within the sick belly of the ship we tossed back and forth so violently that sometimes my small body was lifted off the bunk, as if I flew.

Papa and I shared a berth. We could not do such a thing without scrutiny in England, he said, but they had trapped the air of France inside the boat when they closed its doors.

21

"You are the daughter of a whorehouse, Adèle," he said. "You will not be a respectable girl until I make you one, and I will do so by making you English. You shall have new clothes and English books before you get your English fortune when I die—oh yes, never fear, I will honor my promise to your sly mother, and richly too. I have never broken a promise to a woman, no, not even vows I would have done better to break long ago. I have kept my vows to the letter, damn my soul." His expression darkened, and though he still looked toward me, his gaze seemed to turn for a moment entirely inward.

"You will learn quiet and gentle habits and to be a quiet and gentle person. If indeed I am your father, you will have too much darkness in you from me; far too much, I fear. As for your mother and your mother country, you have too much of both in you as well."

My mother's heart gave a great angry thump in my belly. I clutched it, pretending I felt seasick, though I did not. While Papa's face was white and slick and I could tell he was resisting the urge to vomit only through his strength of will, the rocking of the sea was a thrill and a comfort to me.

He looked me up and down in my pink dress, the one Maman's friend Cecile had made, fluttering all over with lace. She could have used that finery herself, but she'd used it on me. She'd said Maman would far rather have seen me in such a dress than in mourning colors. And Papa had not demanded that I formally mourn my mother. We had left, in fact, before her funeral. He had said it would disturb me.

22

"Yes," he repeated. "Far too much."

He turned away to rest on his own narrow bunk.

I let the waves lift and drop me, and I breathed the stale air he had said was French. I twisted Maman's ring on my thumb and wondered what would ever feel like enough trouble now to make me give it up.

Papa barely looked at me for the rest of the passage over. I did not understand what he was so afraid to see.

Thornfield was a wet, hulking monster of a house. Its windows watched the barren landscape with a cruel and sleepy gaze through heavy curtains and age-pocked panes, and its outer walls shone black with damp even on rare sunny days. Its crenellations bristled. When I saw it from a distance, I always expected Papa's house to unfurl, to unhunch its stone shoulders and crawl off across the moors. When I first went inside its doors, I felt like I'd been swallowed.

Papa had barely dropped me off there before he left it again.

In fact, he was almost always gone. For the first months, I was mostly alone, with only Papa's servants to mind me during his frequent trips away, and they did not seem to desire my company. The weather rarely allowed me to stay outdoors as long as I wished. Although I was often confined, I amused myself with the books in Papa's library; he had quite a few in French. I briefly struggled with a few English texts but found that as much as I could speak and understand the language, reading and writing in it was a challenge. English books with illustrations, however,

I adored. These I tried to copy onto the drawing paper that Mrs. Fairfax amply provided; I'm afraid I left half-finished sketches scattered around the house like fallen leaves, which could not have endeared me to her. If I was wild or indecorous to the staff or on Papa's rare visits back home, you must remember it was because I was a child, a frightfully lonely and bored one. With servants fulfilling my needs but refusing my company and usually no Papa around to discipline me, I began to think of myself as almost the lady of the house.

But there was another lady of Thornfield. A chatelaine of Papa's heart, or at least his mind. The woman to whom he referred when he told me he'd never broken a word of his vows.

Thornfield's true mistress was a ghost.

She screamed and laughed from secret places, and she haunted the halls at night.

I woke up several times my first night at Thornfield convinced that *I'd* been screaming. But Grace Poole, the sad-eyed servant who smelled like gin, told me that she heard nothing.

The next night I woke again, but I thought the screams must be someone else's. Once more, though, Grace informed me that the night had passed in peaceful silence.

"And you'll tell the master so when he asks you how you slept," Grace said, a warning in her eyes and on her juniper breath. "He doesn't like to hear of anything strange in his house."

"Even if something strange is happening?" I asked.

Grace Poole looked away. "He doesn't like to hear of it."

Whether he liked it or not though, Thornfield's ghost was always there.

She watched me for a long time, I think. Gradually I started waking up at night and knowing she was there. At first she was a kind of imaginary friend.

One night I dreamt I saw a woman in white hanging from the huge oak tree that grew outside the house.

When I woke up screaming the screams that I'd call silence come morning, I saw a real woman at the foot of my bed, dressed in white with wild hair.

Staring at me.

Even in the shadows, her eyes gleamed in a way that reminded me of Papa's glistening darkness at the theatre—but while his darkness drew me toward him with that irresistible force that I later learned to compare to gravity, this woman's blaze repelled me.

"What are you, then?" she asked, her voice low and fast. "What are you—another me? Come to be Daddy's new doll, then, precious girl?"

She stepped up onto the bed as if it were a low stair; she was tall and strong enough that the stride was nothing to her.

"Papa brought me here from France," I said, my voice soft but very clear. I still had half an idea that I was dreaming, and though I was frightened, it was only dream fear, and my voice did not shake.

"Oh, yes," she said, "all his best things he collects from realms abroad. I suspect he'll put you up next to me on the same shelf once he's done. Can you guess where he brought me back from, poppet?"

She took one great step across the bed and squatted down by my pillow in her long and dirty nightgown, and she dug my hand out from under the covers and pressed it against her cheek. "They don't make skin like this in England, girl, nor France. Dear Edward says he should have known from it how dark I was within."

At the touch of her strong, hot hand and of her burning cheek, I knew I was awake. I opened my mouth to scream—how I wanted to scream—but the sudden knowledge that I wasn't dreaming had stolen my voice.

Nonetheless this woman clapped her other hand over my lips. My braids had come undone during the night and some of my hair was trapped between her hand and my open mouth. I felt it scratch my tongue and grow damp, and I tried to swallow.

"No screaming, darling, or he'll put you away before he's even played with you. Don't want to get yourself shut up on that shelf, believe me." She looked up at the shadowy molding on my ceiling. "All kinds of cobwebs and big fat spiders up there, and no one ever dusts. Not even Grace."

She smiled, and slowly she took her hand away from my mouth. She gently pulled out my damp hair and tucked it behind my ear, where it lay cool and wet like a slug.

"Gracie does take the doll down off the shelf though, now and then," she said, "when Daddy is gone or deep asleep. He mustn't know."

She slid down from the bed, her movements still sinuous and strange enough that I think older children than myself might have believed her a ghost too.

Yet she was living. She was a real woman, with an eeriness to her that was so different from my own lost mother . . . and yet there was something in her that I recognized.

I wonder now if I might have seen in her not my mother but myself. I wonder too how many women of Thornfield saw, or feared to see, themselves in her.

"He mustn't know," she said again.

And she was gone.

It was frightening, of course.

She was mad.

Of course.

And yet . . .

I was suddenly not alone in that house, not so alone as I'd thought. Not the only strange thing.

So it was that I met Bertha Antoinetta Mason Rochester.

It was several nights before I saw her again, and weeks or months before I learned that she was truly Papa's wife. It took many of our secret meetings—in my room at first, and then whispered conversations through her bolted door when I was finally brave enough to climb up to the attic—before Grace Poole would admit that there was a reason she sat in her narrow chair by the attic stairs so often, that I was not the only lady of the house she served, that she let her ladyship out at night sometimes.

It was in that drab corridor, sitting on that narrow chair, that she finally told me so. "I couldn't bear it, otherwise," Grace said, quietly, looking down into her gin-dosed cuppa.

I thought about the times I'd seen her carrying food up the stairs, always better food when Papa was gone than when he was home. I'd thought she was taking it for herself, and I'd hardly blamed her.

I settled down on the floor next to her. I had a little sketch-book in the pocket of my pinafore, and I took it out and began to draw—just nothing pictures, little sketches of butterflies and birds to pass the time.

After a long while, she spoke again, softly. "It'd be like I was another . . . I couldn't bear it."

She never spoke quite as much to me after she admitted to letting Bertha out. It was as if once she gave me the secret, we both had to swallow it to keep it safe.

It might have seemed to someone watching as if I were lonelier in that big house than ever. But we found there was much that we could bear together.

On the next of his rare visits home, Papa told me that he'd put out an advertisement for a governess.

I had yet to become sufficiently English, he told me. "I had been hoping that the land itself would sink into you, get its cold, fresh fingers inside your hot French soul and turn you into something like itself," he rumbled over tea. "It was entirely unfair to you for me to expect it, and I am sorry. Nonetheless"—he looked me over

28

with a gaze that seemed to suggest his certainty that whatever he discovered about my body would also be true for my soul—"you cannot be allowed to go on as you are. You are in great danger of turning out just like your mother—or like . . ." His eyes flicked briefly upward, and I wondered if he was thinking of Bertha or of himself.

Bertha had been trapped all alone in her attic since Papa's return, even at night; I didn't dare to visit her when he was at Thornfield. When he was home, she was alone, her arms tied in a horrid self-embrace, in the straitjacket Papa believed she always wore.

At least Bertha could hug herself in that jacket. I tried to tell myself that might make her less lonely at least.

Papa tipped back the rest of his tea in a quick swig. When he put down his cup, a few cloudy brown drops stuck indecorously to the stubble on his upper lip. It still baffled me that English people took milk with tea, and I did not think I could ever manage to learn to like it myself. Still, I knew enough to drink milky tea when Papa was there to watch me.

"May I sing for you today, Papa?" I asked as he stood up from the table.

He raised a hand as if deflecting an attack.

"I have no desire to be charmed, Adèle," he told me sternly. "Especially not by little imps who know more about womanhood than is proper in girls twice their age. You are going to learn to be proper, to restrain yourself and your worse nature. This is something we all must learn. I learned it too late to save myself." I knew by then that he meant marrying Bertha and, later, meeting Maman and women like her. "Or to save you from the life you've had so far . . . to save you even from coming into such a world as the one we live in. But by God, I will save you from it now. By God, I will save us both."

I felt myself wanting to cry and was ashamed of it. I was ten years old by then after all; I should not care so much about such trifles as whether the man who had the care and keeping of my whole life took pleasure in anything that I could do for him.

But he was a sharp one; he stepped closer to me and peered down into my face. "I am sorry, child," he said, his voice quite gentle. "I am not used to minding female feelings. All my life I have been a selfish man, thinking of no one's interests but my own. The habit is a hard one to break." He cleared his throat. "Perhaps you could read to me, Adèle. I should like that."

I looked up at him, knowing the movement would flick small withheld tears down my cheeks like scattered pearls. I was not the small seductress he thought me, but I had learned more than a few of the Moulin girls' ways. I'd learned very early, for instance, the effect that the smallest tear on a pretty girl's cheek can have on the heart of a guilt-ridden man.

I saw him flinch away from the pearly tears, and we walked to the library together so he could choose an English book for me to read. I still struggled with reading in my father's language, but for his sake, during those early Thornfield years, I would have done anything he asked.

I kept singing the songs that Maman and her fellow showgirls had taught me as I stood in front of the narrow mirror in my bedroom every night. I tried to mimic the way they held their heads, their postures, their walks, the liquid, suggestive movements of their hands—all the little mannerisms that their patrons found so fascinating. I had always found them fascinating too, for their own sake and for the power they provided.

Sometimes, as I moved, it was as if I saw a ghost, my mother's limbs so briefly inhabiting mine. I was growing up to be beautiful, as she had been, and I was relieved, and grateful it would give me the ability to survive, and proud—and afraid. I felt the weight of Maman's heart in my gut and I trembled, hungry for her, and I hugged myself with the arms that I was training to look like hers.

Sometimes, when Papa was gone and she was lucid enough for Grace Poole to let her out, Bertha danced with me in the dark mirror too.

THREE

THERE WAS NO POSSIBILITY of taking a walk that day. After I met Bertha, I'd started forcing myself to go outdoors even in the rain just to feel my own freedom, and I'd gotten into the habit of roaming the moors; but the morning Jane Eyre arrived, the sky shrieked and wept, and I could only watch it from my bedroom window.

She came looking so much Bertha's opposite that I knew Papa would be pleased—although it was clear Miss Eyre *tried* to please no one. She was a small, thin, pale thing no taller than myself. She was the smallest grown-up I'd ever seen outside show business.

She would never have made a career of it, though: there was nothing showy about her. Her skin was watery as buttermilk, so pale that it faintly glowed; her hair was straight and brown. She had a small, thin mouth, although it might not have been so thin were her lips not held so tightly together. Her teeth were good, which was unusual for someone without money; I'd learned from the Moulin girls that one could often judge a person's wealth by their teeth. Her pale eyes were large and sparsely lashed; not beautiful but strange, both deep and sharp, as if her gaze cut through one's flesh to the soul beneath—but part of that gaze was always reflecting back, too, on herself.

"Miss Eyre is to be your governess here, Adèle," Mrs. Fairfax told me when she arrived.

The lady gave a nod, trying her best to look imperious from her diminutive height; her head barely came up to Mrs. Fairfax's more naturally imperious bosom.

I curtseyed in return.

Miss Eyre blinked, and Mrs. Fairfax bent down to murmur to her, "It is the only way she knows, and I am sure it comes from her mother—but I have no doubt that you will teach her better soon."

I felt my cheeks burn. The girls at Le Moulin, not to mention Maman, had all praised my elegant curtsies.

"Il n'y a pas de bonté en moi?" I shouted at Mrs. Fairfax before I could stop myself. My voice came out shrill and shaking; my nails bit into my fisted palms.

Is there nothing good about me?

I felt Miss Eyre's cool gaze on my hot face. I bit the insides of my lips to keep from screaming again. My teeth met the earlier wounds and scars they'd made inside me. My whole mouth stung with echoes.

When I dared to meet her eyes I saw a sharp, unsentimental kind of understanding in them, laced with that inward turning, as if toward memory. Instead of replying to Mrs. Fairfax, she spoke directly to me.

"Mais si, Adèle," she said, with an impeccable accent, *"tu es pleine de bonté, exactement comme tu es."*

You are good, Adèle, just as you are.

I did not know when I'd last heard any word of approval about myself, let alone in my mother tongue. I staggered as if from a blow.

I think she switched to English then because she saw the look on my face, although perhaps it was just that she was there to teach me English ways. "You and I shall learn all sorts of useful things, Adèle, as well as curtsies; worry not. As long as you apply yourself with diligence, you shall do well." She did not smile, but a line appeared on one pale cheek.

Her voice was stern, her manner serious. She did not present herself as an easily likeable person, and yet somehow I found I liked her straight away.

That night I stayed awake until near dawn with Bertha, playing cat's cradle and chanting a Caribbean rhyme she'd taught me, and when Jane swept into my room and pushed aside the heavy curtains at the window, it hurt my head even to open my eyes.

"Good morning, Miss Varens," she said in her crisp voice. "It is a fine day, and well past time to be up and making use of the hours God has given us."

I looked out the window: the light was abundant, but cold and gray, the sky covered with thin clouds like hammered tin. The moors around Thornfield stretched out to a heathered horizon.

I smiled at her from my bed. Before I'd come to Thornfield, I'd always shared a bed with Maman or, when she had a man in, with one of the other children in the red room. I'd never known how lonely a large bed in a cold and empty room can seem, with no one you trust to hold you; I think that is one of the reasons I welcomed Bertha so quickly, and was not more frightened of her.

So it was a relief to see Miss Eyre there on my waking, which used to be so lonely; a woman who was there, in her way, to take care of me.

Miss Eyre did not return my smile, but that awareness was still in her eyes. "Quickly now, Adèle," she said, and I jumped to obey.

I knew Papa wanted Miss Eyre long before she knew it herself. I knew it from the day he met her.

She had lived with us, made a home for herself in the odd shelf of women at Thornfield, for a few months by then. I had come, in that short time, almost to love her. It was not hard for me to understand why Papa, or anyone else, might feel the same way, even though Jane never tried to make herself an easy person to love—at least not in the ways that I understood, back then.

She was quiet, almost to the point of sullenness sometimes; although her intelligence burned with a fire that was obvious to me even at ten years old, she shared her thoughts with others only when she felt their own opinions were wrong.

Of course this might not have made her a perfectly suited governess, but after our first few lessons, she and I began to feel a good deal of sympathy with each other.

I believe she found me a bright pupil, and eventually an attentive one—after all, I had little else to attend to at Thornfield, and her lessons provided the first real challenge to my intellect since I'd arrived. I admit to some naughtiness at first, a little caprice; I was so young, and had grown used to being nearly my own mistress in that house. But Jane was strict, especially about my paying attention during her lessons; this I quickly decided was understandable, for she undertook so much effort to make them productive and interesting for me. And when I overheard Mrs. Fairfax warn Jane of my bad nature—which she said Papa had told her of, my very first day at Thornfield—I was so hurt and angry that I determined to prove them wrong.

I found that I quite liked the challenges Miss Eyre set. Some of them I rose to easily, and some I did not; I excelled at mathematics and technical drawing, but it took a long time for me to learn to read and write well in English, for all that I could speak and understand it. I labored over the task so much that perhaps it is part of why I am setting down this story now; I still want all my struggles to amount to something.

"But, *Mademoiselle*—ah, miss," I exclaimed one afternoon, throwing my quill down in frustration and sending a little spatter of black ink across the page, "why should I learn to write at all? Maman is dead, and Papa would never let me write to my friends in France. I have no one to write to!"

Miss Eyre set her lips tightly and picked up my pen. "That was a waste of paper, ink, and breath, Adèle," she said. "Writing is one of the most useful tasks to which a woman can put herself. We have voices just as men do, and our words hold just as much wisdom and weight as theirs—perhaps more, for the physical restrictions of women in the world, unjust as they are, grant us more time to devote our minds to intellectual pursuits. When you write, your words survive even your death."

As it did so often during the day, the image of Bertha alone in her attic room, talking to herself, rose suddenly in my mind. I wanted to run up all the flights of stairs in Thornfield and find her there, like a princess in a tower, and—do nothing, perhaps, for I knew there was little enough I could do. Only press my ear to her door, and give her ranting voice a listener.

"What is the use of a voice," I said, "when you have no one who will listen?"

Jane Eyre flinched at my words, and that interior look came over her face again. I have seen that look in her eyes many times over the years. I know she would hate to hear how much it always reminds me of Bertha.

"We must find you someone to talk to, then, Adèle," she said. "You are right. Someone your own age—someone well chosen, of course. You may be lonely here, child, but you are lucky in your loneliness, if it keeps you from knowing how horrible your fellow children can be."

I thought of the friends I had left behind in Paris, all the roving packs of us, sticking together and minding each other because we knew it was how we survived. I knew more of other children than Miss Eyre thought I did, and yet I did not contradict her. I knew she was thinking of my own best interest, as she saw it, and I further knew that I could never convince her to see my old Parisian comrades as suitable correspondents. Besides which, many of them could not read French, let alone the written English she desired me to practice.

She brought the question to Papa at dinner the next time he returned.

"I am afraid there are no suitable playmates for Adèle among the children of this parish," he said drily over his meat, "or rather, she would not be a suitable playmate for them. God forbid she should teach any of those . . . mannerisms of hers to these pale and proper Yorkshire daughters!" He smiled. "Their mothers would raid Thornfield with pitchforks. Nor can she play with the local boys—no indeed." He seemed to be restraining laughter. "God help them if she did." He dabbed at the side of his mouth with his large white napkin, all propriety on his surface. He glanced at me, as briefly as he always did, and then back to Jane. A light came into his eyes when he looked at my governess, a light that was more than half darkness. Even then I knew to call it desire.

For a long moment they regarded each other. I was a little awed to see that Miss Eyre never flinched from his gaze.

"Ah," he said suddenly. "I've hit upon it. I've a solution, Miss Eyre, never fear. A cousin of mine still lives in Jamaica, where I spent the worst years of my . . . misspent youth. He has somehow managed to settle happily in that sweltering country, and he's produced a brat about Adèle's age. Why not write to him, Adèle, and ask for correspondence? He can tell you about his exotic adventures among the, ah, sugar canes, and you can tell him how you hate these English moors."

I felt a catch in my throat, and I opened my mouth to tell Papa that I loved the landscape here—although even as words pushed against the bitten insides of my lips I did not know if they were true. Whether I loved or hated the bleak purples and grays of heather and grass, the vast lichen-covered rocks and nearly barren fields with their sudden green-eyed bogs that spat out sheep skulls, I had known them to be gorgeous in their bleakness.

But Papa did not love Thornfield, nor the moors around it. He was still watching Jane with that look in his eyes that I had seen in so many men's in the audience at Le Moulin, or when they entered the showgirls' boarding house—although never when they left.

Jane flushed like a green-red rosehip under his gaze; I wondered if she knew she blushed. It was obvious to me that she was not used to feeling the weight of the kind of look that Papa laid against her then.

Supper was soon over, and after dinner she set me at practicing my writing again at one end of the long study, while she and Papa read books by the fire, looking up at different times so they did not know they watched each other.

The writing came no easier to me than it ever had, and yet I felt a fresh determination to master it. I was beginning to understand, through Jane's example, how a woman's thoughts formed into the right words could make people listen to her, could make meaning from the inexpressible longings of her heart. I was not yet sure that I knew what my heart's longings were, but I was beginning to believe that writing might help me get there.

Whether that desire to make my life mean something is my savior or my doom, I do not know. Yet here I am, still writing, and still speaking with my own voice as long as I have you to listen, even if it may be that you hear these words after my death.

Here we are, reader, you and I. Holding hands, here on this page.

FOUR

SO PAPA WROTE a letter of introduction, and I began my correspondence with Eric Fairfax.

My own introductory note was shy and fumbling—but Miss Eyre's idea was a good one, because I suddenly had reason for wanting to improve my writing. A child growing up in Jamaica would lead a fascinating life, perhaps even more interesting than my own life had once been in Paris, and I longed to learn about it.

I wrote:

Dear Master Fairfax,

I am sorry for calling you "dear" because I do not know you, but I am told it is the polite way to begin a letter in English. I am writing to you because my governess and my Papa say I must improve my English writing and reading, and I have seen no reason to before I learned about you. I was born in France (I must no longer say that I am French) and I speak and understand English well enough to get by here at Thornfield, where there are not many people.

Papa says I will not always live at Thornfield (although sometimes I do not believe him). I must go out into the world someday and be a credit to him. I thought credit was to do with money, but it seems that many English words have double meanings.

Thornfield is a big dark house in the middle of a moor. Trees grow sideways in the wind, and rocks stick out of the earth like teeth. There is a plant called heather that is simply everywhere, and it is ugly for a flower but it smells good. I have enclosed a dried sprig of it so you may catch its scent for yourself.

Please tell me what Jamaica is like.

Until I hear from you I remain,

Yours faithfully,
Adèle Varens

I did not like to say I was his faithfully either, but Miss Eyre said my other choice was "your servant" and I liked that even less.

I started running out to the mail coach the day after I sent my letter, even though Miss Eyre told me it could take a month or more to reach Jamaica, and even if Eric responded immediately—which was not likely, she reminded me, since young gentlemen often had more rigorous schooling schedules than young ladies—it might be another month before his letter's return.

It was two months later exactly that I received Eric's first reply. It was a rainy day, but I was so thrilled to get an envelope addressed to my own name that I didn't even go back inside the house before I pulled apart the red seal and opened it.

The letter read:

My dear Miss Varens,

I feel more confident in calling you "dear" than you did: I must confess that your letter made me like you very much. You sound like a—well, like an interesting, lively person, full of life. One would think there would be plenty of liveliness—joie de vivre, I think you'd call it—in Jamaica, from all the adventure stories they tell about the Caribbean back in England.

I wonder if my Uncle Edward has told you I lead an exciting, adventurous life in an effort to interest you in writing to his lonesome cousin? Uncle Edward is kind, Adèle, even though at first his manner might not seem so. He did my family a great favor once, and someday I should like to tell you about it.

But let us become acquainted with each other first.

You already know my name, Eric Fairfax, which I share with my father and grandfather and innumerable male relatives before that. I am thirteen years old, and I have lived here in Jamaica all my life. The cold wild moors you wrote about are just as exotic to me as Jamaica might be to you, and I am glad for the chance to hear about them.

I must confess, however, that my life here at the sugar plantation is often dull. For instance, I have never even seen a pirate. Much as

I've begged my father, he refuses to take me on board one of his trading vessels for the chance of meeting one; but I believe that finally this will change after my fourteenth birthday, in only a month's time. After all, as I've often argued with him, his ships regularly take on cabin boys younger than I—younger than you, too, I wager, although I know it is improper to ask a lady her age. (But how old are you?)

And will you tell me more about yourself, Miss Varens? What are your favorite ways to pass your time at Thornfield, when Uncle Edward isn't there? Is it terribly lonely for you?

I ask because, although I do not dwell on it, I am often lonely myself. My mother and younger sister both died of a fever last year, and since then my father spends little time at home. I miss my sister's company most especially—hers was almost a twin soul to mine—and I am happier than perhaps is rational at the prospect of knowing you, no matter how distant we might be in relation, geography, or indeed any other particular. I find myself full of a very foolish hope that I can be a kind of brother to you now, and that we can be companions in our lonely homes and countries.

Thank you for writing to me—merci.

(I know it would not please your governess, but perhaps I should use our correspondence to practice my French.)

Until then, I eagerly await your next letter & remain:

Your servant,

Eric Fairfax

I was so happy to have my letter at last, and so relieved at its friendly contents, that I hugged it briefly to my chest. When I took it up to read again it left a blurry ink print on my pinafore. I suddenly saw myself as if from outside my body, a girl standing in the rain with ink on her hands and her breast, hair straggling out of her braids and sticking damply to her neck and forehead.

I don't think I have ever truly managed to stop watching myself from outside, not ever since that moment. I wondered what Eric would think if he saw me bedraggled like that, and I scurried out of view of Thornfield's nearest window, in case anyone *could* see.

If there was one thing that the Moulin girls never tolerated, it was notions of romance. Not one of them ever kept letters or flowers or any tokens at all from the men whose admiration made their living—except for jewelry, which they either sold or kept as a kind of insurance, like the ring my mother had given me. All of those tough, gorgeous women would laugh to see me smiling over a boy's letter, I knew, even if he was a cousin.

Third cousin.

Of a man who, after all, might not even be my father.

For the first time I found myself vaguely wishing he was not— but then such a sting of disloyalty to Maman shot through me that it made me shudder.

I rushed inside, feeling as if someone was still watching me after all. I pulled my hair into a braid so tight it made my scalp hurt. I scrubbed the ink from my dress as best I could.

But even though the letter was rain-smeared almost beyond the point of rereading, I couldn't quite bring myself to throw it away.

Soon I adored Miss Eyre, even if I could not adore our lessons. I missed the glamour of the haphazard teachings I'd received from Maman and her girls—there was nothing glamorous about anything Jane taught me, and indeed it was clear that she deplored the very concept. Even the way she taught me to curtsey was plain.

"If you are a good soul, Adèle," she said, "that goodness shows through in the simple honesty of your manner, the way you present yourself. No man—no person—should be able to accuse a good soul of deception."

Deception, I soon learned, Jane Eyre despised almost above all things. She told me that what was called glamour at Le Moulin was simply a feminine form of lying. "It did not please God to make me beautiful," she said, "but He gave me a mind and a soul that are equal to any man's, and those gifts I value far more."

She was showing me how to do my hair in the low bun and severe part that she wore every day, and so we were regarding each other side-by-side in the mirror.

I watched her for a moment. I looked into my own eyes, and then into hers. "God made me beautiful, miss," I said. "I have very good hair and pretty skin. The dancing girls always said it was like roses, and fretted over me, and told me theirs was never so fine, for all they were paid to be pretty."

Miss Eyre looked at both of us in the mirror too. Red patches appeared all at once on her cheeks, as if our reflections had slapped her. "God did indeed make you prettier than most, Adèle," she said. She looked away from her own image.

I hadn't said a syllable about her hair or skin, and I'd seen enough petty unkindness pass between the girls at the mirrors in Le Moulin never to say anything cruel about another's looks, but Jane made me feel as if I had.

"But beauty matters nothing," she said suddenly, looking up again. "One might use it to—to make someone long for you, but their longing will soon wane. Even the most beautiful lose their beauty very soon. In truth beauty is a burden, Adèle: it keeps a man looking at your face, instead of into your soul."

We heard a lovely giggle from downstairs: Blanche Ingram, a fashionable woman who was visiting Thornfield with some friends. The deep rumble of Papa's rare laughter followed the sound like thunder after lightning.

Jane's cheeks faded into paleness again. "You'd best go down to them, Adèle, to be polite," she told me.

She pushed me toward the door. As for herself, she retreated to the shadows.

Dear Eric,

I am going to be unladylike again, which is the opposite of Papa's and Miss Eyre's intention for our correspondence—but you see at least that I am writing in English, so it is all right.

I keep having dreams about you and Jamaica. Maman always said it was a sure way to secure a man's fascination if you told him you'd had dreams about him, and I must admit that is my intent, for I think if you were fascinated your letters would come faster and more frequently, and I am often bored at Thornfield.

Having fascinated you, I will go on to admit that my dreams do not focus on you, but on what we do together. We are pirates, you and I, sailing the Caribbean in search of treasures to plunder and maidens to rescue. These dreams are most satisfactory and thrilling, except that the high seas in my mind's eye persist in sharing the gray tint of the moors where I find myself stranded on waking.

I implore you to tell me more about the color of the Caribbean Sea, so that I may dream it properly.

Yours sincerely,
Adèle

Dear Adèle,

My mother had a sapphire brooch that my father buried with her. It was finely made, large and oval in shape, and its every facet glittered and sparked as if it were made from dozens of stars stitched together. But the heart of the stone was a deep, roiling blue shot through with green, so deep that looking at it was more like hearing a musical note, the low hum of a cello perhaps, than seeing a color. My sister and I used to take turns holding the brooch up so close to one eye, and closing the other, that the whole world turned to a lagoon of sparkling, deep blue-green.

Stars stitched together over blue and green gemstone shadows, and cello music: that it what the ocean looks like here. No one will ever see my mother's brooch again, but I hope I have conjured it for you a little bit.

I return your confession with one of my own: you have fascinated me from the start. I tried not to write to you too often because I did not want to seem too eager, nor to bore you; but I am glad to hear that you look forward to my letters as much as I do yours. And I am pleased that you dream of us as pirates: dreams of you have crept up on me, too, since I read your first letter.

I propose a game: begin a story of you and me as buccaneers, and I will add to it. I would like to think that between the two of us, over a course of years, we might perhaps write a whole book's worth of adventures.

I await your first chapter.

In fascination,
Eric

Jane told Papa my written English was improving faster than she could have hoped. Papa smiled with an open approval that he had never before shown me, and my efforts redoubled.

One midsummer morning I awoke without Miss Eyre's prompting, something that had never occurred since she arrived at Thornfield. I found myself mimicking her in her absence, throwing open my curtains hard enough to shake off the dust—although they were not dusty any more, with such daily shaking—and I marched as smartly over to my water jug to wash my face as if Jane had been watching me.

When I came downstairs, my face still stinging from the frigid water, I found her sitting at a thin wooden chair in the kitchen. She was staring at the back of her left hand.

There was nothing different about that hand that I could see: still small and thin and pale, with no obvious mark or injury.

I walked up to her and put my hand on top of hers. They were exactly the same size.

She looked up and her gaze met mine. "We are going to marry," she said. Her voice sounded uncertain, as if she were making a comment about a painting or a passage of verse that she didn't think she understood, or as if she were speaking about someone else's life than her own; the life of a long-ago saint, perhaps. "Mr. Rochester and I are betrothed."

Her eyes held a few large, clear tears; their expression was so wondering, so happy, that I almost began to cry myself. All the sad gravity that had been in her expression had vanished, and I only realized then that it had been loneliness. Her eyes shone now like a child's, like an angel's in a painting, and even though I was still a child myself my heart broke for her, that she'd borne up against such loneliness for so long—and borne it so well that I only saw it once it was gone. In her face I saw a lonely child who suddenly had reason to hope she would never be lonely again.

I knew that child well.

"Oh, miss," I whispered.

We smiled tremulously at each other.

She pulled me into an embrace. When I felt the shaking in her small body, and the beating of her heart, I began to cry in truth. "Oh, *Mademoiselle*," I said through my tears, suddenly unable to remember any language but my first, "*que c'est merveilleux*."

But already I was thinking of Bertha.

Why did I not tell her?

How much pain could I have spared her? Spared them both?

Bertha, alone in her hot, dark, dirty attic room—for I could spend so little time with her ever since Jane Eyre arrived, my days so full of lessons even when Papa was gone, and so tired at night, that I think there must have been many times that she came in to see me and I did not wake—Bertha spiraling ever deeper inside herself, twisting and twisting into her aloneness, like a vine that strangles its own stem when it can find no other support.

And Jane, whose cool, pale face burned with such love when she looked at Mr. Rochester that it was just the same as the fervor I saw when she read her most beloved books, or when she prayed to her beloved god. How could I take that passion, that ardor, from her?

Yet how could I betray Bertha by pretending, along with Papa, that he owed her no obligation, and was free to marry another? How could I bear to cause the pain that my silence, or my speaking, would bring to both of them?

I confess I did not think of sparing Papa's pain.

Dear Eric,

You awake one night to find yourself bound and gagged, carried out the front door of your plantation house by two strong and fearsome pirates. They walk you as easily as a piece of luggage through the hot and humid night, toward the dark and sparkling, humming sea (I can picture it so much better now).

You try to struggle and scream through your gag, wondering if they plan to drown you, wondering what on earth they plan to do with you at all. Will they hold you ransom? Do they know something dark and terrible about your family, something you yourself can only guess at, and are they seeking their revenge?

They place you in a rowboat, taking surprising care not to injure you even though they do not remove or loosen your restraints. They row you out to sea, approaching a beautiful black ship that had been hidden just out of view of the bay. As soon as you come aboard they march you to the captain's cabin.

The captain's large and exquisitely fashionable hat conceals his face for a moment as he writes something at his desk. As he lifts his head you see that "he" is a girl, about the same age as yourself and quite stunningly beautiful (a vanity I am allowed as narrator). Her face looks mischievous, but kind and brave; you feel sure she does not mean you real harm . . . but this only adds to your confusion.

As she walks toward you and removes your gag, the most treacherous thought of all begins to cross your mind: If revenge against your family is this lovely pirate's desire . . . could it be justified?

I started bleeding the night before the wedding. I woke to the sound of thunder, my thighs and sheets stained dark. I washed myself in the basin; at least I knew from my Moulin education what was happening, and I did not think myself injured, the way I later learned so many girls did when their first courses came on them.

I was pulling the reddened sheet off my bed when lightning struck just outside. I jumped and flinched, and when I looked up again I realized I had pressed my own blood onto my nightgown. I saw myself like Bertha for a moment, frightened and wild and stained, and I filled with a horror unlike any I had felt before.

I replaced the sheet with a clean one as best I could on my own, tucked a handkerchief between my legs, and slept the rest of the night on my side, curled up tightly so it wouldn't budge, my widening hipbones digging into the mattress. When I woke in the morning, I saw that the lightning had split and burned the great oak tree outside.

I was not welcome at the wedding, but I know from what Jane and Papa told me later how it went: the objection just at the crucial moment, the appearance of Bertha's brother like a malevolent ghost, the bridal party's rush back to Thornfield. The harrowing reveal: Papa's demon Bertha and his angel Jane, facing each other at last.

And Jane Eyre's flight.

I know I was a selfish child to think of it, but it was true:

It was not only Papa that she left.

FIVE

EVERYONE KNOWS what happened next.

The fire at the great house. The lord of the manor who nearly died, running back into the rubble to save that woman—the madwoman who started the fire.

That much of the story, at least, he couldn't change. The townspeople had gathered to try to help douse Thornfield, and they saw him look up at the roof and cry out and run back in.

They thought they understood what he was doing. They thought they knew who was mad in that house, because the house's master told them.

But let me tell you this now, and remember it well:

We are not the mad ones.

PART TWO
THE WEBSTER

I soon asked and obtained leave of Mr. Rochester, to go and see her
at the school where he had placed her. Her frantic joy at beholding
me again moved me much. She looked pale and thin: she said she
was not happy. I found the rules of the establishment were too
strict, its course of study too severe for a child of her age: I took
her home with me. I meant to become her governess once more,
but I soon found this impracticable; my time and cares were now
required by another—my husband needed them all. So I sought out
a school conducted on a more indulgent system.

—Charlotte Brontë, *Jane Eyre*

SIX

READER, SHE MARRIED HIM.

Jane Eyre came back. After the fire. After all that loss.

She found my blinded Papa, and she loved him.

He loved her too; she had finally saved him, as he'd always hoped one of us would, from the life he'd always found so miserable and lonely, so incomplete.

And then Jane came to Ashfield Academy, and she saved me too.

Papa, blinded and crippled in the Thornfield fire, had retreated in his misery to a smaller estate called Ferndean and sent me to the first boarding school that would take me. He intended to live at Ferndean as a kind of hermit, he said—except of course that even before Jane returned to him, he still kept a brace of servants. A real hermit would have to cook and clean for himself, and Papa had never done that in all his life.

By then he was truly a broken man; he never spoke to me, refused even to touch me—although I sometimes tried, once it was healed enough, to hold his hand.

In my loneliness for Jane after she fled, I'd plunged myself into the pirate stories Eric and I wrote. But after the fire, after Bertha's death, I found I wanted to talk to my friend about what was really happening in my life. I wrote:

I want to offer some measure of comfort to Papa, angry as I am at him for failing to save Bertha's life—sometimes I am still not convinced she started the fire, you know, or at least not on purpose—but it seems Papa does not want anything that I can give him.

For the first time in all our correspondence though, he did not write back promptly. Silence from him hurt even more than Papa's silence, his retreat inside himself; it was strange, but although I'd never met him, I felt far closer to Eric than to this man whose home I shared. When Papa sent me away, part of me was glad to leave him, but it hurt not to have Eric in my life, even more than I could have guessed it would.

Over six months passed before I received his reply. By then Miss Eyre had come back, and she and Papa were gone on their wedding trip. It would be mere weeks until Jane came to Ashfield to rescue me, although I didn't know it then.

I opened Eric's letter with breathless relief. He apologized for his lengthy silence, but told me he had a good excuse for it: his first adventure at sea at last and his first sight of a pirate. A horribly frightening experience, he said, and not nearly as full of derring-do as he had imagined it might be.

But do not worry too much about Uncle Edward, Adèle, he wrote. *I have no doubt that your presence was a comfort to him—after all, your letters have been a comfort and a joy to me.*

That was the first time Eric made me blush.

When Jane came for me at last, I was thrilled to leave the school where Papa had sent me after she'd left him. It was not a place where any child could be happy. Barely enough food to keep us living, and thin, burnt gruel at that. Girls dropped from weakness and fevers like flies.

I made the mistake of saying once, when a teacher mentioned my past, that the children in the French brothel where I was born were treated far better than the students at Ashfield. I was punished both swiftly and soundly for my lies—with a paddle, so that I could not walk properly for days.

Yet there were worse punishments. Things done to disobedient girls in broom closets or in our own beds late at night.

One night, indeed, I woke up to see a pale face looming over my bed.

I thanked God for Bertha then, because I had learned not to shy away in fright from nocturnal specters. I was not frozen with fear, and when I recognized the face of our headmaster leaning over me and felt his fingers on my counterpane—

I grabbed his hand where it strayed over the blanket, and I bit him.

I bit him as hard as I could.

I tasted his warm, soft skin and his blood. I watched him swallow his cry of pain—he had reason to stay silent in that room—but I locked my jaw like a dog and would not let go. I bit down with the good, strong, straight teeth the Moulin girls had prized in me. I heard and felt a tendon snap.

He grabbed my hair with his other hand and wrenched me away from him. His adult strength bested mine, and I let him go.

He stared at me, his bloodied hand showing the deep crescent gash of my mouth upon it, his breathing quick and shallow.

I spat his own blood back at him.

He fled.

I stayed unmoving in my bed until I was sure that he was gone, and then I rushed to the basin and filled my mouth with drinking water from the jug and rinsed it out, over and over again. I washed my face of blood, then kept washing until my dry lips cracked.

I didn't stop until another girl came to me, took my hand, and led me back to bed. She tucked the blanket over me as gently as any mother would, although she was surely younger than I. She didn't say a word; perhaps she already knew better than I did how little good it would do for girls to use our voices there.

In the morning I went to another teacher, a woman I thought I could trust, and told her what had happened. I knew exactly what the headmaster had been doing at my bedside—no child of Le Moulin could not know. I was sure he had done it to other girls too but that they might not have the knowledge, the words, to understand it.

I was hit for telling lies. With a belt that time.

The headmaster came to watch my punishment, his white-bandaged hand tucked into his pocket. A thin and innocent smile on his face. "I shall have to patrol the dormitories twice as often now," he murmured, "to ensure there will be no more girls telling lies."

It was only a few days later that Jane came to rescue me.

When I saw her, I hugged her as if she were herself and Maman and Bertha all at once, all the women I had ever loved.

She returned my embrace just as fiercely. She had been at just so cruel a school when she was young, she told me as we traveled back to the new home she had made with Papa. Her dearest friend, a girl named Helen Burns, had died while they were there, a preventable death that she attributed to the horrible conditions in which they lived.

She mentioned no dark closets, no dormitory secrets.

When I told her, her eyes filled with a deep pain like a bleeding wound. The wound spilled over, and a few silent tears slipped down Jane's cheeks.

"Oh, Adèle," she said. "That is so horrible, I cannot fathom it. It is beyond even cruelty." She gripped her handkerchief and twisted it so hard I thought it would rip.

And then she asked me: "Are you sure?"

Something about the wound in her eyes, so deep, made me hold her hand and tell her I was not.

"Well, it doesn't matter, then, if you're not sure. Perhaps it is just a confused memory from your terrible years in Paris; Edward has told me all about them." She sighed, unable to keep herself from shivering with the relief of not having to believe what I had said. "It doesn't matter in any case. I'm taking you home, and you shall live with us now, my dear, with my Edward and me. You will be safe at home with us." She closed her eyes again, nodding. "You will be safe."

Jane and Papa seemed to think of Ferndean, their new home, as a kind of haven, an earthly paradise. It was a smaller estate than Thornfield, a house of ivy-covered gray stone among a concealing thatch of strong old forest. It was a private little world, an Eden, and that was just what Jane and Papa wanted.

For me it was private unto suffocation.

I hated Ferndean. Hated it. Something was haunted in the air of that place, in a way that Thornfield, with all its specters, had never been.

When I wrote to Eric again, I spoke only of pirates.

Jane and Papa talked about Bertha more than one might think they would, given that she once had been the obstacle between them. They spoke of her regularly, purposefully, and there was a quality about it that reminded me of Jane's ministrations to Papa's healing injuries from the fire. It was as if there was some task they were accomplishing through those conversations. Eventually I saw that there was: they were whittling her down, slowly and steadily. Shrinking her, turning her flesh into words. They both spoke of her with sympathy, but it was a kind of diminutive sympathy, as if by making her someone to pity, they made sure they were above her and she far below.

It started to work even on me—until I realized one day, as I listened to their virtuous, pitying discussion of her at the dining table, that she was starting to grow smaller in my memory, that if I conjured a mental image of Bertha and one of Jane, Jane had become the larger woman, even though I knew well that Bertha had been as tall as Papa.

No one buried Bertha's body. She burned, and fell, and burned again until she was all burned up. Papa ordered a headstone for her and installed it over an empty place in the ground. The work they were doing now was her real burial: they were burying the truth, the ugly, painful, complicated truth of Bertha Antoinetta Mason Rochester, until there was nothing left but a poor madwoman whom Papa had tried to keep safe for her own good and who nonetheless had almost killed him.

"You would have a far easier time killing me, Jane," he told his second wife on the day I realized that they were burying Bertha. "You would only have to leave me again, and I would die."

A little worried crease always appeared between Jane's eyebrows when Papa told her he would die without her. "But I shall never leave you again," she would say. And the crease would vanish, and with her own dry, mincing humor, she would add, "You may depend on it, for you are so much older than I. You will certainly die long before I do, and I will be with you until the end of your life."

They clasped hands and looked into each other's eyes as if into mirrors.

I let my own eyes close, for one brief moment, and pretended I was looking into the eyes of two dead women I loved, who were neither so small nor so mad as Papa made them.

SEVEN

BY THE TIME I left for boarding school again, Ferndean had become as oppressive as a tomb.

Jane—Mrs. Rochester—would take me to school, just the two of us. Papa would never leave Ferndean again, he declared, for fear it would be like leaving Paradise and an angel with a flaming sword would block his way back in.

"I must clutch tight to the miracles I've found here," he said from his favorite chair in Ferndean's library, as Jane entreated him one last time to go with us to London. "I could hardly believe you were real, Jane, when you returned to me. I'll waste away for want of you every moment you are gone." There was teasing in his voice, but only a little. "I would not blame you if you found that London held greater temptations and you left me."

Jane's expressive eyes filled a little bit with tears, and she bent to look her husband in the face. "I could never ever leave you," she said. "Not only God's law but my own heart forbids it." She smiled, the smile that turned her plain, thin face into something remarkable in its sharp clarity, and she stroked his cheek just where the scars pulled most brutally across his skin.

They kissed, not briefly; his hand gripped hard at her bodice. I looked away.

There were many things I wanted to ask Jane about the new school she had chosen for me, but she spent the first hours of our carriage journey staring out the window in such a deep reverie that I didn't feel I ought to rouse her from it. Instead I watched the changing landscape: the moors that once felt endless vanished as if in a fairy tale, and fields of faded yellow, then gold, then green, gradually replaced them. I felt lighter and lighter with relief the farther we went from Ferndean: the place had seemed to shrink around me in the last months, the walls tightening like laced corset stays, the windows closing like eyes, as if there was something there they did not want to see—or to show.

By the time Jane declared she needed to focus on caring for her husband and couldn't teach me anymore, and that I should be sent back to school, I nearly felt I couldn't breathe at Ferndean. The farmland air we traveled through was delicious in contrast; for all that it was tainted by our driver's pipe smoke, it tasted infinitely fresher than the air inside the house had been.

"Do you know I haven't left Edward since we were married?" Jane said suddenly. "It is . . . unexpectedly hard. As if I have left a part of my flesh behind." She looked down at her hands in their

67

fine gloves and flexed and stretched her fingers. "Or one of my bones."

I tried to smile at her. I'm sure she meant it to be romantic, yet the idea struck me as gruesome.

"Indeed—oh, Adèle, I have not been sure if I should speak of it to anyone yet, but . . ." She made a little gesture toward her belly. "He is flesh of my flesh in truth now. We are to have a child of our own." She did not blush, but her face glowed with a pale, worshipful radiance. She was only just far enough along to know for sure; she hadn't yet told Papa. She didn't have to say that he'd never have let her travel if he knew.

A child of their own. I wanted to laugh—or cry; I could not make my face settle into one expression. "You'll be a wonderful mother, miss," I said, hoping that only happiness for her would show in my voice.

Jane looked at me queerly then; perhaps she guessed at the longings in my heart. "Thank you, Adèle," she said. And more gently: "I do wish you'd remember to call me Jane now. I am no miss anymore after all."

I smiled at her in truth then, but for the moment I did not trust myself to speak. Indeed we spoke no more for some time, each of us nursing our own thoughts as we watched the changing landscape outside. It was less rural now, and both busier and dirtier. Soon we would arrive at a city I'd never visited, but I was born and raised in a great city, and there was a part of me that sensed I was returning home. I felt myself pulled toward the miraculous cacophony of London, where there would always be crowds of people everywhere and no room for anyone to keep real secrets, or to feel alone and afraid, the way I had so often felt in my room at Ferndean at night. I could never explain, even to myself, why I felt less safe there than in the room where Bertha used to creep in on me. But it was so, and I was never gladder to quit a place.

As we left the countryside behind, Jane's mood seemed to lift. She began to chatter more eagerly than I'd ever heard her do; she was usually such an observant, discerning person that she had little use for talking for its own sake. But I realized as she spoke that she was talking to reassure herself far more than me.

"I wrote to all the best schools in London, Adèle," she said, "and to the families who have sent their daughters there and to the alumnae themselves. It was of great importance to me to save you from an education like mine, wherein human kindness was conflated with sin and indulgence. The Webster's headmistress is strict, I am told, but she is not a tyrant. If God grants you half-decent girls for your classmates, I hope and believe that you might find yourself quite happy there, so long as you apply yourself. You are receiving an education not only in Latin and mathematics and music, not only in sewing and dancing and the proper management of an estate, but in how to do all these things in the English way. For you are still French, Adèle, quite French, and as charming as you are, it was the original object of my employment to teach you how to be otherwise, and I know that I have never quite succeeded."

I knew that by "French" she, and Papa, really meant "what Maman had been." But what had she been? A dancer, a prostitute, an unwed mother. Unladylike, glamorous, beautiful and possessing an intimate understanding of her beauty and how to use it to her advantage. Perhaps they had not succeeded at all, Jane and Papa, for I still could not, in my heart, regret my resemblance to her in form, figure, or manner. It was true enough that I had never put my full effort into unlearning her ways or forgetting the little songs and dances and elegant habits of movement that I had learned from her and the other Moulin girls. True, too, that when speaking with anyone but the two of them, I let the ghost of Maman's Paris accent linger in my speech.

So I stayed silent, wishing I could truly listen to Jane talk but finding it too painful—both because I could not agree with her words and because I knew how much I would miss her voice when we were parted. I wondered if she would miss mine.

In London, smoke and tall buildings darkened the sky, and crowds of people and animals and carriages colored the streets as we moved farther into the city. At one point, as we waited behind a tangle of mail coaches, a small girl in a ragged dress ran up to our open window, where I was staring eagerly out at the city.

"Buy a posy, miss?" she asked.

I blinked in surprise. It was surreal, as if I had returned to Paris and met my past self.

She was not half as pretty a child as I'd been—it might sound cruel to say it, but everyone raised at Le Moulin knows beauty is currency and can weigh it to the last grain—but she knew well how to arrange her clothes and hair and the expression on her little face in order to squeeze the most sympathy from her mark. From me.

I smiled at the girl and nodded, reaching back for my purse, but Jane caught my hand. "The way to help such creatures as that one is through social reform, not encouraging begging, for that is all she is doing; you know as well as I that her flowers are merely a token. If you simply give her money, she'll only bring it back to whomever is minding her, and I can promise you it won't be spent on good honest food or clothes or schooling for the child. If you want to give your money to the poor, Adèle, we can drop it in the poor box at the next church we pass. Lord knows what use it would be put to if you give it to her directly."

"It will be put to what use is most needed," I said sharply—the words had been pushing at my lips since Jane started speaking. "I remember that quite well from when I sold posies on the street myself."

I pulled my purse out of her hand and gave the urchin her penny. She snatched it and tossed her dingy posey into the carriage and then ran back into the street. I felt myself soften, and I looked at Jane in apology; the fact of all Papa had given me, was still giving me, was obvious after all. Jane's mouth had tightened so much that her lips had vanished, but her gaze told me maybe she understood at least a little.

And yet, turning back to watch the child hand her penny to an older girl—a dark-haired, freckled girl in a brown dress and shawl, of maybe sixteen, who pocketed the coin with a quick, hungry, approving grin—I still couldn't help missing Maman.

71

At last we arrived at the Webster School for Young Ladies, a gray stone building on a quiet, tidy street. Ivy grew in artful curves up and around the blue-painted front door. In its lightness, its tall and narrow façade, it reminded me of a bird only just alighted on the London ground. I thought it might take flight again at any moment, and was surprised to realize that I already wanted to be inside it when it did. I had not liked any prospective home on sight since I'd left France, but I liked the Webster straight away. I couldn't quite believe that this would be my home for the next nine months—long enough that by the next time I saw Ferndean, Jane and Papa would have their baby.

We were ushered inside the school by a girl about my age, wearing a white shirtwaist and pale blue skirt that glowed with cleanliness. She blushed mightily as she curtseyed and led us to the headmistress's office, but she held her head high and her movements were assured; she'd clearly done this job many times.

She wore the same uniform as the clusters of girls in the sitting rooms that we passed, talking quietly together over their sewing, or practicing piano or singing or painting, or reading books or writing letters. I realized she must be not a servant but a student.

As we walked through the main hall, I heard a multitude of soft girlish voices, like a susurration of birds' wings.

Now, of course, I can describe the Webster blindfolded: its tidy and demure pink-and-white carpets and striped cushions, its wall-paper in soft yellow florals, its dark wood floors and stairs and banisters. The smell of old books and new paper, ink and soap, communal tea. I can reel off the names of the role models and patronesses whose portraits lined the walls.

Strange how much smaller a space becomes once it's familiar. The Webster only loomed on that first day; by the morrow its walls already felt intimate.

Not Thornfield nor Ferndean was ever like that.

The girl showed us into a high-ceilinged office where a gray-haired woman sat writing at an old cherrywood desk.

"Mrs. Rochester and Miss Varens, ma'am," she said, dipping a curtsey.

Hearing Jane's married name never failed to startle me.

"Thank you, Miss Norfolk," the woman said, finishing the line she was writing before she looked up at us. When she did, her face surprised me; she looked scarcely older than Jane. Her skin was pinkish and smooth, her mouth as round as a child's. The iron-gray hair was pulled back in the low, severe bun all English ladies wore. Her eyes were blue and stern.

"Good afternoon," she said. "I am Mrs. Webster, and I am pleased to welcome you to my school." She gestured to two uncushioned chairs before the desk, and we took them.

"Thank you," Jane said, sitting down with evident relief. I worried suddenly that her new pregnancy had made her too weak for the journey—but then I remembered Moulin girls who worked right through their ninth month, and I told myself not to be foolish. Still, I watched Jane closely as she spoke. "The Webster has received the highest recommendations from everyone to whom I've spoken. I've been repeatedly assured that you teach your girls the very best of English womanhood, and that is exactly what my husband"—she still glowed a little with disbelieving pride when she said *husband*, more than a year into their marriage—"and I hope for Adèle."

Mrs. Webster smiled. "Yes," she said, "I've read your letters. I can assure you that here, Adèle will acquire the best kind of English manners and the best kind of English mind: a sharp, wise, and rational one."

Jane smiled back.

They talked particulars for a few moments, and I found myself entranced by the portrait hanging on the wall behind the headmistress of a pale-skinned, dark-curled, long-nosed woman in an elegant dress at least thirty years out-of-date. The natural assumption would be that this was one of the school's founders, and yet she bore not the least resemblance to the youthful, gray-haired Mrs. Webster. There was something about her expression, so fierce that it felt exhausting just to look at the painting. What must the woman herself have been like?

Mrs. Webster caught me staring. "That is Mary Wollstonecraft," she said. "One of many role models we venerate at this school. You shall come to know her very well, through the best medium—her own words—before your first year with us is out."

I couldn't suppress a little "Oh!" at the name. I'd listened to more than one heated debate on Wollstonecraft's writing between Papa and Jane, and I could scarcely believe Papa would allow me to attend a school that enshrined a woman he'd called a whingeing harpy.

And yet he might not have meant it at all. I knew that, for Papa and Jane, arguments about books were a kind of flirtation, a prickly romancing, and Papa especially relished saying shocking things to Jane just to get a rise out of her. He might well admire the lady after all.

That did not help me know what I made of her myself.

"Miss Norfolk!" Mrs. Webster called the girl back into the room. She appeared immediately, smoothing her skirts with thin red hands. She had clearly been waiting outside the door.

I'd listened outside enough doors myself that catching her at it made me smile, but at my smile, she only blushed. That wash of red across her face and neck made my heart clench—because I hated to cause her embarrassment, I told myself then. Because I didn't want to start off on the wrong foot with the girls here. Only that.

"Show Miss Varens to the dormitories," the headmistress said. "Her things will be brought up later. Now, Mrs. Rochester, shall we finish with the accounts?"

Jane nodded, and she looked at me tremulously. And then, "Just a moment," she said, and she stood and rushed to me and hooked her arms hard around my waist. She leaned her small head against my collarbone and I returned her embrace.

It lasted only a brief moment; Jane had told me she'd never thought much of long goodbyes and that it would be easier for everyone not to make a show of our farewell.

So she pulled away quickly and gave me a terse smile. "Be well, Adèle," she said. She returned to her seat and picked up the papers the headmistress placed before her.

She did not look at me again, even when the girl—Miss Norfolk—bobbed another little curtsey and tipped her head to me, indicating that I should follow her. I left the room, forcing myself not to look back at Jane, the second mother I would leave behind.

But I glanced down at the place where her head had rested, and I saw a tearstain there.

I touched it gently, feeling its dampness, its fading warmth. And for a moment, there was nothing in the world but my knowledge that Jane would miss me. Really miss me. Even when she was back with her true love, with her longed-for baby: she would miss the girl I'd been when she met me, and the girl I had become under her care. She had tried to change me, to be sure, but she had loved me even before I began to change, and she loved me still.

I had never once seen Maman cry. Not once.

I did not cry myself then, but I touched the wetness of Jane's tear to my cheek before I squared myself and followed Miss Norfolk away from the headmistress's office.

She didn't look back again or speak to me, and I found myself feeling too shy, at first, to speak to her. So I simply followed her up a wide stairway with more portraits of women lining the walls. As we ascended, the stairs narrowed and the artwork changed to amateurish landscapes and still lifes—the students' own work, I was sure. I was relieved that I could already produce drawings about as good as these, as well as pencil portraits, because of my studies with Jane. No matter what else my classes had in store, I wouldn't be working frantically to catch up in one subject at least.

Miss Norfolk finally looked back at me and smiled as she opened a door at the very top of the stairs: the attic. Bertha flashed through my mind, and my heart gave a hard little twist.

I was so focused on looking ahead into the room where I would sleep for the next nine months that I didn't notice how low the door was. I cracked my forehead on the lintel and, not for the first time, cursed my height. I had grown several inches in the last year alone; although my sixteenth birthday was not until November, I already towered over Jane, and I thought within a year I might be as tall as Papa.

"Watch your head," the girl said a beat too late.

"I wish I had, Miss Norfolk," I replied, rubbing my crown. "It nearly took my head off."

"Oh." She stepped toward me and took my chin in her hand, then turned my head to the side. "You've got a little scratch there, all right, although the skin's not split. You might just get a bump or a bruise." She inspected me for another moment, bolder than the shy and blushing girl I'd met downstairs—although I saw she was still blushing. "And call me Hannah, if you please."

I could feel her warm breath on my neck as she looked up at my forehead. The whole pose felt shockingly intimate.

I quite liked it.

"Hannah," I said quietly. "I'm Adèle." I looked down at her; she was a few inches shorter than I, but then, so were most women. "It caught me by surprise, that's all," I said. "I left France long ago, and I'm no aristocrat; I did not expect to be guillotined in London."

She gave a surprised laugh. Her wide brown eyes turned to crinkled lines as she smiled, making her whole face merry.

"You won't be telling us . . . to eat cake, then?" she asked.

"I wouldn't presume that far," I replied, beginning to smile back. I lowered my voice and added, "I've stashed some contraband fruit-cake in my luggage." English roses couldn't be so different from Paris urchins that forbidden sweets did not join them under a united banner of friendship, I had reasoned. I did not know if I could make friends on my own strength but felt sure that cake always could.

Hannah looked faintly scandalized. "You'll be the most popular girl in school," she said, but as she spoke her smile faded.

I wondered if the other students were cruel to this shy, rosy girl. At once I was determined that I would be kind enough to her to make up for anyone else's mistreatment.

She led me into the dormitory, a narrow hall with a sloped ceiling (I'd been right that it was the attic), lined on either side with slim, iron-framed, white-painted beds. They shared white sheets but had mismatched counterpanes that I knew had been brought from each girl's home; the school's introductory letter had instructed that I bring one too.

Most of them were rich looking, brocade or even velvet in beautiful colors. A few were cotton patchwork. I wondered if it was an intentional display, that everyone would know, even in the egalitarian world of dreamland, who the scholarship girls were.

I remembered my time at Ashfield and wondered if there were a darker reason still, to make it clear which beds belonged to the girls who had least in the way of power or family protection.

For a moment the cozy room seemed to shrink until I felt as if I couldn't stand up straight.

But the Webster was not Ashfield. It was not even Thornfield nor Ferndean. Nothing bad had yet happened to me in this new, narrow room.

I knew which was to be my own bed, for it was the only one without a counterpane. Hannah sat down on the bed next to the empty one; it was covered in the most patched over of any of the patchwork quilts. *With Love from M* was stitched into the hem by the pillow in a faded, smooth yellow thread that looked as if it had been stroked about a million times. She touched it fondly.

A porter arrived and pulled my heavy trunk over to the end of my bed, then nodded at us and silently left the room. I opened it immediately and put aside my own counterpane, a fine, heavy golden thing Jane had sent away for; I dug through my clothes and sundries until I found the cake I'd hidden at the bottom.

It was beautiful, dark, and spicy, each slice shot through with candied fruit like stained-glass windows. It was meant for far-off Christmas, but like the other Christmas cakes, it had been baked in July, soaked in rum, and stored in the back of the pantry to wait for December. I took out the biggest, most almond-studded piece and offered it to Hannah. I'd planned to bring it out after hours, but . . .

"I'd prefer to begin making friends right away," I told her.

She looked from side to side, and then her thin red hands darted to the cake like birds. She brought it to her mouth, breathed in the cinnamon-and-clove scent, and took a tiny bite. I watched her tongue retrieve an errant crumb from the cupid's bow above her lips. I chose a slice for myself and took a luxurious mouthful, my senses filling with sugar and spices and rum.

We grinned at each other, conspirators.

"That is wise of you," she said. "I have the bed next to yours, and that means we're to share a desk in the study too. It's *my* good side you want to be getting on."

I nodded happily. Getting on Hannah Norfolk's good side sounded like something I would very much enjoy.

EIGHT

THAT MOMENT with Hannah in the dormitory was the only quietude I found that day. She brought me back to Mrs. Webster's office, and I spent the rest of the day following the headmistress to so many classrooms and meeting so many mistresses and students that my head swam with new information. Jane and I had arrived during the dinner hour, and before I knew it I was being directed back up to the dormitory with the other girls, most of whom I had only made brief eye contact with as Mrs. Webster showed me around.

The bedtime regimen at the Webster Academy for Young Ladies was so strict and efficient that I had no time to feel awkward with several dozen girls I barely knew. No one spoke to each other as we changed into our nightdresses—I was glad that mine was a similar white flannelette to the other students', and even a little finer than most—and we cleaned our faces and underarms in basins full of an unexpected luxury: warm water. It even carried a faint, familiar scent. When it took me a moment to identify it as rosewater, I wondered at myself, since so many of the Moulin girls had used it on their clothes and hair.

Warm, rose-scented water: this place was no Ashfield. I felt a little stiffness leave my spine.

A short, thin woman, Mrs. Jones, handed out birch twigs and tiny pots of charcoal dust, and she walked among us, observing and correcting our techniques as we scrubbed our teeth. When she stopped next to me, she beckoned me to open my mouth.

I hesitated for a moment, remembering the headmaster's demands at my last school. But we were not alone; I glanced around at my fellow students, a few of whom were idly watching me. I opened my mouth for this woman, feeling a bit like a filly at auction.

It was not the last time I'd feel that way at Webster.

"Your teeth are good," she said, "but for that unfortunate gap." I'd inherited the little space between my front teeth from Maman, and I valued it for both the remembrance of her and, childishly, the ease I had at whistling. "Mind your smile well. Nothing is less attractive to a young man than a girl with teeth twice her age."

I thought of a great French courtesan Maman once told me of who was famous for having reached the age of thirty with all her own teeth.

Ever since I'd crossed the channel with Papa and dropped my last milk tooth into the dark sea like a pearl, I dreaded leaving any bones on English soil. I cleaned my mouth assiduously at least three times a day, often until it hurt too much to go on.

It wasn't what the lady had in mind, but I just nodded at her and spit out my frothy charcoal. I was glad she had only looked at my teeth and did not see the scars inside my lips.

She inspected every other girl's teeth just as closely. Each moment was accounted for and observed, right up until Miss Jones doused the dormitory lamps. I'd had no chance to offer my cake to anyone but Hannah, and it was the only card I'd planned to play. It felt a bit absurd to realize how much I'd been relying on the ambassadorial power of sugar and how frightened I felt at the prospect of having introduced myself to my peers with nothing to sweeten the deal.

Mrs. Jones led us in the Lord's Prayer after the lights were out. "Now, into bed, girls," she said, and I heard a chorus of counterpanes and linens all turning back, of girls' knees pushing against mattresses, even as my own movements added to the sound.

I had become used to reading in bed before I fell asleep, thanks to Jane's influence. It gave my mind a chance to wander off the well-worn path of my own life's worries and find someone else's path to walk. But now I was faced with darkness too deep for reading and lying in a new bed, in a new room, and the quiet breathing of strangers all around me. There was of course another way I knew to help myself fall asleep, but *that* was not available to me in a shared bedroom either. I was sure I'd lie awake all night.

Miss Jones stood by the door, her left side silhouetted in hallway lamplight, for several minutes before she finally left.

I stared up at the inkwell of the darkened ceiling. I wondered if I still talked in my sleep, as Bertha used to say I did. I started to think it might be best that I couldn't fall asleep, for I didn't want to embarrass myself with strange ramblings or divulge any secrets to these unfamiliar girls . . .

After a while I began to hear a soft murmuring sound by the window. I thought it was the wind at first, but then a giggle burst out.

Thank goodness. Girls whispering and laughing in the dark— that was a world I remembered. Backstage at Le Moulin, at home with Maman and the other dancers, at Ashfield, where we had only each other's whispers and laughter to keep us safe and warm, or at least to give us the illusion of warmth and safety. Even with Bertha, and her strange, lonely, reaching fits of frantic, humorless shrieks . . . girls laughing together has always meant home to me.

I sat up; my nightgown's neckline slipped down around my shoulder and I was instantly chilled. I righted it and went quickly to the trunk at the foot of my bed. I noticed that the blanket on the bed across from mine was tented, and a faint glow came from under it: a girl reading by candlelight. A dangerous practice, to hold the flame under the fabric, near the pages, but one I'd done myself more than once. I made a note to ask her what she was reading when morning came.

I found my dressing gown and, hidden underneath it, the hastily rewrapped fruitcake Mrs. O'Connor had made back at Ferndean.

I looked for a long moment at Hannah's bed; she lay on her stomach, her eyes closed, her limbs so still that she could have been sleeping—except for the tension that was obvious in the lines of her shoulders and the arms that clenched tight around her pillow.

"Let us eat cake, Hannah?" I whispered.

She didn't answer, or even move, until I decided she was sleeping after all. I marveled at her ability to fall asleep so fast, a skill that has always escaped me, but I supposed that she must be exhausted every day, performing her chores in addition to her studies.

I would have felt better approaching the whispers at the other end of the room with an already-won friend in tow, but I couldn't bear to wake her if she needed sleep so much. I touched Maman's poison ring and let it give me strength. I had mettle enough to do anything that needed doing by myself—my years at Thornfield and Ferndean had given me that, far more than my years in Paris, whatever anyone might think.

I held the cake before me like a Eucharist and walked across the room. The wool rugs scratched at my feet. At Ashfield there had been only cold, bare floors.

My eyes were adjusting to the dark, and I counted nine figures huddled together on just two narrow beds. It was hard to make out their features or even the colors of their hair, but I recognized the gleaming white-blond braid of a girl I'd noticed while we were preparing for bed, and the abundant black curls of another stood out in silhouette.

I stopped a step or so away from them; their heads were drawn so closely together that I wasn't sure if they knew I was there. Finally a lull came into their conversation, just long enough that

85

I could insert my own voice without interrupting any of theirs. I remembered the importance of that from the dressing-room pecking order at Le Moulin—interruption was always, always an attempt to dominate the speaker. Even among veteran dancers who'd known each other for years, it was a risk. For a newcomer, it was unforgivable.

"Hello," I said, smiling through the dark, though I wasn't sure they could see. "I've brought you an offering." I held out the dark, spice-fragrant cake.

They all turned their heads to look at me. Their eyes gleamed in the windowed moonlight like a pack of indoor wolves.

The white-braided girl grinned and reached for the cake, and then we all descended on it together. By the time I'd doled out the slices, I'd learned each of their names: the curly-haired girl was Charlotte, the towhead Felicity. There were three Janes, an Elizabeth, two Marys, and an Emmeline in the laughing group gathered on the two beds.

And by the time the cake was finished, I was one of them.

NINE

Dear Eric,

The pirate queen finds herself sailing a new ship: the SS Webster
Academy. *I am pleased to report that the crew is a stalwart passel
of lasses, and they have accepted your queen into their crew with
alacrity . . .*

*No. I can't go on like that; the metaphor will flounder, as will
the ship. I want to write to you of my real life, Eric, for at last—at
last!—it is not something I want to pretend away.*

*My first weeks at the Webster have passed with unsettling speed.
I was surprised, after the cold, hungry, frightening stretch of time at
Ashfield, and after the creeping, clasping reach of the days I'd spent
at Ferndean and at Thornfield, that time still has the capacity to
pass quickly for me. I'd thought that feeling—of being carried on a
smooth, fast-flowing river of time—had been one of the things I'd
left behind forever in my Paris childhood.*

*But our days here are so full of lessons and activities that I
find myself plunging through them from the moment I wake and*

pleasantly exhausted at their end, barely able to stay awake to join the cheery gang's after-bedtime gossip for more than a few minutes. I value that time, though, for the girls are charming and lively companions, and hearing their whispered stories and dreams brings a special kind of glow to my heart. I sometimes wish Hannah, the girl I share a desk with, would join us, but I have not pressed the matter with her too much. She always says her chores make her far too tired to do anything at night but sleep. But she avoids the other girls at mealtime too; even when she isn't serving, she usually sits with a girl named Catherine Essex, who keeps her nose in a book all the time and rarely speaks to anyone—this is a girl who even reads with a candle after hours. I have not tried to join her at those times, for I've had the sense her book is a more welcome companion than I would be.

I suspect it is Hannah's scholarship status that keeps her shy. I wonder sometimes if it is the reason the other seat at her desk was free, instead of any other girl's. I wish I could show her how often I feel different from them too, as only a ward and not a true daughter of a society family. But my guardian is wealthy, and Jane remembers her own childhood poverty so keenly that she makes sure I always have the best of everything. I know that our situations are materially very different indeed, and that stops my tongue when I want to tell her I know how she feels.

I PAUSED in my writing, looking across our cherrywood desk at Hannah, who had also finished her schoolwork and was reading a novel with a worn cover, glancing up at the grandfather clock by the door every few minutes. Her chores intruded on her study hours, and I knew it was only through great determination and no small cleverness that she found time to read for pleasure at all.

She tucked back a curl that had come loose by her ear.

I looked down at my letter.

I had spent more than a little time those first weeks plotting to bring Hannah into the group of girls that I had found so easily lovable, so kind. When I mentioned her to Charlotte and Felicity, they showed no malice or even dislike; they merely said that she preferred to keep to herself, and they didn't mind if that was what she wanted. There were other girls, like bookish Catherine, who preferred their own company, and for the most part no one bothered them.

Yet even though Hannah kept herself apart, there was something in her that I recognized and cared for deeply, something I could not quite name, as if my soul looked at hers and saw itself. I kept chasing that surprised laugh she'd let out the day I met her. Though it came only rarely, and Hannah more often blushed or shook her head when I said something funny or shocking, I found I longed for her company more than that of the other, more boisterous girls.

But I struggled to express to Eric why it bothered me so much that Hannah kept herself apart from us. From me. And I worried I had already written too much about her.

That drew me up short. It was true that I dreamed of Eric sometimes, that I still felt a little thrill in my heart when I opened one of his letters. It was true that I hoped we'd get along as well when we met as we did in our letters—that our meeting was a *when* in my mind, not an *if*.

But why should Eric mind if I wrote about another girl? Was I afraid he would be jealous?

I took a deep breath and glanced again at Hannah, immersed in her novel. She was nibbling on a fingernail as she read, something she'd be chided for if the study-hour mistress saw it, but the unselfconscious movement, the little worrying of her mouth over the short, pink nail, charmed me. I bit the insides of my lips, my own nervous habit, in sympathy, and I realized I was wondering what Hannah's fingers would taste like in my mouth.

I was not naive about such things. A few Moulin dancers had enjoyed each other's company more than any man's; a few of their customers had been women too. I knew I was not alone in such feelings . . . such longings . . . as I had for her.

It wasn't that I feared Eric would be jealous. It was that I knew quite well he'd have good reason to be.

My admiration of Hannah did not erase my feelings for him though. He had been my only friend for years, and a hope I only sometimes dared acknowledge—the hope so many of the girls at the Webster shared, that our futures might hold a love match, and not simply a marriage that would enrich or ennoble our families.

Hannah looked up and met my eyes, and I did not know whether to feel pleased or embarrassed when she flushed under my gaze.

I smiled quickly at her and refocused on my letter, on Eric. I would simply write about something else.

Our classes are almost all fascinating: we study history, geography, poetry, mathematics, or philosophy in the mornings, and our afternoons are devoted to learning the running of a grand house, etiquette, embroidery, drawing, music, and dancing. I love all the morning classes except for history, which I find unsettling. We learn there all the ways that England is superior to every other country—and especially, it feels to me, to France—from its culture to its military prowess. I feel disloyal to my mother country as I memorize the dates of all the battles it has lost to my adopted one. Yet Great Britain is the greatest of all nations, we are taught: a fact that is both an honor and a burden for good English people, since their society must act as a role model and a savior for all the rest of the world.

But do they want to be saved? I wonder. Jane and Papa would scold me for such thoughts. I hope you will not, Eric. What history have you learned, in Jamaica?

Our teacher, a pretty widow of middle age named Mrs. Holcombe, is passionate about the virtue of the empire; her late husband was a captain in the British army. Most of the girls are swept along in her enthusiasm for her beloved country's past and her faith in its glorious future.

And yet my French heart persists in feeling that Mrs. Holcombe is only giving us part of the story.

I enjoy the afternoon lessons too, although they rankle many of the girls. Etiquette is mostly just politeness topped with charm, and I already learned the latter during my time at Le Moulin. The rest is just fiddly little rules, but I find I can memorize them easily and replicate them quite naturally, almost as if I'd been curtseying in that stiff, pretend-I-don't-have-legs way and choosing the correct fork from among dozens all my life. I knew a bit of pianoforte as a child in France too, and I learned a bit more from Jane. I have no great talent at embroidery, but I find that my fingers like the delicate, repetitive movements: they keep me just busy enough to focus on the work at hand, and just calm enough to be able to pursue my own thoughts, or to join in conversation with the students next to me.

Whenever possible, that girl was Hannah, but I thought better of saying so to Eric.

When I looked up again, she was still watching me.

I swallowed; I had become such a habitual watcher of the ever-busy Hannah that I hardly expected to find her closely observing me too.

I didn't look away. I'd learned early on from the Moulin girls how much one can say with an unbroken gaze at those times when words won't do.

So I steadied my gaze against hers, and as her cheeks warmed, I felt mine do the same. She bit her lip softly, and I wondered if she did it on purpose. I let myself focus on her mouth for a long moment, on the wet patch that she'd bitten, and then I looked in her eyes again. When the color washed higher over her freckled cheeks it was as if I could feel the heat of her blood on my own face, and I knew I was blushing too.

I held my ground, looking in her eyes, thinking about her mouth. Any moment now, I thought, she'd look away.

The grandfather clock chimed and made her flinch. She closed her book quickly and began gathering her things, her whole face ruddy with blushing. She bit her lip again, but whether to keep from smiling or frowning, I couldn't tell.

Not knowing how to read the moment didn't sit well with me; I didn't say anything to her or try to catch her gaze again.

I let her leave and turned back to my paper beau.

I wondered how to sign off; I had never worried about revealing too much of myself to my beloved correspondent before.

I hope that your father will let you go to school someday soon too, Eric, and that you will be as fortunate in your circumstances there as I have been in mine at the Webster. And many of my new friends' brothers attend Oxford; perhaps your uncle, my guardian, might persuade him of English education's superiority, since he believes in it so passionately for me. I would be thrilled to know you were here on this gray island, instead of in warm but horribly far-off Jamaica.

Yours sincerely,
Adèle

It was too bold, I knew, but I had said nothing untrue. And I did still harbor dreams of Eric. I did want him to be here. I felt longing, wanting, pulsing in my body every day.

The mistress rang her handbell for the end of study hour. As I walked past Hannah's empty chair, I let my hand brush its back, to catch the ghost of warmth she'd left there.

I simply didn't know whom I wanted more.

TEN

AS TIME WENT BY, the Webster and its routines became my home in a way no place that I had lived since Le Moulin had ever been. No one at the Webster, of course, would have liked to hear how much a finishing school is like a boarding house for dancing girls and "fallen women," as Mrs. Webster so primly called them. I wondered if respectable wives were their opposites: risen, like angels. I wondered whether angels should be called risen or simply unfallen. I could never bring myself to believe the attentions of men, whether the kind sought at Le Moulin or the Webster, capable of defining a woman too much one way or the other. I had seen many prostitutes leading happier, freer lives than Papa's first wife, for instance. Even Jane was consumed by her respectable marriage.

She did not visit me when she was pregnant, which I understood; her body, unlike the rest of her, had always been frail, and taking the long carriage journey to London and back was not a risk I could ask her to take again. I missed her, but her pregnancy let me forgive her. I couldn't help but think that even if she were not pregnant, though, she might not visit as often as she claimed she would; her husband, as she often said, required all of her attention.

I knew Papa liked it that way, and what I truly couldn't stand—what truly kept me from visiting Ferndean whenever I could help it—was the wholly adoring way Jane looked at him, as if her heart lived in his body. And the way his gaze would slide to me, as if awaiting the same attention.

No. Much better to stay at the Webster, under the gray and sooty London skies, than to endure the sylvan shades of Ferndean and the love between Papa and Jane that crowded out anything but the thought of itself.

Besides, I grew to love London. That very soot reminded me of the smoke-belching ship we'd sailed on during our crossing and made me feel as if I might be borne on the same air again back home one day. I felt closer to France in the city than I ever did in the country.

We took constitutionals every day, either in the morning before classes began or after lunch, depending on when the perpetual London rain seemed most likely to lift. Our capes and bonnets were soaked as often as not, but Mrs. Webster was stringent in regard to exercise. On truly miserable days we marched up and down the stairs of the school itself, chattering to each other or singing in the round until the stairwells echoed. We had dance classes too, for exercise as well as to prepare us for our entrance into society. I had always been good at dancing, and since I knew many of the dance steps already and was taller than most of my fellow students, Madame Green usually had me act the man and lead a less proficient dancer about the floor. I found I liked that very well indeed, especially when Hannah was my partner, and I could whisper something mildly scandalous that would make her blush in my arms.

When the weather permitted, we went on Saturday excursions to the country, for long walks and for sightseeing. It was important to Mrs. Webster that we see what she called "the extant rural way of life. For," she said, leading us down a bucolic country drive one late-autumn Saturday, "as factories draw the common people ever closer to our cities' beating hearts, there may indeed soon be no one left in the country but the aristocracy and the landed gentry— among whom you girls, once married, may well count yourselves, if you do not already—and what servants they can pry away from London to join them. You may well find yourselves the managers, not only of your husbands' estates, but of all the countryside itself, the very heart of England."

"She makes it sound like we're to get seats in Parliament when we leave school, or officers' commissions," Felicity murmured to Charlotte, who laughed.

"Well, I might as well be," she replied. "My parents plan for me to wed Colonel Bailey when I turn eighteen, and he's told me already his wife must be as staunch a patriot as himself. That's one of the reasons my parents chose this school. I must learn enough to hold the colonel's interest and support his views, whenever I see him or write to him, so that he does not forget me. He's only thirty-eight and handsome; I know I'm lucky."

I felt my mother's heart flinch inside me, but the other girls around us were nodding, speaking up to share stories of the men they planned to wed—or that their parents had planned for them. None of us were out yet, meaning that we had not been formally presented to English society as eligible for marriage. Yet more than half the girls were already spoken for—most by men as old as Papa or older still.

Maman and the Moulin girls had made their living on old men. I knew that much. I knew plenty about the world, and the men it contained, that would shock my innocent schoolmates. I had fancied myself the worldly-wise one of this group.

But they were all so . . . resigned . . . to spending their whole lives tethered to the kind of old men whose company Maman and her friends would not tolerate for a moment after sunrise.

My sorrow grew slow and heavy inside me, as I listened to them speak of their unloved intendeds; I felt as if I stood before their tombstones while they still lived. Like my sleeping classmates at Ashfield, they did not know what crept in the darkness around their maidenly beds. I felt a premonition, as Juliet did in her story, that they were married to their graves.

I think it was then, walking through the sun-speckled country-side with my friends, that I knew in my heart I would do murder if I needed to in order to protect them.

The night after that walk, I could not bear to join the "shadow cabinet," as Felicity had begun calling the after-bedtime gatherings on her and Charlotte's beds. Instead I stayed in my own narrow berth, lying stiffly on my side and watching Hannah lie stiffly on hers. I couldn't make out any individual words from the murmurs on the other side of the room, and I was glad. Something about their quiet laughter, the freedom of all of them piled in bed together, made me sick; it was like they were already ghosts, the fond memories of the married women they'd soon be, lying awake in beds they shared not with each other but with husbands, old or cold or cruel.

Every married woman was a ruined garden. Wasn't that what my mother had said?

I remembered Bertha again, shut up in her husband's attic until she died from it, until her own endless, inward turning loneliness turned to fire and burned her up.

In that moment I felt sure that all of us would burn.

Hannah turned over in bed and looked at me. Her wide eyes shone even in the darkness.

"I can't bear it either," she whispered.

"What?"

It was the first time she'd given any indication that she did not fall immediately to sleep when the dormitory lights were doused.

"They talk of their husbands-to-be, and I know the least I owe my family is to find a match like theirs; that's why I'm here, working near to the bone just to help pay my way, and my parents and brother at home doing the same. Do you know I weighed two stone more when I first came here?" She gave a hard little laugh. "Can't afford to buy new clothes, and I don't have time to take in the ones I have. Our fine embroidery classes don't teach a straight seam.

And they talk of their future safety and wealth as if it's assured because it is, because it will be assured even if they never marry, if they're old maids. Adèle, I have to marry for my family's sake as well as my own, and I'll never get the chance if I must compete with them."

It was the longest speech I'd ever heard her make.

She gave a sudden shuddering breath and buried her head in her pillow, her thin braids whipping around her head.

I slipped out of my bed and rushed onto hers. I wrapped my arms around her over her counterpane.

I felt her skinny limbs flinch, and then she turned and hugged me back.

Not thinking—of anything—I pressed my lips to her cheek. Her skin was so warm that I suddenly could not bear to move.

"Oh, Hannah," I whispered, and heard my voice shake.

She pulled away.

She gazed at me in the moonlight, and there was something in her face that made me let her go at once. I felt sure it was horror, disgust, that she'd seen into my heart and known I longed for her, and had been repelled.

Writing this, through the lens of years, I wonder if that was true . . .

It doesn't matter now, and it didn't then. Whatever she'd seen or recognized in me, if she didn't want it too, it was no good at all.

"I'm frightened all the time," she said quietly. "I'm so frightened I won't make the match my family deserves. My father gambled away more than we had before his death, and my mother needs shelter and food, and so I need a rich husband. But I'm not charming or pretty enough, and heaven knows I work so hard here I'm too tired to even hold a good conversation." She paused for a moment. "You—you seem to like me, Adèle, to care for me."

I nodded slowly. I did not trust myself to speak just then, for fear I'd tell her how much I really cared.

"You're beautiful and clever," she went on, "and you made friends here so easily. You seem to understand men too, more than any other girl here. You will . . . help me, won't you? Please?"

I bit the insides of my lips that longed to kiss her again. I twirled Maman's poison ring on my finger.

"Of course I will help you, Hannah." I made myself smile. "I learned how women catch men before I learned to walk."

I felt her exhale, her ribs moving under the counterpane, her breath against my skin. "Thank you, Adèle."

I kept smiling, not sure if she could see me but hoping she would hear it in my voice. "First thing is getting our beauty sleep." I climbed out of bed, then tucked the covers snug around her. "You just drift off into sweet dreams, now, and worry no more about it."

She closed her eyes. Her fingers poked out and touched the yellow stitched heart on her patched, worn counterpane.

I climbed into my own cold bed.

Dear Adèle,

Imagine young Eric Fairfax's surprise when the pirate queen removed her feathered hat and dashing military coat and transformed before his eyes into the fair maid Adèle Varens, a young lady attending the Webster School in London. She seemed chagrined to appear, now, only as herself, but he wished he could find some way to assure her that he found her voice and company as fascinating as ever, and that he was sure her adventures in London would be as intriguing as those on the high seas . . .

Adèle, this story crumbles in my hands, and I will let it go. I mean only to say that I don't mind if we write about pirates or schools or any other subject on God's earth, so long as I may be permitted to keep reading your letters and to send you mine. You have become one of my closest friends without my ever seeing your face (though I have often imagined it) and I think that is the purest kind of kinship two people can have: it is our souls that have met through our letters, Adèle, and mine has grown to care for yours very much, if you will permit my saying so.

At your request I have determined to speak with my father about attending Oxford; he is a strict man with his own ideas about how to prepare me for running the plantation when the time comes, but I will do what I can to persuade him. I confess I wish to be close to you in person someday, not just in spirit.

So tell me only of your own life, if you wish, dear soul. I ask merely that you do so soon.

Your servant,
Eric

P.S. I have included a small gift here; I know your birthday is the second of November. It's a locket portrait. I humbly ask, even though

I suppose it negates the purpose of a gift, that you send one in return. I should like well not to have to imagine your face anymore, and I hope my own is not too sharp a disappointment.

It was quite the opposite. I was reading the letter at breakfast, when all the girls received their mail, and hardly had a moment to open the flat silver locket and look at the dark-haired youth inside before Felicity, to my left, snatched it and gasped.

"Oh my, who's this handsome gentleman?" she cried, and then of course everyone at the table had to see. Even Catherine Essex took a moment to lift her head from her poetry book to admire the face inside the locket. She was a romantic, of course—every Webster girl was but me, it sometimes seemed. The locket was passed around the whole room before I finally got it back—from Hannah, who smiled at me as she handed it over.

It was true that the likeness was handsome, if you could call a two-inch portrait such. Curly dark hair, the tanned skin one would expect in the tropics, a strong and stubborn chin. Black eyes that seemed to burn. His clothing seemed somehow old-fashioned, the way he'd tied his cravat not the way English dandies did this year, but I supposed it could be one of many things done differently in Jamaica.

His face stirred something in me. I was not alone in that opinion, as the giggles and whispers at the table told. But it was not just because he was handsome; I felt repelled as well as drawn to the person in the little painting. It took me a moment to realize that it was because in his countenance I could see the family resemblance to his Uncle Edward.

I pushed away the thought; after all, Papa was not handsome, as he often said himself. They could not look that much alike. Indeed the more I looked at the miniature, the more I convinced myself the resemblance was only something I'd imagined.

I put the locket on a pale pink ribbon from my embroidery class basket and wore it around my neck, first over my dress and then, when the girls began to tease me, under my shift, against my skin. It made me happy to think of my longtime correspondent next to my heart.

I loved him, by then, dearly; his written voice had long been a balm to my soul, and his affection a hope for my future.

I tried to forget I'd ever wished I had not seen his face.

ELEVEN

WHEN JANE WROTE to me asking if I might obtain an invitation to the home of one of my school friends for the Christmas holidays, my stomach twisted with something like betrayal. God knew I had no strong desire to return to Ferndean, but I had missed my old governess, the closest person to a mother I'd had in years. I had believed that she missed me too. I didn't blame her for not visiting me while she was pregnant—or at least, I called myself selfish when I did—but I thought that at least she'd been looking forward to seeing me.

All is well with my health at this point, thank goodness—I knew from a previous letter that she had been nearly continuously ill for two months—*but Papa and I are both, in our ways, in fragile conditions, and he continues to demand all the attention I can spare. I was so pleased when you wrote to us about the many friends you've made at the Webster, and I know from my own less happy student days how many girls stay at school at Christmastide. Papa and I have no doubt you'll enjoy yourself far more with your new friends than you would in our nest at Ferndean.*

I moved my thumbs over the letter's smooth paper, sucking in a deep breath slowly and then letting it out. I was in the Webster's green sitting room, where several of the other girls had retired after teatime to read mail or visit with relatives. In the gentle murmur of conversation, I hoped no one could hear my unsteady breathing.

I didn't want to go to Ferndean for Christmas. It wasn't my home; it never had been.

It just hurt to know the only living woman I loved didn't want me there.

I stood, suddenly feeling too warm in the cozy room with its soft seats and large fireplace. My winter petticoats swung heavy against my legs. I quickly stood and walked out, past the curving wooden staircase, past Mrs. Webster's office, out the front door, and down the gray stone stairs onto the London street.

The first snow had fallen a day before, and it had been reduced to a few icy brown smears on the street now; the clouds in the sky looked dark and sick with smoke, and the city air hardly smelled sweet. Still there was something in it that I needed, that was better, if not fresher, than the stifling air inside. I stood in the cold, taking deep breaths as if I could clean out my throat, my lungs, and make them new. I looked at the letter in my hands, and in a sudden impulse that I knew was melodramatic even then, I tore it up and ground the pieces into the slush under my feet. I watched the ink bleed and fade into the dirty, cold water until the paper dissolved.

When I looked up, someone was watching me. I knew it with the sense, long unused but not forgotten, that every child of Le Moulin had gained, an ability to feel another's gaze like a soft graze along the skin. It was a survival tool back then, and it still was, I supposed.

So I looked for the looker more quickly than most people would, and I got a glimpse of a face wreathed in curly hair, a brown skirt and shawl as whoever it was vanished around the town house across the street. If I hadn't had my Moulin instincts, I wouldn't have seen her at all.

A dark-haired girl about my age, short and stocky, wrapped in a dark shawl; her skin tinged golden, even in winter; and her round face starred all over with freckles as she looked back at me—and then she vanished.

Only a flash, and she was gone, but the ghost of her, dark-golden, round, stayed in my mind's eye longer than it had a right to do. A flicker of warmth, her face, her gaze, on that cold day.

I don't know why it was enough, that small moment, to make me decide I wouldn't let Jane break my heart.

I went back inside and asked Felicity if I could go to her family's estate with her for Christmas.

Allen Manor glowed all yuletide long with the light of what seemed like, what might have been, ten thousand candles, fine white tallow candles that barely flickered, gleaming on fine damask and oak furniture and faded Turkish rugs and the intricate white moldings that curled in the corners of every room like marzipan. One's overall impression of the house was of great pale sweetmeat.

And when I think back on the holiday I spent there with Felicity and her family, I remind myself of all that light, that sweetness—the taste of sugarplums and puddings and rosy-centered roasts with mint jelly, taking tea in the little glass-walled orangery, warm even in the dead of winter, looking out at the wintry landscape around us.

Those are the things I choose to think of, you see. These memories of Allen Hall glow like little gems, perhaps because I have polished them. I chose what I looked at, what I focused on, while I was there, and I choose what I remember too.

If you knew what I've left out, you may despise me for it—but perhaps not. There are stories no one has a right to hear. Can I tell you I have secrets and still ask you, reader, to trust me?

I will not share these words with anyone else for a long time. Not until those for whom I care most deeply are safely beyond hurting. Are dead. And still, I think, there are stories I will never have the right to tell.

I will tell you what I can.

While there was not much snow that Christmas, the estate grounds we saw from the orangery were faded to a wintry beige. The dark splotch of an occasional evergreen stuck out like a bruise. There are those who could find beauty in that landscape, I suppose, but it reminded me too much of the moors at Thornfield. I'd once believed I'd loved their barren starkness, but with time, and with another, sweeter home at the Webster, I thought that must have been only because I had nothing else to love.

I tried to look only at the forced orange trees and to pretend that they would grow here on their own.

We spent a lot of time in the orangery. I suppose that was because of Felicity's family.

When we arrived at Allen Manor in one of their carriages, Felicity and I were both exhausted. It had been a long day's journey from London, and we both kept drifting to sleep and then being jostled awake every time the wheels hit an uneven bit of road, and the roads became less even the farther we went from London. When we stepped out at last, limbs stiff, eyelids heavy, the frosted-cake look of the big pale house pleased me, and I turned smiling toward my friend—only to find her glancing warily from one window to the next, her lips pulled into her mouth in a tight line, as if she was looking for something she did not want to see. I wanted to ask her if she was well, but her expression was so different from what I had expected that it momentarily stopped my tongue.

In that brief time several footmen appeared around the carriage, as if conjured there, to take our bags, and a thin woman with graying red hair, clearly a senior housekeeper by her dress, opened the door and invited us to come inside.

"If I may say, Miss Felicity, it is so wonderful to have you back," she said, smiling. "The household is so quiet with only your mother in it, what with your father still in town and your brothers at school."

Felicity's mouth relaxed, and she returned the housekeeper's smile warmly. "Thank you, Mrs. Fahy," she said. "I am glad to see you too."

We followed Mrs. Fahy through the tall doorway.

The grand sweep of the hall that we entered drew my eye immediately up the walls, which were hung with fine old tapestries and family portraits, up and up to the ceiling. What I saw there took a moment to understand: a huge fresco, a painting of two figures in a background half dark, half light. The ceiling on the right side of the room was painted with a profusion of flowers, a whole field blooming like a hothouse, while on the left the ceiling was painted with stranger shapes, dark and craggy, deepening almost to pure black at its far corner.

And the two figures: one was a young girl of about my own and Felicity's age. The other was a man. The man, dressed in dark Grecian robes, grasped at the girl's legs and pale garments with a grip that tore through them to the flesh of her thigh; the artist had rendered deep shadows where his fingers dug into her flank. The man's face was half snarl, half laughter, the girl's mouth and eyes open wide, her empty hands reaching for the blooming landscape from which he had pulled her. Far off in the painting's background, at the edge of the field, near the corner of the ceiling, was another female figure, her hands, her mouth, open and empty and frightened.

We had studied classical mythology at school that term, and it was a scene I recognized at once. The rape of Persephone.

I felt a nauseous chill run from my belly up through my throat to my forehead, and for a moment I thought I might vomit. I searched for something else to focus on, quickly, before the painting made me feel sick enough that anyone would notice.

I steadied myself by retelling the story. What had I learned in class? There was Persephone, the goddess of spring, and the man was Hades, god of the dead. In the girls'-school version we read, he saw her picking wildflowers one day and *captured* her, bringing her back to his home in Hell, where she was forced to remain after she ate six pomegranate seeds. That word, *captured,* was all we ever read, but the paintings we'd studied all called the encounter rape. Our teachers never elaborated on the meaning of that word, but I, at least, understood it, and I couldn't imagine that none of the other girls did. That woman in the corner of the painting was Demeter, Persephone's mother, the goddess of harvest; after Hades dragged her daughter to Hell, she mourned so fiercely that the earth plunged into perpetual winter. When he saw that the people were starving and freezing to death, Zeus, god of the sky, struck a bargain between Hades and Demeter: because Persephone had only eaten six seeds, she would remain with her captor for six months of the year and with her mother for the other six. Zeus sliced her in half, as Solomon had offered to cleave apart the baby claimed by two mothers.

But in the version I told myself, staring at the horrible fresco, Persephone gathered up the flowing excess of Hades's rich robes in her empty hands, looped them around his neck, and strangled him. She seized his horses' reins and drove his carriage up out of the gaping ground, back to the field of spring flowers that had been her home. And when her mother would have kept her there, Persephone refused, and she rode Hades's carriage up into the sky itself, to tell Zeus he had no more right than her mother or Hades to determine the course of her life.

It was pure fantasy, of course. But so was the version we'd learned in school. Looking up at that fresco, in that moment, I began to despise, with all my being, the fantasies of men.

My reimagining of Persephone's fate, the little story I told to keep myself from feeling sick, took all of two heartbeats to do its work; only Felicity, I think, had noticed that I faltered at all. Mrs. Fahy did not even turn around.

I held the image of Persephone ascending to Heaven in Hades's chariot to confront Zeus in my mind, and I was able to meet Felicity's gaze unwavering.

"I never look at it," she told me later, when Mrs. Fahy had installed me in one of the hall's guest rooms and Felicity and I were drinking tea and eating little ginger biscuits in front of the fireplace in her own chambers. "Honestly, I hadn't thought about it in years before I saw you looking up."

"I can't imagine forgetting it," I said. Worse than that was knowing the rape of a young girl was the image, the idea, that someone in her family had wanted to impress upon every guest who walked through the hall's front doors—but I could not quite say so to her, for all the late-night whispers we had shared.

Felicity shrugged. "You can forget almost anything, if you live with it long enough," she said. "It becomes just . . . part of the everyday world around you, and then it . . . fades away. And then it's gone." She was looking into her teacup, where the dark liquid reflected firelight. Her voice had gone low, and I remembered suddenly the way she had relaxed when Mrs. Fahy said her brothers and her father were away.

"I know."

Felicity's mother was a vision of her daughter in eighteen years' time: a touch taller and broader, but with the same strong nose and chin, the same startlingly pale hair. She made little conversation but watched her daughter with a quiet adoration glowing in her eyes; it made me like her right away, and envy my friend, and despise myself a little for that envy.

We ate dinner with her, those first days before Felicity's father and brothers returned, in the library; housemaids brought us little individual folding tables and we sat in the comfortable chairs by the fire, the tall, dark bookshelves looming benevolently behind us. We ate cold meats and jellies and cheeses with bread and fruit; Felicity's mother said she didn't like to bother the servants about hot meals in the dining room when the lord of the manor wasn't home, but I didn't miss the formality at all. The night of our arrival, Felicity and her mother had reunited while I changed out of my traveling clothes and bathed; they were both waiting for me when Mrs. Fahy ushered me in.

I couldn't help glancing up at the ceiling, as I'd done in every room of the manor since the grotesque revelation of the entrance hall; my bedroom ceiling was plain enough, and if there was anything painted above us in the library, it was too hidden in shadow to make out. So I turned my attention instead to the mother and daughter by the fireplace—I think I shall always picture Felicity and her mother standing close to a fire—and I smiled and joined them.

Lady Allen asked me a few polite questions in her soft voice, if I liked school, who our other friends were, if they were kind to me and to her daughter. Her care was genuine, but I could nearly see her counting out the number of questions she thought it correct to ask me. Then, to my surprise, she picked up a book that I hadn't noticed resting on the arm of her chair, splayed open to save her page.

"Mother and I like to read during meals," Felicity told me. "It's something we've always done—since she taught me to read, at least."

Now that I thought of it, I remembered Felicity reading at supper more frequently than the other girls did, but since most of us needed extra time to study now and then, I hadn't thought much of it. "It sounds delightful," I said sincerely. "I wish I'd brought my book down with me."

She and her mother laughed the same laugh, low and gentle. "This is the library, you goose," Felicity said. She waved me toward the closest shelf, which I was pleased to find contained mostly poetry. I selected a volume by Sappho. We spent a warm, silent, and perfectly happy meal together, the Allens, the poetess, and I, and I relished the taste of oranges and verse on my tongue.

The first days at Allen Manor passed in that atmosphere of cozy gentleness. I started to think I'd never want to leave. We spent our days talking together, gossiping harmlessly about the other Webster girls. Having been there longer than I, Felicity knew more about them, their families, their prospects—and she knew more about the society men who courted them at the school-sponsored teas and dances. It was through Felicity that I learned so much about the etiquette of courtship, things I'd never have otherwise known: a subtle language of fans and flowers and sidelong glances that was so different from what I'd seen my mother—or indeed my father—ever do. Felicity spoke little of her own experience with those men; she told me briefly about the admiration she'd felt for a young officer named Farrow, but just before my own arrival at school, her opinion of him had fallen. Now she held the unwavering attention of a much older man named Lord Winton, for whom she felt nothing, she said, but who was wealthy and powerful enough to be worth marrying and old and frail enough to be safe. Looking back, I should have asked her more about both men, but we had our tacit agreement about the importance of leaving certain painful things unspoken. We took such easy pleasure in each other's conversation that I barely noticed when she steered our focus away from herself and toward our classmates again. The whole first week with her seems like one long, sweet day in my memory, full of talk and laughter, quiet reading with her mother in the evenings, the scents of orange trees, and snow.

Then her father came home.

Lord Allen wasn't a large man—he was barely taller than I was— and his long face and wan coloring gave no impression of strength. When I saw him, I realized I'd been picturing him like Hades in the fresco, and I had to cover my mouth so he wouldn't see me trying not to laugh. His pale blue gaze snapped toward me as I did so though, and the emotions that chased each other through his expression—self-consciousness, annoyance, disdain, anger—were forceful enough that suddenly I didn't want to laugh at all.

"Felicity, my dear." He held out his hands, still gloved in leather from his travels, and his daughter took them.

"Merry Christmas, Father," she said. "It's good to see you." She told the lie easily and well, but I who had heard her tell the frivolous schoolgirl lies we all told to our teachers now and then knew it for what it was. I watched my friend carefully as she held her father's hands, and I saw some part of her . . . retreat, inside herself, far into some inner country, away from the fingers her father grasped in his. I saw some little part of her—some unnameable aspect of the friend I cared for—vanish, like a ghost.

Her mother had not come out of the library to greet her husband.

Felicity was only most of herself for the whole rest of our visit; that little, untraceable part of her was gone. I didn't ask about it; I knew why she had pulled that part of herself inside. She was keeping it safe. She was surviving.

We ate all our meals at the long, white table in the formal dining room after that, Felicity's father at one end and her mother at the other. No book in sight. Felicity told me her father always locked the library over the holidays, so that they could focus on the festivities at hand instead of polluting their brains with too much reading.

There were more fires lit in more rooms when her father was home, but it felt as if there were fewer people in them.

Felicity and I spent our days with her mother, in her little sitting room, reading the books she'd hidden there long ago, for the times when the library was locked; none of us spoke much, but we passed many a pleasant hour. Or we wandered the estate together, Felicity and I, or spent hours on end, as I have said, in the orangery.

It was a beautiful place. It was a prison.

It was only during our journey back to school that Felicity told me she had started sleeping outside her mother's bedroom when she was eight.

"On the nights when he had friends over and they were drinking," she said. "Only then. I'd heard them too many times—him and Mother." She spoke so quietly that I could barely hear her over the rumble of the carriage wheels. "One night I decided I couldn't let him keep . . . so I stood outside the door, and when he came upstairs into the hall and started to move toward her door, I just . . ."—she took a deep breath—"watched him. Stared at him. He told me to go to bed. I said I'd had bad dreams. He told me to find my nurse. I said I wanted to be near my mother. He wasn't quite . . . He left us alone."

I was filled with a reverence, looking at her, that I imagine is how the faithful feel when looking at their idols, their crucifixes and icons. Their saints. "How often did you do that?"

Felicity gave a little shrug and waved one of her hands, as if it didn't matter. "Often enough that I don't remember how often." She blinked; two tears slid quickly down her cheeks and into the lace of her high neckline, absorbed at once. Her hand was still raised, as if she was going to wave it again.

I touched it, as gently as I could, and her fingers twined themselves with mine. "You're a heroine, Felicity," I said.

She flinched. "I hate that I'm not there to do it now. To guard her door. But she wants me to go to school, to . . . She wants me to be taken care of." She swallowed. I knew we were both thinking of what it meant to her father, to take care of her mother.

I thought of the fresco in the entryway, Persephone and Hades, the empty hands, the screaming. I think I'd pictured Felicity in Persephone's place when I had seen that horrible painting, more so when I had met her parents and felt the horrid secrets in that house long before I'd heard them spoken.

But Felicity was not the helpless maiden nor the grieving goddess. What I thought of at that moment was Cerberus, the three-headed guard dog of Hell. And when I imagined my friend at eight years old, staring down her drunken father, I could feel her fierce protectiveness, the strength of her refusal—and I could see the beastly gleam in her child's eyes.

I spent the Easter holidays that year with Charlotte, and the two-week summer holidays with Catherine Essex, who was sweet beneath her solitude and whose unexpected invitation made me suspect she knew as much about loneliness as I did. We didn't speak much during the time I spent in her cavernous and quiet home because that seemed to be what she desired, but the companionable hours we spent reading in her gardens are memories I will always cherish.

I still felt a selfish bitterness hard in the pit of my stomach whenever I wrote to Jane, telling her of yet another friend who had invited me to her home, and received replies that were tinged invariably with relief. In response, my letters grew both briefer and more emphatic about my own popularity, a sentiment that I believe Mrs. Webster echoed in her reports about me.

And the other girls—not a single one of them had a home devoid of darkness, of some secret pain. I'd mourned my school-mates' futures already, had done so ever since that day in the sunny countryside. I didn't tell any of my Webster friends about my past at Le Moulin; I was sure it would frighten them, make them think less of me, although looking back perhaps it was I who thought less of them for making that assumption. But in their family homes, I began to mourn their pasts too. I mourned the lives they'd never had, the freedom they had never tasted. I met too many raging or drunken or leering fathers, too many mothers sunk so far into melancholia and submission as to be walking ghosts, too many bullying or sneaking siblings, too many family secrets too horrible to speak out loud, but only to be whispered, or gestured toward, or communicated in strange, sideways rumors. I met, in short, too many haunted houses, and I began to think the childhoods of my new friends, as privileged as they had been, were graveyards too. The secret of my urchin past, my dancing, painted mother and her friends, began to glow in memory like a gem. I do not know when I began believing that the air in France was always warm and bright or to expect every day in England that it would rain; I only know I still believe it now.

But haunted as my friends' houses were, I still preferred them to Ferndean.

So it was that I spent my first year at the Webster without ever going back to the place that should have been home; so it was that so quickly school, punctuated by brief sojourns with my friends, became my home instead. When Jane wrote to me about the birth of her son, her and Papa's son, enclosing in her brief and jubilant note (*you would forgive my brevity, Adèle, if you knew the strange elations and exhaustions, the soaring and the suffering in the heart of a new mother!*) a deft sketch of her baby's sleeping face, I felt more pushed away from her, from so-called home, than ever.

For as selfish and as foolish as it is, I wrote to Eric in my next letter, *I had hoped that Jane did not quite think of herself as a new mother. To see it expressed so clearly and thoughtlessly in her writing wounded me more deeply than I could have guessed it would.*

Perhaps I am wounding her in return by staying away. Part of me hates the thought of that. I do love her, Eric, as I hope has been evident in the way I've written about her to you before. She is the closest thing to a mother I have known since my own died.

But part of me is cruel enough to want to wound her. To want to know that she misses my presence, for right now, from both her letters' content and their infrequency, it truly does not seem that is the case.

All the Webster girls were invited to a coming-out ball that winter. It was sponsored by one Lady Shadley, a hostess whose parties were a legend at the school, in the society papers, and throughout London at large. She also happened to be Charlotte's aunt. It was a great honor to be invited to one of Lady Shadley's parties, even more so to make one's debut as a marriageable young lady there, and it was the first real opportunity for us to practice all the skills and charms we'd been learning in our classes, as Mrs. Webster frequently reminded us. And no one needed to say, it was our first chance to court the kinds of men who could provide the lives that we were being groomed to lead—at least, the first chance to court them openly.

When Charlotte returned from tea with her aunt a month before the ball, the girls crowded around her in the sitting room, eager to hear every detail of the preparations. As the girls plunged into excited talking, I watched Hannah stand silently by the door in her apron, waiting to help clear the tea service. Her cheeks were pale, but her eyes were very bright; in fact they were wet.

I chewed the inside of my lip. I knew she needed a gown, and she was too proud to ask to borrow one from her wealthy classmates. Besides, secondhand dress would mark her as plainly as a signpost.

But I was to have a fine new dress. Jane had already placed the order with a London seamstress, and I had only to visit the lady's shop to have my measurements taken. Who would ever know if I sent Hannah in my place and borrowed a secondhand gown from Felicity or Charlotte? I could not imagine meeting anyone I wanted to impress at this ball; for though I had been sent to the Webster for the same purposes as the other girls, I felt only a claustrophobia verging on horror at the prospect of marriage to a wealthy Englishman.

Besides, I had been raised by showgirls, hadn't I? I knew how to make an old, threadbare costume seem new again, or a cheap fabric look expensive. Altering a simple evening dress to look like those currently in fashion would be the work of a few hours; I was no expert seamstress, but I could do enough to keep myself from standing out.

And I had promised to help my friend. Even if it meant sending her into the arms of a rich man and away from me forever, that was what I was going to do.

It was only what my mother had done for me.

I walked quietly over to Hannah, nestling myself between the doorway and one of the oak bookshelves that lined the wall. "I have an idea," I told her, "and I think you're going to like it."

So I played the mother's ghost to Hannah's Cendrillon—her Cinderella, as they said in England. And Hannah went with us to the coming-out ball, with more to gain or lose than any other girl.

I only wish I'd known what was truly at stake.

I received a letter from Eric just a day before the ball. Hannah brought our mail up to the dormitory, where many of us had gone following our afternoon classes to air out our own gowns and admire one another's. The long room turned into a diaphanous tunnel of lace and silk, delicate skirts flicking and shimmering in the air like mirages as the girls rushed back and forth to look at each other's finery.

"Two for you today, Adèle," she said, smiling, and she handed me a large box tied with twine and an envelope addressed in the handwriting I'd come to know so well.

I took them both hungrily, but though I was eager to read Eric's letter, I opened the box first. Inside was something soft, wrapped in delicate white paper that rustled as I pulled it out.

"Not so, Hannah," I told her. "This one is for you."

Hannah's ball gown, paid for by Papa via Jane, made to my friend's measurements instead of mine. The fabric was so fine it nearly floated between my hands, the color a soft pink that I knew would echo and intensify the rosy glow I'd so often admired on her cheeks.

When I looked up at my friend's face, that glow was already there. I held the dress out to her and she stroked it lightly, the calluses on her hands catching a little on the silk.

"There are gloves to match, and slippers, in the box," I told her. "Try them on; if there's any trouble with the fit, we must know today, so we can order replacements if need be."

"Adèle—"

I shook my head. "Go air it with the others," I said. I didn't want to hear her thank me. "I'm going to read my letter."

Hannah cradled the dress in her arms like an infant as she walked shyly toward the group of girls at the far end of the room, near the gable window. I heard a little gasp of pleasure, and as I opened Eric's envelope, I looked up and saw Felicity spring at Hannah and her dress. "That color!" she cooed. "Oh, it's perfect for you, Hannah." And Hannah, blushing more than ever, managed to smile and say, "Thank you, Felicity," with only a trace of shyness in her voice.

I think it was in that moment that I realized I loved both of them. With a heart full of love, I settled down onto my bed to read my letter.

Eric wrote first of his new tutor, whom he found too strict, and of the distant relations who were visiting his father and who had brought a colicky baby that kept the whole house awake at night. I wondered if Jane's baby had colic, and I felt not a little pang that I didn't know. I had been so hurt by her rejection that I hadn't wanted to hear anything about the child that had seemed so thoroughly to have stolen any place I had in my stepmother's heart.

But Eric, with his usual insight, addressed the worries about my bond with Jane that I had described in my last letter:

I cannot imagine that Mrs. Rochester, whatever the nature of your relationship in her eyes, does not miss you. I miss you without having met you. Sometimes it feels like a fiction that we have never been in the same room, the same house, the same country—more of a fiction than our pirate tales, indeed. My mind has met yours— dare I say more than my mind—in these pages.

I cannot imagine a soul in all the world who would not miss a girl like you.

TWELVE

THE BALL was a lush assault.

Every one of us had dreamed of that night, of course—even I, who cherished no sweet illusions about finding either romance or security in such a place, had looked forward to it, to dressing up and looking beautiful, to seeing and being seen. I'd had glimpses of this kind of London society through my visits to my friends' homes, but this would be no peeping through a keyhole; tonight we would be, all of us, in the thick of it, true players in the game.

And when we approached Lady Shadley's towering home for the first time, it was as if the dream place all the girls had made of it (and even I had dreamed of) were shimmering only halfway into reality, the dark outer walls of the building and the cobblestones of King Street faintly luminous in the streetlamp light, the tall glass windows on the top floor glowing golden from within like a painting of heaven. Here was luxury, here was decadence, and I could see in the reflecting light on each girl's face that she felt that hope of heaven, of never knowing want, if only she met the right man inside those walls.

I walked in arm in arm with Felicity on my left and Hannah on my right. I could feel each of them trembling a little bit, Felicity with excitement and Hannah with trepidation. I offered each of them a little squeeze of my hand and a smile, and the two sweet smiles they gave me in return . . . each was so different, yet both seemed to feed my soul.

I took a deep breath and looked around the room; there was enough luxury to overwhelm my senses five times over. I could smell sweetmeats and champagne and candle smoke, coating the air with something heavy and sticky. The white marble floor gleamed like ice, but scores of candles turned the room bright and the throng of dancing, laughing, chattering bodies made the ball feel as close and hot as the tropics that Eric described in his letters.

I felt a brief longing for him to be here with me, the boy I'd never met. I had a frustratingly romantic notion that I'd like to dance with him.

But then I felt Hannah squeeze my arm. I crushed my thoughts of anyone or anything but her. I was determined that Hannah should have her chance tonight, or if nothing else, that she should simply have the good time she so often was denied.

On my other side Felicity gritted her teeth, grasped her skirts, and swept off elegantly in the direction of an elderly man who I assumed had to be Lord Winton. The other Webster girls dispersed out through the room in their pale, pretty dresses; most of them tried their best to seem as if they didn't mean to wander close to the gentlemen who'd caught their eyes, although Catherine Essex walked straight to a fainting couch at the edge of the room and opened a book she'd brought with her. Mrs. Webster frowned and headed in her direction. Charlotte, a beauty as well as our wealthy hostess's niece, already had a few young men swarming around her like moths around a lamp, but as we walked out of the fern-shaded entryway and into the full light of the ballroom, they eyed me and swarmed in my direction instead.

Suddenly they seemed less like moths than wasps.

Yet this was what I'd trained for long before I had any other schooling, what I'd watched Maman and her girls do every night of their lives, for every night of mine until I left for England and another life.

Thinking of Le Moulin made the ball seem less overwhelming; it too had been a hot and heavy-scented place, where dancing was a kind of facade, an advertisement for other transactions men and women could make. I had better training for this than any other girl there. I just had to remember it, and then use my own charms to show off Hannah's to her best advantage—something the Moulin girls often did for each other when one of them was having a slow night.

I smiled and tilted my head close to hers, murmuring to her in a quiet, intimate voice that no one else could overhear. "How are you feeling?"

"Only slightly terrified."

I put my arm around her. "It's all right. You'll be fine. And you look beautiful."

She shook her head, ringlets dancing around her slim neck and shoulders, which were suddenly splashed with pink like a rising

127

tide of petals as she blushed. Her gown was petal-colored too, pale pink and deeper rose, the wide neckline showing off her shoulders. It did not dip as low in front as most of the girls' did—as mine did—in the current fashion, for Hannah was more conscientiously modest than any of us, but the seamstress had added delicate lace ruffles to the upper part of the gown's bodice, to its puffed sleeves, and to its hem. She wore white and pale pink flowers in her hair too—I'd bought them from one of London's seemingly infinite supply of young flower sellers that morning and done her hair myself (and then helped three other girls with theirs, even though their hair had already been curled by hired lady's maids—another Moulin skill that never left me). The blossoms made her light brown curls seem darker and made you notice the darkness of her brows and lashes against her blushing skin too.

She blushed more, I thought, than anyone I'd ever known; even Jane's transparent skin had not reddened like that. I allowed myself to wonder how much of her body blushed and how one might chase or waken that pinkness by stroking a finger along her clear, responsive skin.

She hardly needed to do any showing off—I was sure there would be many men in that room whose thoughts would follow the same lines as my own as soon as they saw her.

"You look lovely too, Adèle," she said softly, and while my own cheek stayed cool, I felt a heat like the blush on her skin slide down my belly. How I wanted, wanted—not her, but to give her . . . something.

I could make her blush, but I could not give her the gifts I wished to give; I knew that much from the kiss that she'd refused, all the other little moments when she'd turned her body away from mine. Anyone could read those signs as *no*. I knew that to care for someone was to try to give them what they wanted, not what you wished you could give. So I was giving her the help that she'd asked for, that she needed tonight, and nothing else. I reminded myself, my body, of that quite sternly.

I pulled her gently close and put my arm around the smallest part of her waist; she would look slim and dainty next to me, tall and buxom as I was, and I knew that plenty of men would admire her all the more for her smallness. Besides that, my own gown was much simpler: stark white, when a softer white would have suited my own complexion better, with an empire waist that did much to obscure my figure, and a red silk sash under my bust. I still felt pretty, and I enjoyed the feeling, but I was happy in the knowledge that my work for the night was helping Hannah, not myself.

I looked away from her for a moment and saw at least one of the young men's gazes locked on the place where I touched her.

It was like casting a lure into a well-stocked pond. I led Hannah to the buffet table, walking slowly with my arm still around her waist, and we each received a crystal tumbler of lemonade from a serious-faced servant. Hannah's gloved hand shook a little as she raised the glass to her lips.

I looked in her eyes, and when I took a deep breath, she matched it, as I'd meant her to. We swallowed our lemonade.

She said something, so quietly I had to lean in again to hear it. "I'm afraid one of them will ask me to dance."

"Indeed, we're threatened with it every moment," I said drily. Several shy-looking men were inching closer to us.

I laughed a little—I learned early how to laugh at men—and winked at Hannah. "Heaven forbid, one of them might even fall in love with you. But isn't that the game?"

"Stop it!" Hannah's eyes glittered, and I realized she was close to crying. "It *is* a game to you—with your rich family and your plantation heir Eric—but I only have a few chances to find security. I thought you understood that. And I'm so afraid of—of falling short of what I need to be here, now that I'm about to freeze where I stand, like—like a rabbit in front of a fox. I don't think I could dance if someone did ask me." Her gloved hand trembled as she took another sip of her lemonade.

"Oh, Hannah." I set down my tumbler, every part of me feeling sober and quiet and regretful. "I'd hoped to make you laugh, to help lighten your mood. I am sorry." I looked away. My gaze fell on Catherine Essex, still reading on the fainting sofa she'd found when we walked in; it seemed Mrs. Webster had decided to let her be. And she'd been wise to do so; a handsome young officer was sitting next to Catherine, leaning close and pointing at a line of text from her book. The usually reticent Catherine laughed at something he said, nodded eagerly, and began to speak; he looked at her with what I could only describe as worship in his eyes while she talked. I was glad that quiet Catherine would get this chance;

although I mostly wanted to help Hannah, I hoped the ball would prove lucky for as many Webster girls as possible.

Felicity walked up to Catherine and the officer as I watched; she wore the pleasant and composed expression of a society maiden, but I thought for a moment that her eyes looked angry. I remembered what she'd told me over Christmas, and I saw that flash in her eyes again as she looked at the officer; she turned to Catherine and took her hand, clearly asking her to come out onto the floor and dance with her.

I thought a little less of Felicity in that moment, I admit. She had no reason to be jealous; she'd never lacked for male attention, and she had a bigger dowry and more family connections than Catherine did. Let the quieter girl have her moment, if a man had sought her out.

But Catherine had not asked for my help, and Hannah had. Besides, Felicity's pulling her out to dance had given me an idea, one that appealed for a whole multitude of reasons I didn't feel the need to enumerate just then.

"Hannah, what if that first dance was with me?" All the girls danced with each other at lessons often enough, and I'd led Hannah around a Webster floor more than once. It wasn't unheard of for girls, whether sisters or friends, to dance together at a ball.

I could see those same thoughts move through Hannah's mind, and then she nodded. "I think that would help actually, Adèle," she said. "Thank you."

She put down her glass on the table and I led her out into a waltz.

In a waltz, you barely touch your partner. But the feel of Hannah's hand in mine, even through both our gloves, and the whisper of warmth where my other hand grazed her waist, made me feel I'd never touched anyone before in my life. I hummed with an excitement I couldn't fully express. In spite of myself, I was thinking, wishing, that one night in the dormitory when I had left my bed for Hannah's she had welcomed me under her sheets and shared the heat of her body with mine, not just against my hands, but my breasts, my belly, my hips, all warm and close . . . We were spinning together in a bright, hot, crowded space, but my mind kept bringing us somewhere dark and private until I was breathing heavily, my head reeling more than the dance could explain.

I tilted my face just a little downward, my gaze on the smooth slope of her neck, and breathed in the soapy-clean scent of her skin. *She doesn't want me, she doesn't want me,* I warned myself again, but her hand tightened around mine, and in the midst of the music, I thought I heard her tiny sigh . . .

The music ended, and a man's hand touched her shoulder. It felt like a ghost image of what my own hand wanted to do, and for a moment I blinked, disoriented, as I felt a similar tap on my own arm. We stopped our dancing. Two suitors had seen us, been charmed, and come to ask for the next dance.

There was no reason to resent them.

This was why I'd asked Hannah to waltz. It was what I wanted.

I couldn't look at the man who'd touched her. I turned instead to the one who had taken my arm. He wasn't much more than a boy—attractive enough, I supposed, about my own height, pale, brown-haired, but hardly different from any other young man in the room.

I allowed him to lead me out into the quadrille that was just beginning. I missed doing the leading, and as we offered bland small talk to each other, I forced myself to look at Hannah's new partner. Hers was taller than mine, with gleaming blond hair, dark eyes, and ruddy cheeks. Hannah had admired fair men before, I knew. I thought of my own blond hair, my dark eyes, my skin that I'd so often heard compared to cream. The man she danced with might have been my brother, I thought, not without bitterness. I knew I was beautiful, I had always known, and a quick glance at my own dancing partner's face revealed his obvious admiration too. But Hannah didn't once look back at me as she waltzed with her lanky boy; her eyes were full of stars shining for him. She wasn't frozen, as she'd feared; she was glowing.

I had never before found my beauty quite as useless as I did in that moment.

But then she smiled at him, so guileless, and happiness for my friend and hope for her safe future swelled up in me and consumed the jealousy and longing I felt. What could I offer to Hannah, except the help and guidance I'd already given? I had no real protection I could offer her, no way to help her keep her family safe, even if there were some way for girls to offer that to each other.

She was in the arms of a richly dressed, harmless-looking young man. She was sweet and pretty. She had as much of a chance as any girl in that room.

The dance ended. I curtsied halfheartedly to my partner, who bowed and smiled in a slightly annoyed way, clearly chagrined that he hadn't been able to hold my interest. I could hardly keep from rolling my eyes as he walked away.

I tore my gaze away from Hannah as her partner bent over her hand and asked her for a second dance. I looked down at the fan that dangled from my wrist. I seized it and twitched it quickly open and shut a few times, like a snapping jaw.

"I assumed when I saw you, miss, that you'd already promised all your dances to luckier men than I," said a husky voice near my ear. "When I noticed that you were free just now, I had to risk asking for a dance of my own."

I looked up from my fan and into a face that I was sure, for a moment, I recognized.

Black hair was combed back smoothly from a sharp widow's peak, although it seemed to want to curl; golden-brown eyes gazed at me with amused confidence from under bold brows. A full mouth above a cleft chin, still smooth where some of the young men wore the beginnings of beards, held the barest trace of a smile. His nose, by its look, had been broken and reset. His light brown skin was dusted with freckles.

No, I could not place him after all, I decided. How strange that I felt I knew him.

"Will you, miss?" he asked, in a voice that was nearly a whisper.

I blinked, unable to remember for a moment what he was asking. I had never been one to lose my words around men—not ever. But this freckle-faced boy . . .

I nodded slowly. "Yes," I said.

He gave me a smile in return that was as sweet as any girl's and that belied the seriousness I had seen in his eyes.

He led me out to dance, and I hate to admit—fickle heart!—that I stopped thinking of Hannah at all.

He wore kid gloves, but I could feel calluses on his fingers under the suede, and I wondered what such a well-dressed young man could have possibly done to earn rough hands. I wondered what they would feel like without gloves.

I had always thought I'd be more loyal in my longings than it seemed I was turning out to be. Eric, Hannah, this yet-unnamed dancer . . . presented with each of them, my mind cast the others in shadow. Yet I knew they were each there still, somewhere in the vast landscapes of my heart.

But I had never touched Eric, and I didn't think Hannah had ever wanted to touch me—not the way I wished she would. I focused on my partner.

He was not as tall as I was, though he was much broader; I had to look down a little bit to meet his eyes. Still there was something in the way he looked at me through his thick lashes, with his warm, dark eyes, that made me tighten inside the way I did when I read Eric's letters or when I touched Hannah's hand. All of me seemed to pull taut into a thin, glowing line, like a horizon just at dawn.

When the dance ended, I saw Hannah's dandy leading her in the direction of the refreshment tables by the balcony. Felicity and Charlotte were watching her too, their faces full of surprised admiration—and perhaps a little jealousy. I was relieved for her, so relieved. I let that feeling fill me up and let my interesting new dance partner help me forget I'd wished I could have been the boy on Hannah's arm.

He looked at me and then out at the floor again as the first swell of the next dance's music began.

"Yes," I said again, with the fleeting, absurd thought that it was the only word I ever wanted to say to him.

The song passed in timeless, breathless warmth. I barely noticed the music or the feeling of my dress on my skin or the floor against my feet, for that matter; it was as if every nerve in my body had rushed to the few places where we touched and quivered there like a crowd waiting for a door to open, so they could rush in. When at last we stopped and he bent and kissed my hand, the crowd of nerves gave a cheer I could feel all the way to my bones.

"I would ask you for another, miss, and for every dance tonight, but I have less pleasing obligations to attend to now," he said, looking up at me through those sooty lashes, his lips still so close to my hand that I felt the warmth of his breath through my glove, on my knuckles, as he spoke.

When he turned and left, my hand felt cold. I clenched it into a fist and opened it again. The crowd vanished, my body an abandoned room.

I remembered Hannah, and I turned to look for her and her dandy.

They were gone.

They weren't at the punch tables, not in any of the well-lit corners of this large, bright room. There weren't even any dark corners to hide in and steal a kiss, like in the novels the Webster girls passed around.

My stomach twisted.

We'd been explicitly told to stay in the main room; not every Webster girl could have an individual chaperone, the way mothers looked after their daughters at many society balls. We had to do our part in looking after ourselves, Mrs. Webster had told us.

And looking after each other.

I made as quick a circuit around the ballroom as I could without betraying my concern, thinking of course they could be hidden behind another couple or seated on a low chaise longue somewhere, couldn't they?

But something told me they had left the room together. Hannah was so hopeful and so trusting. She had trusted me after all—and I'd spent years listening to Papa tell me how untrustworthy I was by nature.

As I passed by the refreshment table, I heard a muffled sound from the balcony beyond. Not quite a breath, not quite a struggle. I don't know how I heard it over the music and the chatter, but I did.

And I knew. Whether it was some hidden memory of a similar noise I'd encountered at Le Moulin or at Ashfield, or even—

It didn't matter. I knew it was Hannah, and that she needed help.

I slipped through the crowd, hardly noticing those I pushed past to get by. Yet some part of me made sure I was discreet enough not to draw attention; if my fears were founded, I had to get to Hannah before anyone else could see what was happening. She had no money, no important family, nothing to fall back on, and nothing to barter with but the quiet sweetness and innocence that shone from her like a golden halo.

Outside was much darker than the sparkling ballroom, and the shallow balcony seemed to stretch out into the cloudy night like a shoreline, shifting and unsteady. There was just enough light that I could see Hannah's pale gown and her gleaming hair—and the hand of her dancing partner in that hair, pulling it hard enough that her chin was forced up and her neck exposed, his other hand tight on her throat and his head buried in her bosom.

I thrust myself between the two of them before I could even think.

"What the hell—" came her assailant's rough voice.

Sharp pain hit the skin of my shoulder and I couldn't comprehend it for a moment. It was Hannah's nails digging into me as she clung to me for safety.

I pressed my back against her, shielding as much of her small body with my own as I could, and I looked up at her attacker just as he pulled his hand back to strike me. He reeked of gin, a smell I thought Hannah might not even recognize.

What I did next happened quickly, but I cannot claim I did not know what I was doing or that I acted without thinking, the way I'd rushed out of the ballroom and placed my body in front of Hannah's. Nor was I acting solely in self-defense.

I hated him in that moment, and I acted from hate.

Reader, I was never innocent.

As he swung at me, I gripped his broad shoulders hard; he looked down into my face with nothing more than annoyance that I was keeping him momentarily from his aim. Not even any real anger, and certainly no fear.

He saw no threat in me. I saw only threat in him.

And beyond him, in the clouded moonlight and the shifting shadows, I saw the intricate ironwork railing of the balcony.

I planted my feet wide apart, set my gaze on the empty air beyond the railing, and pushed.

His face still showed nothing but smug annoyance, right up until his center of gravity pitched over the ironwork. Then I saw one second of understanding, of fear, before his body tumbled backward and he vanished.

My ears were full of the pounding of my own heartbeat, Hannah's gasp behind me, my own harried breath. I did not hear him hit the ground.

I stepped to the railing and looked down. I could hear the blood pulsing through my body and see the blood running from his. The flickering light of a gas lamp illuminated only half of the scene below; the rest was filled in with darkness and shadow. We stood in even deeper shadows above him, thank goodness, though no one was on the street to look up at us. I knew that it wouldn't be long before there was.

"Don't scream," I told Hannah, even as I turned, but it was clear she was incapable of doing so. Her mouth opened and closed silently; she had her gloved hand pressed over her throat, in the same place his had been, almost as if she wished to keep strangling herself now that he had stopped doing it.

We have only a moment before we're discovered, I thought. "Hannah. People will come out here soon, any moment now, and neither of us look hurt." So many horrible memories threatened to surge over my mind's floodgates, the dam that kept certain images out, from Ashfield, from Paris, from everywhere—so many girls and women, the things they endured, the things they did to themselves from shame. The ways they hurt themselves when they were blamed. When they knew that no one believed them.

"Hannah, I need you to hit me," I said.

Her hand came down from her throat. Her mouth formed the shape of the word *what*, but still no sound came out. She just kept staring at me, still unable to speak. Slowly she shook her head. Her whole body was starting to tremble.

I raised my hand to reach out and touch her, my intention only gentleness and comfort, but I thought better of it even before I saw her wince.

Over the music from the ballroom, I thought I heard a gasp in the street below.

"It's all right," I told Hannah softly. "I can do it."

I gripped my bodice in both hands and pulled—once, twice, until the layers of fabric tore—exposing the chemise that lay under my gown and corset. I tore that too, then held my breath and, bracing myself, dug my nails into the skin of my own chest and raked them down, so that deep scratches welling blood followed in my fingers' wake.

I suddenly found myself in a world all made of crystal: bright and glaring with refracted, shining, horrid clarity. I understood how unlikely it was that Hannah and I would be believed that the young man was attacking her. I knew how little two ladies' claims about a well-bred man would matter—especially a dead man.

A man whom I had killed.

I heard a gasp behind me.

I raised my chin and turned to face my judgment.

My last dancing partner stared at us, at my face and Hannah's, at the blood on my breast. "Mother of God," he said in quite a different voice than I'd heard him use before. "What happened?"

I looked into his dark eyes, thick lashed and lovely as a girl's. I saw something honest there, something that I somehow believed I could trust. I remembered that feeling of connection, of already knowing him, that I'd had just a few minutes before.

Against all my instincts, I told him the truth. As Hannah shook silently beside me, I told him everything I had seen and everything that I had done.

Against all expectations, he believed me.

And when the rest of them came out, he told the story for us. "I saw Mr. Hamilton attack this young lady," he said, by which words I learned my victim's name. "I saw her friend come valiantly to her aid, but of course his strength was too much for both of them. In his drunken lunging after them he stumbled, and he fell . . ."

Time and details had begun to run together for me, my world of crystal turning muzzy and dark, and so I cannot recall his exact words. But I knew then, as I still know now, that a man's story is more easily believed than any woman's.

And I knew that the degree to which we were cooed over and coddled, the degree to which our story was believed, did not entirely rest on his corroboration.

Our own standing as genteel young ladies helped too. If a dancer from Le Moulin claimed that a patron had attacked her, the police would call her *menteuse,* liar, to her face—or would say that such risks were part of the life she had chosen, and she deserved no better, nor ought to ask for help.

Mrs. Webster was there moments later, gathering us to her, putting her arms around us, the skirts of her demure dove-gray gown seeming to cover us like protective wings. Her authority, her reputation, helped us too. She was the one who brought us out of the room, to the street, and it must have been her who called for the carriage to bring us home. I struggle to remember her words too, but I know that once we were sitting in the carriage, she said nothing; she seemed to know that nothing could be said. She only watched us, carefully, without judgment, and with care. It seems obvious, looking back on that moment, that it was not the first time she had had to care for a student after an assault. After all the cruelty I have seen, it would surprise me if she did not find herself in such a situation every year. A good schoolmistress, I suppose, must be a more fearsome protector of girls than I have ever been.

Hannah stayed silent too. She sat next to Mrs. Webster, leaving no room remaining, so I sat opposite them. After a few moments, her trembling slowed, and she leaned her head on the older woman's shoulder. I was facing backward from the motion of the carriage, with no one to lean on, but my spine felt rigid and cold as steel, so that I do not think I could have bent it enough to rest on another person if I'd had the chance.

Mrs. Webster pulled the carriage curtains shut, and we rode in darkness back to school. When the wheels hit a bump, the occasional glare of a gas-lamp light flickered between the gaps in the curtains, and the two women across from me showed as bodiless faces for brief moments before they were consumed by darkness again. In those flashes Hannah's once-rosy face was white, so white and shocked, so robbed of its sweet innocence. So haunted.

And *they* haunted me, the other girls I'd known who hadn't been believed. The Moulin girls, the street women, the dancers. I felt them trailing and drifting and twirling behind us on the hushed ride back to the Webster, beautiful ghosts.

I twisted Maman's ring. I had to wear it on my pinky now, since all my other fingers had outgrown it. The metal had gone cold and it spun loose around my finger. I had heard of people going cold with fright or horror, but I hadn't realized it was happening to me.

I made myself feel my cold hands, the set of my jaw, the rigid length of my neck and spine, and the stiff weight of my limbs. It came to me, slowly, that mine was now the body of a murderess. A body that had ended another body's life.

I felt no regret. I was glad that such a man was dead. But I knew, somehow, that I had to let my body feel its shock and shame.

I felt Maman in my body too, as we went back to the Webster. Her heart beat low and fast in my gut like clapping hands.

And Bertha, dancing in the dark mirror, tucking my hair behind my ears with the gentleness Papa claimed she never possessed, laughing in her singular way that snapped from kind to mocking in a moment. Bertha, screaming as she burned and fell.

So many ghosts.

I had promised Hannah I would help her, and I had. I wanted to help all of us. In the carriage back to the Webster, my cold, shocked body warmed to that knowledge, to a vow that I made to myself anew, that made me anew with it. My guilt did not matter as much as their lives.

I knew then that I would damn myself to save as many of us as I could.

PART THREE
THE VILLAINESS

I'm gonna raise, raise hell

There's a story no one's telling

—Brandi Carlile, "Raise Hell"

THIRTEEN

I WOKE IN THE DARK before sunrise the next morning, staring into the blackness of the dormitory ceiling, a sick and bitter taste inside my mouth, every muscle in my body cramped and aching. I lay listening to the sleeping breaths around me, and I had to keep myself from trying to tear off my own skin.

Hannah's bed was empty. Sometime after we arrived at the Webster, the headmistress had swept her away, while I'd still been frozen with shock. I heard my own voice asking where she'd gone and another answering that she would come back in a few days, but I couldn't find a place or a name to go with that exchange. The uncertainty was only another kind of horror.

I washed myself from a jug by the window that was scrimmed with frost, but I still felt hot and cramped and frantic. I kept my movements quiet and controlled, but I felt sure that at any moment I would start to shake and scream. I chewed at the scars inside my lips, at the softer insides of my cheeks, until my mouth filled and I spat bloody spittle into the basin where I'd washed. The taste made bile rise in my throat.

The idea of breakfast with everyone else, in only a few hours' time, was unthinkable. I was sure my mouth would always taste of blood and bile.

As soon as the first gray, murky light began to seep through the dormitory windows, I dressed and fled downstairs, quiet as I'd learned to be backstage in Paris. Those memories seemed impossibly distant, as if I were reaching out for every other day of my life and they were pulling, running, away. No other moment could touch me now; I had only the last horrible evening and the blank night and this morning.

A lone scholarship girl was awake to stoke the fires. I made sure she did not see me.

I hurried out the front door and down the slippery stone steps, and the first gasp of winter air seemed to hollow me out. For a sweet moment I was no one, nothing. I did not know why I was standing on the step of that gray building at the very break of day, where I came from, or where I wanted to go. The air heated in my lungs, and I let it out in a cloud that hung before me in the cold.

Then I was Adèle Varens again, and I had killed a man.

It seemed unreal; it seemed too real. I looked down at my hands and couldn't bear that, looked at my dress and cloak, pulled on crooked in the dark, and couldn't bear that either.

I made my eyes focus on the farthest-away part of the street that I could see. A figure in a dark dress and shawl stood there, facing the school.

I started marching toward her, determined that I would find the next farthest-away thing as soon as I could see it, and so on, and on, and on, until I had gotten far enough away from the Webster that I could breathe air no one else I knew had breathed. I wanted that just then—just my own air—more than I had ever wanted anything else I could think of.

But as I walked toward the girl in the shawl, I couldn't quite make myself look for the next faraway thing. I kept watching her. Her face called to me somehow, a face that I vaguely felt I should be able to place.

She turned and fled as I approached, vanishing around a corner by the grocer. A flower seller pushing an overflowing cart walked through the space where she'd just been, an early riser from the ranks of street vendors who would crowd this lane before long.

The heat and pain had left my skin; my mouth tasted like nothing now. The fierce longing for distance from the Webster, from myself, had vanished as quickly as it came.

I went back inside, surprised at how simple it was to leave and return to the dormitory unnoticed. I pulled off my dress, petticoats, corset, and stockings and climbed back into bed in just my shift; my sheets had not yet fully cooled. I could not begin to understand myself or the vast changes in feeling that hurled through me from moment to moment.

I stared at the lightening window, unmoving, for the next quiet hour until my peers woke up. My mind felt empty except for the faint sound I could hear in the silence: the rush and beating of my blood inside my head.

None of the other girls stirred until the morning bell rang. I wondered how they could bear to sleep; they must have heard what had happened by now. When they woke, none of them spoke to me, not even Felicity or Charlotte; although each of them watched me as I dressed.

But as we filed down the narrow stairs together and along the pink-papered hallway to the breakfast room, I felt a presence at my back, and then a gentle hand touched my shoulder. I recognized her before I turned to look: Felicity. When I saw her eyes, I remembered the young girl who had slept outside her mother's room, then in her bed, all those nights just to protect her. She did not smile at me, but she looked at me for a long moment with a kind of steady understanding that was undeniable. I nodded, and she nodded back.

I managed a few bites of porridge at breakfast, sitting next to her; I tasted none of what I ate, but at least my stomach did not rebel. I saw Mrs. Webster watching me. She did not pull me aside to tell me I would be expelled, as I'd vaguely wondered if she might; she did not ask me how I was. She said nothing to me then. I had a cloudy recollection of her office the night before, of a strange doctor she had called for who checked over Hannah and me and asked us a few questions . . . yes, Hannah had still been with me then. The doctor had given each of us something to drink, something that erased any further memories after my first sip and that seemed to reach back through time with murky fingers, clouding out other things I might recall. I wished it had worked better.

Mrs. Webster said nothing.

The night before, it had felt as if her silence was born of understanding, of knowing how much it would hurt to talk of what had happened so soon; this morning it felt like the silence of refusal, of forgetting, of pretending the bad thing had never been at all.

That was a particular English silence I knew well. For my own sake I was glad enough not to have to speak of it just yet; for Hannah's, though, I despised our headmistress a little—but despised myself more, for I could not breach the walls of Mrs. Webster's silence or my own remaining shock to ask where she had gone.

It did seem that she looked at me pointedly when she called for our Saturday walk, but I could not be sure.

I barely felt my own fingers reclasp the cloak about my throat, the same one I'd worn in the gray dawn that morning; I barely felt my own steps as we moved through the streets. The girls talked around me, softly, but I didn't hear a word.

I was grateful to have left the heat and cold of my own shame and horror behind, to walk among the other girls, an empty vessel. I felt nothing, saw nothing, was nothing among them.

Charlotte came up to me on that walk and spoke to me, stumbling over her own speech in a way that was totally unlike her usual ebullient ease. I don't remember her exact words or mine; I think she flinched when I spoke, but did not move away. I think she and Felicity walked with me for the rest of that outing; at least it feels, in my memory, as if they did. But I remember so little of that day, or of the following weeks.

All I knew was that Hannah did not come back.

I kept waiting to be questioned, by Mrs. Webster, by the police . . . something. Even by my fellow students. But it was as if the horror had made that night's events vanish, from the collective tongue and the collective mind of the Webster. One of the first things I'd learned about this country was the English ability to make it seem as if bad things never happened, simply by not talking about them.

I received a letter from Eric three days after the ball, but I couldn't bear to open it. I left it under my pillow, as if his care could cleanse my dreams . . . and then I forgot about it until after the linens had been changed. It is the only letter of his I never read. I still wonder what he said and how the decisions I made next might have been changed if I had opened my heart to his voice then.

I remembered what Grace Poole and Mrs. Fairfax had told me at Thornfield all those years ago: Papa didn't like to hear that anything unusual had happened in that house, and, therefore, nothing unusual happened. Whatever I thought I knew, I was wrong—at least, wrong enough not to speak of it.

I started waking around three every morning, my heart pounding from nightmares I couldn't remember. I would slip outside in the darkness, walking the frosted streets, returning just as the first light slid through the smoky sky. No one stopped me. No one ever cared. Each time, I was a little stunned that we were so much less thoroughly chaperoned than I'd assumed we were, though there were enough reasons most of the well-bred Webster girls wouldn't want to leave the safety of the school in the middle of the night, I supposed. Looking back, I don't know if those risks didn't bother me because I thought I'd learned how to protect myself when I was in Paris, or whether I simply didn't care if I was harmed. I dressed plainly, in black, with a scarf wrapped around my hair, and I kept to the shadows. My old understanding of city streets and danger must have done a little to keep me safe; blind luck must have done much more. Although I wonder too, now, if I was more protected than I knew—but there I am getting ahead of myself.

Those walks, at least, were the only risk I took. I wanted to survive. If everyone else had accepted the truth that the boy who danced with me had told, the truth that I'd told him, then I would accept it too. I would. I would. I'd bite my tongue like I'd always bitten my lips; my mouth had never been so bloody, but I swallowed it all.

I moved through silence and blankness and blood. I had saved Hannah, but she was still gone. I felt as if I was gone too.

Until I saw the girl in the shawl again.

I'd woken even earlier that morning, and the street was a little busier than I usually found it, dotted with people wandering or stumbling home from their own late-night adventures.

I knew as soon as I saw the girl that she'd been following me. All the sensation I'd lost rushed back into my body—the last weeks had sent more painful changes through me than I'd thought possible—and when I caught her eye and began to walk toward her, this time she did not turn and run.

She watched me as I approached; her golden-brown eyes were framed by thick lashes and strong black brows. Freckles that nearly matched her eyes were scattered across her soft cheeks, and there was just a trace of shadow above her full lips.

She held my gaze boldly as I drew nearer. I matched her, filling with an urgency that I couldn't quite place.

And then—the way stars are just points in the sky until you recognize the constellation—her eyes, her lashes, her brows, her mouth, all seemed to connect to each other with thin glowing lines, and I knew.

"It's you." I grabbed his arm so he wouldn't slip away before I understood; but he didn't move. "What are you doing here? And why are you dressed—as a girl?" *And a poor girl*, I thought, which was nearly the stranger disguise of the two. I'd seen men dressed as women at Le Moulin, of course, but never a single person who pretended to be poorer than they were.

I couldn't say women's clothing didn't suit him at least; his rough, brown wool dress and faded plaid shawl set off his freckles and the brightness of his eyes. He pulled his arm from my grip and laughed, a low, husky laugh in a voice I knew. "I thought you might not recognize me," he said, "though I don't know why, since I'm sure I'd recognize you in any getup in the world." He sighed and closed one eye, still watching me cautiously with the other. "I'm dressed like a girl because I am one."

"Are . . . one?"

A quick curtsey. "Nan Ward. Pleasure."

The curtsey was such a perfect mimic of the one the Webster girls learned that I had to smile, and the smile broke something in me, or healed it. "Yes," I said. I remembered how that night I'd thought it was the only word I ever wanted to give to him. To her.

The world was strange and new, and I was made anew in it, in seeing her. I smiled wider. "Adèle Varens," I said, and gave her the gentleman's bow she'd given me when we'd danced. "The pleasure is mine."

"I know it is," she said, then laughed again, a warm and easy sound. "I mean, I know who you are."

"You know?"

She saw the look on my face and laughed. "Sure, I've been watching all you Webster girls. I've been working on the boy you met at the ball for months, trying to figure out how to be someone who would charm you lot. The ball was his birthday, his first outing, like. I was just there to—" She stumbled over her own quick-spoken words and stopped herself. "Mother of God, but there's something about you that makes me want to talk too much, I swear. I was swallowing my own tongue to keep from telling you that night, and I'm right glad that you know now, even though I shouldn't be."

I remembered how I felt when she kissed my hand, and it was suddenly as if the time between that moment and this had vanished, and Hannah had never been hurt, and the man I had killed didn't matter at all. I felt again the warmth of her breath, and I realized I was blushing. I was shy with this girl, as I'd never been with anyone.

"I've been looking," she said, suddenly serious, "for a girl to strike a deal with. At the ball I thought you might be the one. I've seen you wandering in the dark a few times since, and today I know for sure. I have a plan for you, my love."

And all that time came rushing back. Would this never stop, the flood and ebb of knowing, of horror and guilt and vindication and pain?

And this girl—Nan—had defended me. It was only because she'd told my story as a man that it had been taken for truth at the crucial moment. It was because of her that everyone believed Hannah and I were victims.

But his testimony wasn't real because he was not real. The man who'd helped us—if he was shown to be dishonest it could be our undoing, mine and Hannah's.

The French word for blackmail is *chantage*. I'd heard it often as a child. It rang in my ears as Nan looked at me.

"What kind of plan?" I whispered, my voice as hoarse as if I'd been screaming.

She stepped closer, close enough that our breaths mingled and I had to tilt my chin to look down into her eyes.

She smelled like black tea and peat fires. Smoky. Sweet.

"A money-spinning plan," she said. "Sure, what kind of criminal do you think I am? I need a high-class girl I can trust and who'll trust me."

I blinked. I hadn't thought about what kind of anything she was, only that she had been the dancing partner I'd liked so well and then the boy who had vouched for me, and now a pretty girl.

She had saved me, and by extension she'd saved Hannah. I remembered the vow I'd made that night, to save more girls no matter what the cost, and it was as if all the myriad feelings and sensations I'd had in all the days since the ball's horrible end came together. I still felt guilty, and empty, and cold and hot and determined and afraid and enraged, but they were all a part of me, contained inside some whole. Suddenly I was more than the empty ghost of this morning, of all the pre-dawn mornings I had walked the streets; I was more than the killer on the balcony at the ball. Suddenly I was Adèle Varens again, each version of myself holding hands once more with all the others in my soul.

And then I was able to stare her down. "Let me make sure I understand you," I said, and I heard power in my voice and warmed to it. "You admit you lied to me on first meeting—everything from your words to your clothes to your sex was a lie—and you admit even now that you're speaking to me on no honest business either . . . and you want me to trust you?"

Her golden-brown eyes gleamed as she looked up at me. "You're the killer here, girleen, not me."

She said it like she knew a million murderers. Maybe she did. But at least she was able to say it, to speak out loud a word I hadn't yet let pass my own lips.

She called me a killer as if she didn't mind that it was true.

I wanted to learn from this girl who called me what I was, and who called herself a criminal, so casually. I had been only the sweet part of myself for so long, tried so hard to be what Papa and Jane and the Webster wanted of me, and not much of me was sweet to begin with.

"Don't you trust me?" she asked.

"Not at all," I said, and followed her.

She led me to a pub by the East India Docks. It took nearly an hour for us to walk there, but something about her drew me. It was as if a leash were looped around each of us; although who held it in her hand and who was collared at the neck, I could not tell and did not want to know.

She talked of herself as we walked along the dark streets, naming herself as a criminal again without the least bother; a pickpocket, mostly, she said, but one with aspirations. "I prefer stealing from the rich, like Robin Hood," she said, her warm laugh escaping again, "and the very richest keep their riches safe at home. That's why I need an ally who's one of their own—but not their own. And even before you treated the boy to his tumble, I knew that might be you."

I tried to keep my tone casual as I asked: "How did you know?"

"Oh, girleen, from a thousand little things," she said. "The way you pushed your friend forward when every other girl there was only hunting for herself, for one. But I can't be giving you all my secrets before you tell me yours." A smile shifted the patterns of her freckles.

That last line was an invitation, I knew. I smiled back at her and put a finger to my lips.

We walked the last few minutes of our way without speaking more, but it was a companionable silence, not a tense one. I could not push away the feeling that I'd known her a long time.

The pub's front door was closed, its windows dark; Nan led me down the little alley to its left and, after producing a long skeleton key from inside the bust of her dress, quickly unlocked it. I distracted myself from wondering if the key was warm from her body by considering the sign I'd seen above the front door; like so many public houses in London, this one was called the King's

Head. I was still French enough to wonder if the name had a hint of guillotine about it.

Inside it was dark and crowded, all ancient wood and stone and ceiling stains from centuries of pipe smoke. Yet something about it felt cozy, familiar; the smoke and the smell of drink put me in mind of Le Moulin's dressing rooms. How horrified Mrs. Webster, and even Jane, would be to think that such scents still made me feel at home. I felt my shoulders unwind, and I couldn't remember the last time I hadn't held them stiff.

The King's Head did, it seemed, have a king: a tall, fat, black-bearded, handsome man who held court in an ornately carved chair by the inglenook. He had large, expressive, dark eyes that looked so much like Nan's that I knew at once he was her father, even before she called him Da and sidled up to him in a way that no one else in the crowd around that big, strong, smiling man would dare to do.

"Da, this is the girl I was tellin' you about," she said. Her true accent (if this was really it) had a soft, feathery lilt—Irish, but unlike the clipped Dublin speech of Mrs. O'Connor, Papa and Jane's cook at Ferndean.

The big man looked me over in an appraising way that I imagined was meant to be intimidating, but I was a girl born in a brothel, raised in a theatre, and grown up in a haunted house. I was—I tried to use the word in my own mind with as much acceptance as Nan had spoken it—a killer.

No man's mere gaze could frighten me. I stood my ground and looked right back.

I watched the sharp judgment in his eyes, and made some judgments of my own, until his expression melted slowly into warmth.

"Grand," he said. "Pleased to meet ye, girleen." He looked at his daughter. "My Nan, ye've chosen well." And he nodded to an older man in the crowd surrounding him, and he moved forward and began to murmur something in his ear.

Nan grinned, her smile flickering wide and bright across her face before it disappeared again, leaving only a sparkle of mirth in the eyes that were so much like her father's.

"Right," she told me, "you and I have a deal to hammer out betwixt us. And, finishing-school girl, you're buying me a drink."

Most of the Webster girls would have been shocked (and a few envious) to see me in a lower-class pub like the King's Head. And yet it held the same air of camaraderie that I felt so strongly in the dormitory and that I had been born into in Paris—and that I had never felt in my father's company.

Indeed, there was something else about this place that reminded me of my childhood. I did not think it was only the class difference, or the number of people of other countries and races, speaking many other languages. There was an air of benevolent ferocity in the room, of a community that protected each other with passion verging on violence.

That was a passion I knew well.

Exactly what they were protecting, though, took me a few more moments to notice. They worked outside the law, of course; Nan

162

had already told me that. But there was something more. I first noticed two dark-skinned women with their hands clasped on top of the table they shared; one woman's thumb stroked slowly across the other's wrist, and as I watched she raised their hands to her mouth for a kiss. The other woman smiled and stroked her cheek, which I noticed only then was faintly shadowed with the beginnings of a beard. What I had thought were two small-statured men nearby both had, on closer inspection, long hair tucked into discreet buns, and curves under their clothes that most men did not have. The more I looked around the pub the clearer the difference these people shared became, a kind of difference that I'd seen around the edges of my mother's community in Paris, but that seemed to be centered here.

"How did you know?" I whispered.

Nan shook her head, surveying the room with a small smile. "You can't live long in a life like mine without growing some instincts about people."

I wanted to ask if she meant that she knew I shared the same difference as the others here, or simply that I wouldn't reveal their secrets.

It would be incredibly dangerous, after all, for her to bring me here if she had been wrong about me.

But then, I supposed, she still held more dangerous knowledge about me than I did about her.

We received mugs of cloudy cider, and Nan explained the bargain she wanted to strike. Her father was indeed a leader, just as I'd read him; he no longer went on the streets much himself, but he was a master forger, and he led a ring of pickpockets and thieves, mostly Irish and other immigrants. Nan wanted to impress him, and information and access to the upper class was, she thought, the best way to do it.

"We need eyes and ears in Society. We need information: who we can most easily fleece and who most deserves it."

"I can imagine you as Robin Hood," I said, remembering the story she'd mentioned earlier—and wanting to tease her a little bit.

Nan grinned. "First story I heard after we'd left Galway was Robin Hood, told to me by an English girl on the boat over here. I rather fancied myself as the noble kind of thief. Still do."

I met her eyes. "I rather fancy you that way too."

When she held my gaze, I didn't look away. The shyness I'd felt a mere hour ago was gone. I liked her and I knew it, and I wanted her to know it too. It felt so good, so sweet and sure, this instinctive liking, when just that morning I had thought the whole world might always lie bitter on my tongue.

Any sweetness the world handed me now, I was going to swallow whole.

"So you want me to be your eyes," I said, still holding her gaze, "and your ears." I flicked a brief glance toward them; her ears were delicate and lovely, pierced with thin golden rings half-hidden in her dark brown curls. "And what do I get in return?"

She leaned back in her chair and took a breath that pulled the fabric of her dress tighter across her breasts. She waved her hand before her in a casually elegant little shrug that, I swear, was almost French. "What would you like?" she asked.

I let my gaze drift down to her mouth.

I heard her take another deep breath, and although no blush darkened her lightly freckled face, when I glanced at her ears again, they had gone pink.

Sweetness to swallow whole.

But the ball and what I had done there still haunted me. I still felt the ghosts of all those girls trailing behind me—those who had been hurt by men and those who would or could be—and I knew that what I really, truly wanted had nothing much to do with myself at all.

"You disguised yourself so well at the ball that I danced with you and looked deep in your eyes, and I turned to you for help in one of the darkest moments of my life and you gave it to me; and yet I did not know you this morning until I saw your face up close, and I still might not have done if—" *If I hadn't wanted you so much when you were a boy,* I thought but couldn't quite say. "I want you to teach me how to camouflage myself that way." I paused. "And I want to learn some of the other things you know. You said you were a noble thief. I want to learn how to take something from a gentleman's pocket with such a light touch that he won't notice it's gone or that I was there at all. And I want . . ." I paused. "I was born in Paris, and my mother was a dancer and a . . . prostitute." I'd never said that word out loud in England, not out of shame, but to protect my mother— her memory—from those I knew would judge her.

Nan raised her eyebrows, but her expression conveyed only surprise, not judgment. After all, I realized, I had no reason to assume she didn't do that kind of work herself.

I made myself talk quickly so I wouldn't linger on the image that rose in my mind's eye of my pretty new friend in a private moment. "I learned a little about how to keep myself from being hurt, including how to hurt someone else if I needed to, during my years in Paris. The children who really lived on the streets knew far more than me, as I imagine you do; my friends at the Webster know nothing. It's for their sake, as well as my own, that I am asking." I took a breath. "I want to learn to fight."

Nan laughed, just a giggle at first that grew into a big belly laugh the likes of which would have earned her a demerit for unladylike behavior at the Webster. A few of the people around us turned toward her, smiling, enjoying her laughter; I could feel the evaluation in their gazes at me, although they weren't unfriendly.

"You want all my secrets, so," she said.

I couldn't help but smile. "Every one."

FOURTEEN

WHEN I FINALLY LEFT the King's Head, dawn had already broken; it was Nan, in fact, who told me I'd best be getting home. I was sure a world of trouble would be waiting for me back at the Webster. My absence would have been noted before breakfast; even sneaking back in would do me no good.

So when Mrs. Webster herself met me on the building's steps and marched me into her office, I was not surprised. She sat me down and perched herself behind her wide desk, looking particularly severe.

"I told your stepmother when she entrusted you to my care that our institution does not employ corporal punishment," she said, "but I am sure you can imagine, Miss Varens, my temptation toward the switch when it seems that gentler methods will not keep my students obedient and safe." She closed her eyes briefly. "It is your safety, Miss Varens, that has been foremost in my mind ever since I was informed of your absence this morning. Yes, I say *ever since* though it has been but a few hours, because those hours have expanded into what has felt like an eternity of worry for my fellow teachers and me—and indeed for your classmates. We know you suffered a terrible ordeal at the ball, Adèle—goodness knows we have done all we can to make sure neither you nor the other students have further cause to think of it—and none of us knew where you had gone. Can you imagine what we thought?"

Abruptly she stood and walked back around the desk, and before I could react her arms were around me in a tight embrace. "Adèle, we thought you might have harmed yourself," she said, her use of my first name betraying her emotion even more than the break in her voice. "I am so glad that you are back and safe. Miss Norfolk will return this week as well." I gasped a little, and she held me tighter. "How would she have felt if she returned and you were gone? We will help you through this however we can, but you must never, never leave us in the night like that again."

I felt Mrs. Webster's tears against my cheek. "I am sorry," I said, and I meant it and felt shame. Yet even then, I remembered the bargain I had made with Nan and our plan to meet again. I knew that nothing would keep me away.

I had not joined the Shadow Cabinet after lights out in a long time, and they had let me be, which I was sure was Felicity's work, borne of her understanding. But that night she came to my bed while the other girls talked, laid her hand on mine, and gently asked me how I was.

Her friendly touch made me realize how tightly I'd been holding my blanket, and I made myself relax my fist enough that we could twine our fingers together.

There wasn't much moonlight that night, and all I could see of her face was the slight gleam of her eyes. But they were the eyes of a friend, and I looked into them, and they looked into my eyes too. Held in my friend's gaze, held in her hand, I finally found my way to something I hadn't found since the ball and hadn't known until that moment that I needed:

I let myself cry.

For Hannah, first.

For the boy. I still couldn't regret the choice I had made, but I had taken a life, and he had lost the chance that life would have given him at redemption; I mourned that loss.

For Bertha and my mother and all the girls I dreamed of saving, and all those I could never save.

And for myself.

"Ten o'clock, group A to elocution, group B to penmanship," Mrs. Harris read out over breakfast the next day. "Eleven, group A to dancing, group B to French. Noon, luncheon. One o'clock, both groups are to retire to the blue room, where we shall receive our guests for tea."

I choked on the buttered roll I'd been eating but quietly enough that no one but Felicity, sitting to my right, heard me. I fumbled for my napkin, but it had fallen to the floor.

Before I could reach for it, she slipped her own napkin onto my lap, then watched with concern as I dabbed my eyes and took a deep breath. I knew she was thinking the same thing I was: that I'd be punished for the lapse in etiquette of daring to choke on a piece of bread.

I should just let the moment go by, I thought. *Just keep my head down the way all the girls do; the way we're all taught.*

Then I thought of Hannah again. Mrs. Webster had said she was coming back, but I still didn't know where she was, how she was faring.

"I'm sorry," I said, standing up, despising myself a little for beginning with an apology even though I knew it made me more likely to be listened to, "but how can we think of suitors when one of our own was assaulted by one so recently? How can we take tea with young men so soon after such violence, and speak prettily with them, and—and smile?"

Mrs. Harris turned a look of such icy neutrality on me that I thought my tea would grow cold in the cup I held. "None of these young men hurt Miss Norfolk," she said, "nor any other Webster student. They are gentlemen, eligible ones, and we shall receive them as such. If they teach you anything, the events at the ball ought to show the importance of cultivating connections with gentlemen, so that you might find yourself protected at all times."

I found myself shocked into silence. I looked down the teachers' table for Mrs. Webster, but she was conspicuously absent.

Charlotte leaned toward me. "She is wrong in her reasoning, you know, but right in her conclusion; any one of us would be safer allied with an eligible man, a powerful man. Do you think that young man would have attacked Hannah if she were engaged to one of his peers?"

"Hannah is his peer," I whispered. "We were all of us his peers. But we are never safe."

"*Quid custodiet ipsos custodes?*" murmured Felicity, who had always been apt with her Latin. I remembered how she had guarded her mother.

"We'd be safer," Charlotte repeated. "That's all we will get, so we might as well take it—take as much of it as we can. This society is an ill one, girls, but it is all we have."

"Does it have to be?" I thought suddenly of what a wonderful politician Charlotte would make. Sharp, inquisitive, fair-minded, charismatic—she would be elected mayor of the dormitory at once were such a position available. I saw just how aptly her Shadow Cabinet was named.

But she didn't answer my question; she didn't have to. She was already practically engaged to a man who would sit in Parliament before long, whose uncle had been prime minister and who showed every promise of following in those footsteps someday. And even I had to admit that Colonel Bailey worshipped Charlotte, that he seemed really to listen to her. Perhaps she would have some political influence after all, and perhaps she was right to take it in whatever way it was likely to come to her. I knew many of my mother's friends at Le Moulin would have said exactly that.

I felt a hand on my shoulder just then. I looked down at the pale fingers, the bitten nails.

Hannah.

I stood, turned, and saw Mrs. Webster beside her; both wore traveling cloaks.

For a moment I stood looking into Hannah's eyes, unable to move.

Felicity leapt up and wrapped her in a hug. I wouldn't have dared to touch her without being sure it was what she wanted, but Hannah was smiling against Felicity's shoulder. I stood and joined them both, and I felt Charlotte add her embrace to ours, and then more and more girls' arms came around us until it felt as if we were at the center of some infinitely blooming flower, and for a moment all my rage was subsumed under relief and pride in my friend who was standing again under her own power, her blue eyes meeting mine, open and clear.

Dear Adèle,

I was so pleased to hear of your friend's safe return; your pleasure, as always, is mine, if it is not too bold to say. And I'll further risk myself by suggesting I've dreamed more than once, in these past years of our acquaintance, of making your happiness my business in a much more material way. Your letters have made me hope, on occasion, that you might not find that dream disagreeable. I hope you do not.

I hope too that your friend does not fear all men because of her horrible experience with one of us; I feel such shame and rage when I think of him, I wish I could have killed him myself. I am glad the

172

accident occurred which kept him from harming her further or, heaven forbid, you. I have never wished harder that my father had allowed me to come to school in London, as you suggested, but his health is not robust, and he fears I may have to take over his business here sooner than was thought. If that is to be the case, I will be devastated by the loss . . . but I promise that I shall come, as soon as I am under my own power to do so, to England to see you at last. And then you may be a pirate queen in truth, if you so wish, for I will have ships of my own and we can adventure all over the whole world; you can show me your Paris haunts, and I will bring you to Jamaica, and perhaps we could settle somewhere that has never seen either of our faces before and be whoever we like, whoever we feel ourselves to be.

But I grow too bold again. This letter must be brief, for I am called away; I only wish to repeat that I hope neither you nor your friend lose faith in all my brothers, for I count myself among them, and I wish for nothing more fervently than the continued privilege of your confidence and trust.

Well, there is one thing I want more, perhaps.

Your servant,
Eric

I kept Eric's letters in the trunk at the foot of my dormitory bed. I'd kept them all, except the lost one, and this latest I placed crosswise to the rest of the stack, so that I could find it easily again. I knew I'd want to read it many times.

His indications of affection for me had increased steadily, and this letter hinted more broadly than any previous one did about the seriousness of his intent. I was starting to believe I could truly feel safe in the possibility of a future with a kindred spirit, a freer life than many of the girls here would face, if I so chose it. But it was not that which made this letter most precious. It was how Eric, not knowing that I'd intentionally killed Hannah's attacker—I had described it as an accident in a confused struggle, the story everyone thought they knew—still said he wished he'd done the deed himself.

He would understand. There was a darkness in him too. There was someone else, besides Nan, who might understand the full scope of my character.

And after all, what future could I have with Nan?

I closed my eyes as if against my own thoughts. I'd known Nan for such a short time. She'd seen through me, we'd shared some secrets, but that didn't mean she understood me—not the way I'd just caught myself assuming that she did. I didn't let myself linger on the memory of her warm smile, her dark eyes, that had seemed so companionable, so kind.

I wrote back to Eric right away.

The officers who came to tea that day were the usual collection of nervous youths, boorish fools, and lecherous older men; I knew only too well what drew them to the collection of girls at the Webster, and it was not our superior education and breeding, as much as our teachers insisted that it was.

Some people think that men are drawn to younger girls because of the beauty of our youth, but ever since I've known that I admire women, I've also known this to be untrue. I have never in my life seen a woman who was at her most beautiful before the age of twenty-five; I doubt I ever shall. Men like young girls precisely because we are young. We are moldable still in a way that grown women who have formed their own opinions are not.

Lord Winton fawned over Felicity as usual; Captain Farrow sat in a corner scowling and speaking to no one, his customary book propped casually on his knee. I wondered, as I had at the ball, if he was truly a reader or simply trying to look like Lord Byron; yet he had been deep in conversation with the truly bookish and shy Catherine then, so he must at least have read enough to hold her interest.

One of the oldest men, a corporal, sat down opposite me, to my distress.

"Now don't worry, young lady. I'm long and happily wed, and my wife hosts charity breakfasts for this school every year," he told me. "I simply wanted to introduce myself to the young girl who I hear acquitted herself so well during the unfortunate incident at Lady Shadley's ball at Almack's."

"So well?" I echoed him, startled. Every mention of the ball had me still waiting to be caught out, accused, or punished. Even though he'd spoken gently, I feared that his tone would turn with whatever he said next.

"Indeed," he said. "I hear you protected your friend most admirably."

I was stunned. He rambled on, talking about how men like Hannah's attacker have failed in their very first duty as men, to respect the honor and protect the virtue of women.

I nodded demurely. I had watched enough Moulin dancers pretend to find old men interesting that I knew exactly how to position my face and body for that effect, while I let my mind saunter out the window to the misty street beyond. Once it began its journey, I found it wandering in a quite fast and determined direction toward the East India Docks, into a pub called the King's Head, and up to the laughing brown eyes of an Irish pickpocket named Nan.

I was just wondering to myself how many tricks I could persuade Nan to teach me when a low male voice just by my ear yanked my mind back into my body and the Webster's visiting parlor.

"I'm afraid our dear corporal has made you blush, Miss Varens," said a ginger-haired young man I vaguely recognized but whose name I couldn't remember.

I touched my cheek self-consciously and found that it was indeed hot. That a girl, and not the gently smiling man across from me, had caused the blush, I hardly wished to explain; I simply smiled, I hoped demurely, and lowered my eyes.

"He is a rogue and not to be trusted. May I offer you the company of a true gentleman, perhaps on a turn about the Webster's courtyard?"

Outdoors—who knew but Nan might be waiting there again and I might catch a glimpse of her.

I realized immediately the absurd unlikeliness of that happening but still nodded at the young man, who introduced himself as Mr. Griffin. The corporal chuckled and waved us off, and Mr. Griffin took my hand and lead me out of the parlor.

It was cool and foggy in the courtyard, the air opaque enough to obscure the low walls into a suggestion of open space. Mist and unseen borders made me think, as they always did, of Thornfield, and I shivered.

Mr. Griffin saw my unintended movement. "Really, these thin dresses are pretty, but they can hardly be warm enough." He drew closer to me, slipping his arm through mine.

I flinched at his touch—two thoughtless movements, and I usually prided myself, a dancer's daughter, on knowledge and control of how my body moved.

He frowned and pulled me closer, angling our bodies toward each other so he could look me in the eye. "There's no need for that, miss," he said. "Not every man is out to hurt you the way the boy at the party hurt your friend, you know. I'd hate to see you paint us all with the same brush."

"As would I." I tried to pull away.

His grip tightened. "You're not afraid *now,* are you? We are in your own school's chaperoned courtyard! And I am a gentleman, Miss Varens. I would never hurt you. I asked you to walk with me because I like you. I could have asked any of your friends—and I'd never hurt them either—but I asked you. Because I like you. Not because I wanted to hurt you."

"You speak, sir, as if the two ideas are mutually exclusive. Yet most of the girls I know have been hurt by men who liked them too well."

He glared at me, his grip tightening to the point of pain even as he said again, "I would never hurt you."

"You're hurting me now." I pulled my arm away, and it took enough force to do so that I thought if I'd been a slighter girl with less natural strength, I might not have been able to at all. And had I been a quieter, more timid girl, would I even have dared to try? And all the while neither of us had done anything that might attract a chaperone's notice. I wondered how many girls were hurt while well chaperoned, every day. And then I thought of the headmaster at Ashfield, the chaperone who was the least safe one of all.

He finally stepped back. "I do apologize for the misunderstanding, Miss Varens," he said. "I trust you can find your way back to the parlor unaccompanied."

As I did so, I wondered if he really had not known he was hurting me . . . and if knowing or not knowing made him worse.

For all that I had promised Mrs. Webster I would stay home, I found I couldn't bear it—the feeling of confinement, of helplessness, that I felt when I couldn't sleep at night; and indeed sleep continued to elude me, no matter how tired I grew. All the pieces of my haunted heart kept me awake: one part by the boy I had killed and the girls I had vowed to avenge, and another by the face of a dark-haired girl who seemed to touch more of my thoughts and affections with each passing moment.

By the following night, when at last I went to meet Nan at the King's Head again, I was indeed starting to do what Mr. Griffin had accused me of: painting all men with the same brush. There were men who were straightforward in their violence and men who were not, but I did not think I had ever met a man who was not somehow dangerous, even if—maybe especially if—like Mr. Griffin, they were ignorant, or pretended ignorance, of their own menace.

And then there were men like Papa. Papa had never hurt me, and yet there was a coded language of violence that hung in the air all around him, that dark gravity I had felt the very first time I saw him in Paris.

I found myself flinching away from every man I passed on that dark, wet London street, and I hated my own fear. I tried to remember Eric Fairfax and his gentle, thoughtful, playful letters, the stories we told each other about being pirates together in some alternate life where both of us had more freedom. Yet I had never met Eric, not in the flesh; was even he safe only because our friendship was so disembodied?

As soon as I entered the pub a large, dark man pulled me aside. I was ready to scream or to fight before I even looked up into his face.

But when I did, it was Nan's father, Peter Ward, who looked back at me.

Without saying anything, he pressed something hard into my hand.

I looked down; it was a knife. A clasp-knife, closed, but still obviously what it was. It was cool and smooth, made of black-painted wood with a bright steel seam where the blade would slip out. The weight of it felt natural in my palm.

"Nan says you're ready," he murmured. "I wouldn't want a friend of hers to come here undefended."

I thought back to my last time in the King's Head and realized how safe I'd felt and how unsafe in my high-class school's own courtyard.

"I might need it more at home," I said, trying to keep my voice light.

Peter smiled a little. "Aye," he said, "that you might."

I opened and closed the knife experimentally; the second click followed quick and smooth on the first like a heartbeat. "Among other things."

"Aye," he repeated. "Everyone ought to know how to fight, though no one ought ever have to do it. Here, I'll take you back to meet Nan. She's to be your teacher, I hear." He tipped his head, gesturing for me to follow him. "It's a rough world we live in, girleen, you as well as me."

We walked back through the pub, progressing slowly because he stopped to speak with so many people, to ask them about their families or their health in ways that showed a depth of care I hadn't seen since . . . I couldn't remember when. I began to suspect that in spite of appearances, in spite even of his profession, he was a man who wanted the world to be kinder than it was.

I wondered how many of the people he spoke with knew what I'd only seen when he'd grabbed me, my face inches from his: that his thick black beard was false, and the cheek under it as smooth as my own.

"All right, we're going to start. Are you ready?" Nan reached into her left sleeve.

I flinched, then immediately went into the defensive stance I remembered from the lessons of Maman and her friends, where the first and most important rule was to be always prepared for a surprise attack. When they were teaching me, they certainly wouldn't have asked if I was ready.

Nan paused, then came toward me in one cautious step, slowly withdrawing her hand from her sleeve and holding out both hands in front of her. "It's all right, Adèle," she said. "I'm here to help you, right? I'll never scare you on purpose." She frowned, a line appearing between her eyebrows. "I'll never scare you at all. That I promise."

I felt my face and neck flush with embarrassment—I, who always prided myself on never having allowed a man to let me blush, on my coolness before even the handsomest and most charming of rakes. "I try always to be ready for an attack," I said. "It's one of the first things the women in Le Moulin taught me."

"They were wise to do so," Nan said. "But I wonder who will be able to teach you to feel safe again?"

I laughed, but my throat felt suddenly blocked and I could not answer. *I never once in my life met a girl who felt truly safe*, I thought.

And that reminded me why I was there to begin with. Not on my own behalf, but on that of every frightened girl I knew—that was to say, of every girl in the world.

I met Nan's gaze, so dark and thoughtful.

I was there for myself too.

But never, never, for myself first. For every frightened girl; for every attic girl. For every girl who could not fight back.

I nodded at her. When I could trust myself to speak again, I said, "Let's begin."

Nan reached back into her sleeve and pulled out a small, spring-loaded knife. No matter what she said about scaring me or surprises, I still suspected a sudden attack. Instead, she turned the handle toward me and held it out. "The first step toward feeling safe is to know that you are armed," she told me.

I thought of Maman's poison ring, the gift she had passed on to me. My gaze flicked toward my hand, where the gold shone dully, then back to her knife.

The wooden handle was worn smooth, clearly from years of use; the blade was thin, much-sharpened, so that it tapered like the fossilized claw that one of the Webster's visiting scientific lecturers had passed around to the girls. That man had watched Felicity cradle his claw in her gloved hands with a lecherous look that had made me nauseous at the time. I felt sick again just remembering it. And angry.

I flipped the knife over in my hands and felt its weight and heft, and I remembered how I had imagined pushing the claw right through the lecturer's watery blue eyes to his lascivious brain.

I didn't regret killing the boy at the ball. I would do it again if I had to, to save Hannah. In that moment I felt that knowledge with all my heart and soul. If I had to, I would kill again.

"Now come at me," Nan murmured, and I did.

She blocked me easily of course. "You're moving like a hand fighter," she said.

"It's served me well enough before," I said, more hotly than I meant to.

She nodded, holding my gaze, and again that unearned feeling that she sympathized, understood, washed over me. "But a knife is different; any weapon is. You don't need to keep your feet as planted, for instance; you don't require the same force you'd need to plant a good blow with your fist. That's one of the reasons a knife is a right and proper weapon for a girl, Da always says; it evens the field no matter if the man is ten times bigger and heavier'n you. So many men are snakes that a woman deserves to have fangs."

Nan slipped her hand into one of her skirt's hidden pockets and showed me another knife. She opened her right palm—I'd noticed she was left-handed, and later I heard Peter call her *kithogue*—and ran the blade smoothly along it, pressing it into her own skin, but it didn't break or bleed. "This knife is too dull for anything but sparring," she said. "You'd have to work it hard to cut butter."

I nodded, she flashed forward, and I felt the smooth cold slip of the knife's blunt edge—not along my throat, which was the part of me I'd thought to defend and brought my arms up to cover, but across the back of the hand that held the knife.

"If your enemy carries a knife as well, aim for their hands, not their throats or their chests or anywhere else," she said. "One good slice on the back of the hand distracts and disarms them at once. You've defanged the snake, you see? Then you'll have time to run away and take anyone who needs rescuing with you, if you and they are lucky."

"I was always taught that keeping my balance was more important than being able to land a blow, or block one," I said. "The girls at Le Moulin had to know a fair bit about defending themselves." Funny, I had never felt able to speak about my time at Le Moulin to the Webster girls, for all the parallels I drew between them, not even to Hannah—especially not Hannah. Maybe I had internalized shame about it after all. I'd never even felt comfortable writing about it to Eric.

But I could tell Nan. I could tell her all my thoughts, uncensored, safe in the knowledge that we could not shock each other with tales of our dissolute lives.

"It'll be hard to keep your balance if you're bleeding out," Nan replied, and I couldn't argue with that. "Better to go off-balance and land a blow, even a slant one."

She lunged and was on me, and I stumbled backward. In half a second, I was on the ground, my legs splayed and my hands and backside hitting the floor hard enough that they would surely show bruises in the morning. Nan straddled my waist, her knife at my throat. I felt as if all I could see were her brown eyes; all I could feel was her knife and her hips against mine.

As we looked at each other, she lowered the knife, and I felt its cool length replaced by the warmth of her hand around my neck. And even though her touch was gentle, almost not a touch at all, I couldn't help longing for a moment for her fingers to tighten, and her head to dip closer to mine.

"Even if she hadn't pinned you, that stripe from a proper knife would have you dead by now," Peter said quietly.

I had forgotten he was there. I had forgotten how to speak as well, it seemed—forgotten everything but Nan's gaze, her hand on my throat, the sweet weight and warmth of her legs on either side of mine. I shifted under her a little—I couldn't help it—and it seemed to startle her out of some kind of reverie too.

She stood and held out her hand to help me up.

"Thank you," I said, "for the lesson."

FIFTEEN

FIGHTING WAS STILL on my mind when I returned to the Webster early that morning, even as I took extra care to move quietly up the stairs to the dormitory. I'd promised myself that I'd protect the other girls if I could, but I knew that I couldn't be with all of them at every moment. I wanted to teach them a skill that they could carry with them, like the knife Nan's father had given me.

I undressed, donned my nightgown, and climbed into bed for the few hours' sleep I was growing accustomed to, all the while imagining the situations my schoolmates might find themselves in and what I might teach them that could help.

Perhaps that's why the nightmare was so bad.

The dream started sweet: I was with Nan again, pinned under the warm weight of her body, but neither our knives nor her father was present. Nan stroked my cheek with her thumb, moving down across my neck to the bodice of my dress, looking in my eyes the whole time. She touched the locket at my breast, toying with it. Then she leaned into me, the way I'd wished she had when we were training, and I welcomed her . . . and then her form shifted, and it was Eric, the face from the locket, the boy in Jamaica whose sweet, imaginative letters had sustained me through lonely years. I welcomed him as I had welcomed her and pulled his face to mine for a kiss I'd long imagined. And even in dream I felt the kiss deeply, felt the wonderful pressure of his body against mine, and I was glad and grateful that our bodies had found each other after such a long companionship of the mind. I pulled away to look at him and his face was changing once more, into the man his portrait so resembled—into Papa. He pressed his body to me again, calling me little elf the way he had when I met him in Paris, murmuring my name as his lips sought mine—

"Adèle. Adèle!"

I woke up cold and gasping; my nightgown felt wet and clammy on my skin, and it took me a moment to realize I had sweated through the fabric. Took me another moment to understand that I was in my own bed at school, and no one's body was holding me down. The only touch I felt was gentle and soft on my shoulder. As my eyes adjusted to the darkness, I recognized the hand on me, and I paired it with the voice I'd heard calling my name.

"Hannah."

"You were screaming," she whispered. "I thought you'd be glad to be woken—"

"Yes. Yes." I took a deep breath, letting the new air wash out some of the gummy, horrid residue of the dream's last moments from my body. "Thank you."

"Adèle, darling, are you all right?" That voice was Felicity's, and it was echoed by several others. I realized I must have woken the whole dormitory.

"I'm sorry," I said to the room as a whole, trying to make my voice carry a little more, hating the tremble I still heard in it. "It was only a nightmare."

A tut that might have been Felicity or Charlotte. "Don't pretend you're well for our sakes, Adèle, please." Charlotte. "We've all had dark dreams since my aunt's ball, and you and Hannah have more reason for them than any of us. Please, let's none of us pretend that we're not haunted by what happened to the two of you that night."

I swallowed. Of course the other girls were afraid too. I'd been so wrapped up in my own rage and pain and grief, in the vow I'd taken with myself that night, that I had barely spared a thought even for Hannah in her absence, let alone how our other class-mates must have felt.

Charlotte came and sat on my bed, Felicity behind her. "You've been—been wearing a suit of armor since that night, it's seemed to me. I never wanted to press you to speak of it if you didn't wish to. Mrs. Webster told us we shouldn't."

I closed my eyes briefly in shame. I hated the image her words conjured, of our headmistress telling the other girls not to bother me, that I was too fragile, that I required their pity after Hannah's and my ordeal.

"But we must speak of it," Charlotte went on. "What happened to you and Hannah could have happened to any of us."

"Has happened to some of us already," Felicity added quietly. I remembered how quickly she'd stopped talking about her own romantic history over Christmas. I remembered her mother.

Someone lit a candle; as its light flared I saw Catherine blowing out her match. In the new low light, many girls were nodding.

I had promised myself I'd protect them. But I should have known, from my time at Le Moulin, my time with Bertha—all my time on this earth as a female—that for many of us, I was already too late.

"Adèle was wonderful," said Hannah then, her voice steady and calm, "that night when—the night of the ball. If she hadn't found me and hadn't . . . done what she did, I would have fared much worse." She looked down. "I would have no chances left to me at all if not for her. There would have been no reason for me to come back here."

She was looking at me now with fondness and confidence in her gaze, and I thought that if that look were all the requited love I would ever have from her, I could count it as more than enough.

I shook my head. "I only did what anyone would do if they had the chance." And the truth of those words healed a little of the horror of that boy's death that lingered in me, that I knew would always be somewhere inside me.

That healing strengthened the resolve I'd felt walking home just a few hours before. "Girls," I said, "you know that I—that I grew up in a different country than most of you did. I grew up in materially different circumstances too. Vastly different. And there are things I learned there, about men and . . . how to protect yourself from them, that I could teach you. Not—not ladylike things." I hated how I stumbled over my words, but I knew it was better than staying silent.

Felicity laughed, the sound cold and tight. "Perhaps not, but I imagine they are things ladies need to know."

Felicity as a small child, guarding her mother with her body the only way that she knew how. Hannah, pinned by a young man's arms and authority.

"Yes." And beginning with the best place to hurt a man, I started to teach them.

Two nights later, when I saw Nan again, I was so eager for more that she took me on a walk for our next lesson. I'd mastered leaving the Webster discreetly via the servants' stairs, and with each passing night I grew more confident in my ability to avoid notice. I was determined to learn from her—and simply to see her—as often as possible. We left the King's Head and moved away from the docks until we came to a street that I recognized, less than twenty minutes' walk from the Webster. It was populated mostly by gentlemen's clubs, which at this hour were still brightly lit; inside men would be drinking, gambling, and generally whiling away time that they didn't wish to spend at home with their families. Nan took my hand and pulled me to a stop in what I saw, after a long moment, was the deepest patch of shadow on the street, between the pools of lamplight. It wasn't until she dropped my hand, too soon, that I was able to think about why she'd chosen that particular place.

"We're going to wait for a particularly drunken man to come out," Nan said, "and then we'll have him."

A few minutes later a portly man with a truly enormous moustache came out the door of one club nearly stumbling. But as I began to step forward, Nan grabbed my arm and pulled me back. "Wait till I tell you!" she hissed. "That's Lord Barton; he has a carriage waiting! We need one who'll be walking home."

Indeed, before he had stumbled fully down the club's marble stoop, a grand-looking carriage pulled into the pool of lamplight that illuminated the street outside its doorway, and a tall footman rushed forward to hold Lord Barton's arm and help him inside.

I squeezed my eyes shut in embarrassment, but when I opened them again and looked at Nan, she wasn't angry; in fact, by the spark in her beautiful eyes, the dimples flashing among the constellations of her freckles, she was suppressing laughter.

"Just wait until I take the lead, the way I did when we were dancing," she said. My body suddenly filled with the memory of dancing with her, the lush pleasure I'd felt before that night turned to nightmare, and before I could think, I grabbed her by both arms and pulled her close to me.

Nan gave a little gasp, inaudible to anyone whose ears weren't inches from her lips. She recovered quickly, and the beginnings of laughter played around her pretty face again; she let out her breath as I inhaled, and the sweetness of black tea and the sharpness of the peppermint humbugs she'd told me she favored were in my mouth.

I was so close to kissing her. But . . .

For all I told myself how worldly I was, how much more I knew than my Webster schoolmates did because of my upbringing in Paris, I had never kissed anyone before. Not with romantic intent. The closest I'd come was kissing the seal on Eric's letters once or twice and wondering if he'd done the same.

Thinking of Eric, I relaxed my hold on Nan just enough that she tilted her head in confusion, and a little line appeared between her brows. "What are you at, Adèle?" she whispered. The sound of my name in her Irish lilt undid something inside me, and the confidence I'd had a moment ago evaporated completely.

I tried to laugh at myself, and if the sound came out a little weak and breathy, at least Nan did me the courtesy of playing along and laughing too. "I just wanted to show you I can lead as well as you," I said. I swallowed. "At dancing, I mean."

"Sure you can, girleen." She tilted her head up, just a bit, and briefly kissed my cheek. "Maybe I'll give you a chance, some other time." She looked over my shoulder and her expression changed. "But right now, here comes our mark, I think."

My skin felt branded where her lips had pressed against me: hot, marked. Claimed. Like I never wanted anyone else to touch that part of me again.

But that was too much feeling to take in just then—in fact the intensity of it scared me; I didn't know if I'd ever be ready to feel that way about anyone, let alone a girl I'd so recently met.

I let her go.

Turning to face the direction of her gaze, I saw a younger man than the last one walking unsteadily out of the nearest streetlamp's pool of light.

"Lord, he's so drunk I doubt he'll remember his own name in the morning," Nan whispered. "Maybe for this first one, you just watch. That'll be safest. You can try the next one, I promise. I'll come up behind him, and—"

"Nan, I know him." I was startled by it, although I don't know why I should have been; wasn't my familiarity with members of society one of the reasons Nan had approached me?

His name was Christopher Brooksbank, and he had attended more than one of the Webster's afternoon teas. My recollections of him were mostly that he didn't speak to me or any of my friends directly but looked us up and down at length and murmured things to his friends that made them color, smirk, or snort with derisive laughter.

Any guilt I felt about the crime we were about to commit dissipated entirely. He was a cad, and his family was more than wealthy enough that he wouldn't long miss any valuables we relieved him of tonight.

I whispered to Nan: "What if I distract him, while you . . . ?"

She looked doubtful for a moment, then shrugged. "He's drunk enough that we should be able to get away easy if it goes south. Sure, if you think you can play him, pretty girl, I'll let you try."

The brand of her lips on my cheek heated again at *pretty girl*. Thinking that I'd never been so vulnerable to any man's flattery as I was to hers, I walked forward until I was within a few paces of our mark.

Pitching my voice low and soft and a little frightened, I reached toward him, as if searching for safe harbor in a storm: "Good evening, Mr. Brooksbank. I—I wonder if you might help me."

He flinched at the sound of my voice, stared at me, and wobbled where he stood. "I don't . . . that is . . ." His gaze roamed over my face and dress, even less subtly than when he had been sober. "Miss, um, Varens?"

"I am flattered that you remember, sir." I pressed a hand to my bosom, where his gaze had settled—I knew well that my figure was excellent, for all an ample bosom was not in fashion—and gave a little curtsey.

He scoffed. "Who would not remember your—ah—" He cleared his throat. "I mean, how may I assist you?"

Nan gave me a quick signal from behind him. I had to keep myself from showing my surprise; even I had not noticed her approach, and she was directly in my line of sight.

My, she was good.

I turned my little gasp of surprise into a sigh, forlorn, all damsel. "I'm afraid I was separated from my friends on our walk this evening, and I—I can't seem to find my way back to our school. I've been so frightened, all alone, and when I saw you I thanked God for putting a gentleman in my path who could help me back to safety . . ."

Nan's freckled hand was pulling back his cloak now, moving as delicately as a slight breeze; with her other hand she undid the clasp

194

of a gold chain that dipped into his pocket and pulled out something that seemed to glow even in the gloom between streetlamps. Her gaze met mine again for the shadow of a moment, and then she melted into the darkness and was gone.

I quickly looked back at Mr. Brooksbanks; he was frowning at me. "What are you . . . I feel . . ."

I stepped toward him again, so that our chests were almost touching; I could smell alcohol, not just on his breath but seeming to emanate from his whole body. I pushed down my repulsion; I'd told Nan I would keep him distracted, and I wanted nothing more in that moment than to do her proud.

"What do you feel, Christopher?" I murmured, my voice now almost a coo. I bent my knees a little so I could gaze up at him through my lashes, the ghosts of Moulin dancers animating my every movement.

He looked at me wonderingly, opening his mouth a little, and I wondered if I could bear actually kissing him . . .

And then he opened his mouth wider and vomited onto my dress.

Perhaps I should have helped him. But I was nearly sick myself because of it; I backed away as he coughed and retched again, bracing his hands on his knees. After a few steps I heard Nan hiss, "Come on!" and I turned and ran, following her as she hurried away into the darkness.

We didn't stop running for several minutes, and I think she would have preferred to keep going, but she looked back and saw me wheezing, gasping to keep up. I'd thought I was strong because the dancing lessons at the Webster never tired me nor did our constitutional walks, because I'd always had some natural strength.

She came back and took my arm, keeping us moving at a quick pace, but one that let me catch my breath. We kept going for what felt like an endless time, her closeness somehow all I could think about despite the effort of rushing forward to keep pace with her, despite the fact that I'd just committed another crime. Back at the King's Head, we came through the back door and went right to her room from the dark little hallway we found there. Immediately her fingers started working on the buttons at the front of my dress.

"We'll have to go on horseback next time," she said, her voice full of teasing. "You're a brilliant piece of bait, Adèle, but you're not much use at running away."

"I'll improve." I took another deep breath, shifting my hips back and forth a little to try and stretch away the cramp in my side. "The Webster's horses are middling at best anyway."

She looked up at me and smiled. "I may know where to find some better." Her gaze lowered again, her nimble fingers moving as quickly and lightly as they had Mr. Brooksbanks's pocket.

I couldn't enjoy the moment, not when the reason for her helping me undress was so disgustingly apparent. Still, when she'd fully opened the bodice and I'd helped her pull it over my arms, leaving me in corset, shift, and skirts as she bundled up the soiled fabric she'd removed, I wondered if we'd ever have an excuse for such intimacy again.

"You can wash this here," she said, "and leave it to dry here, too, if it won't be missed."

"It won't," I said. "We're meant to wear our uniforms every day, except for when we go to church. I have two other dresses I can wear for that." This one was black cotton, decorated with a little lace and a few tucks, but fairly plain. Jane had said it was better to have something to wear to a funeral than not to be prepared; she'd spoken in a clipped, no-nonsense voice, but now I recalled the dear school friend she'd spoken of, the girl she'd been so close to, who had died.

"I do love a girl in uniform," she said.

As she left the room, I realized I was blushing. When she returned, carrying a tin basin and wooden washboard, she smiled at me in a way that made me wonder if she knew why.

When I found a few spots on my overskirt, I washed that too. As I washed, I decided to leave the dress with Nan: mourning clothes were good for blending into the night, of course, but I also thought they might lend me an especially decorous air, and perhaps make men hesitate a little more to suspect my intentions. With a mourning veil over my face, and this dress, I could be well disguised indeed. And the idea of a murderous widow, I had to admit, appealed to me.

Nan had lent me one of her dresses to wear, a faded brown wool that was patched in several places. It was small in the chest, wide around the waist, and short in the skirt, but it kept me from going out into the pub with my corset and shift showing, and I was grateful; it seemed that my years posing as a proper English girl had more effect on me than I had realized, for I knew I would be embarrassed to go out into the main room partly unclothed.

When I did emerge, I found Nan showing off our plunder to her father: a heavy golden pocket watch.

"Deeply engraved, which will make it hard to pawn," he said, "but I might be able to change the initials; and the mechanism itself is very fine, we could sell that and keep the gold. Solid, both the casing and the chain." He nodded at her and then to me. "Well done, girls."

I smiled, far more pleased with his approval than I could have guessed I'd be, but then, it had been years since I had sought, much less received, approval from any kind of father.

"We'll keep the watch," he went on, speaking to Nan, "and let your lovely lady keep the chain." He unclipped the two, and I marveled at how quickly and delicately his broad hands could move. "Everyone should have a keepsake of their first theft."

Nan took my hand by the wrist and lifted it. I glanced around the pub, wondering if anyone was watching us, but no one except Peter was, and he didn't seem to find anything unusual in the way his daughter touched me; and in the King's Head, I suppose, it wasn't. I had seen more than one pair of loving women in my time at Le Moulin, both between dancers and, once in a while, when a wealthy lady paid for companionship. Until I'd come here, I'd heard only the barest whispers of such things in England: two widows in Yorkshire, lifelong friends whose husbands had died young, who had lived together all their lives and eventually been buried in one grave; small sounds at night in the dormitory, now and then, that made me wonder if I was not the only girl who wished to crawl into another's bed.

But here people of the same sex shared loving looks and touches openly; here they flaunted the strict rules of what belonging to one sex or another even meant. I looked at Peter again, at the beard that was so skillfully, believably applied to his smooth chin.

As I watched him, he stroked that beard and laughed at me, his kind eyes crinkling. I brought my gaze quickly back to Nan's fingers.

She looped the gold chain, warm from her hand, three times around my wrist, then clasped it. "This isn't just a keepsake," she told me in a warm and intimate voice. "I'd call it a trophy."

I swallowed. "I'm just glad I didn't fail," I said.

She looked into my eyes. "As if I'd have let you."

I don't think I stopped smiling the whole way home.

The next day was Sunday, and after the Webster girls attended the morning service at St Paul's—where it often seemed we were there to see and be seen by the good families in attendance as much as to know God—Mrs. Webster took us on our monthly charity rounds. Usually these rounds involved genteel activities that we could conduct in the school's parlor or that of one of its benefactors, like Charlotte's aunt. This time, however, we went to a workhouse. Mrs. Webster and Mrs. Harris had lectured us extensively about the conditions we were to expect there. "It will hurt your hearts to see the pain and sorrow of the souls that you will meet," the headmistress told us, "but remember that we are there to do them good, and we will do all the good we can."

"And keep your hands to yourselves, girls," Mrs. Harris added, "for there will be nothing you could touch in that place that isn't filthy. Don't let them touch you either."

There was nothing to particularly distinguish the building we approached from the outside—nothing material, that is; it was built of brick and had a long facade, lacking in windows, but that was not unusual. Yet there was a creeping sense that seemed to emanate from inside it, a kind of miasma of sadness and anger; I cannot explain it better than that even now. During my years in Paris I'd entered many places the poverty of which would shock my Webster peers, yet none of them had the strangling aura that this place had, even before we went inside.

There was only one entrance to the whole building; Mrs. Webster had told us about this, saying that it kept anyone from entering or leaving undetected. As we walked through the narrow doorway a glowering guard watched us, making tick marks on a grubby piece of paper to record our number. I thought of the nights I'd come and gone from school, so much more easily than I'd imagined I could. Mrs. Webster and Mrs. Harris had both called this place a charitable organization, but it seemed more like a prison.

We had to walk single file down the narrow, low-ceilinged corridor; Mrs. Webster walked in front of us, and Mrs. Harris behind. They guided us quickly to a residence hall whose door was marked, I saw as I passed, "Able-Bodied Women." They had told us too that we would only be visiting that one group. "Your parents would never forgive us for exposing your delicate sensibilities to the other rooms," Mrs. Webster had said, "for the indigent and elderly, and the children's rooms would be beyond your innocent young hearts' ability to withstand."

Mrs. Harris had laughed coldly and added, "And the men's quarters are not to be thought of."

And yet, for all their lectures, there are some things that are impossible to prepare for. Even now, years later, I recoil from describing it and then recoil from my own reluctance; for so many people have had to live in the workhouses, still live in them today.

The stench, first—it was strong enough that it took long moments to notice anything else in that room, even to use my eyes to look. There were open buckets for human waste in two corners; the low, stained ceiling seemed to push the sour human smells of the place back down on us. The walls, cheaply whitewashed, were stained too, with damp and creeping patches of black mold. Narrow cots were lined up so close to each other that there was barely room to walk between them. A bundled-up blanket at the foot of a cot to my left smelled strongly of vomit; the woman resting fitfully on the thin, bare mattress was obviously pregnant and suffering from it. I thought of Jane's discomfort during her pregnancy, but she had wealth and servants and access to doctors, and could wait out her symptoms at her leisure. This was a workhouse, and this woman, for all her obvious suffering, was still in the able-bodied women's room. Today was Sunday, but tomorrow they would be back at whatever hard labor the house's management asked of them: picking oakum, mostly, horrible and wearying work.

The pregnant woman kept her eyes closed; I did not know if she was sleeping or just unwilling or unable to move. The other women in the room were gathered in small groups, speaking quietly with each other, most of them mending ragged garments as they talked. Most of them ignored us too. We had been given baskets containing food—fresh rolls and little twists of butter, apples, small portions of spice cake—and clean and mended secondhand petticoats, which we had once worn ourselves. Our instructions were to give our baskets to the women, to be kind and polite and speak to them only briefly. "You are there for your own education, as well as to offer these women your charity," Mrs. Webster had said, "but lingering will only expose you to more than would be healthy."

To give to people we weren't allowed to really meet or speak to seemed less charitable to me than condescending. Still I was not prepared for the open hostility, even hatred, in the faces of the women whom we approached, one by one, with our foolish little baskets.

But then, I remembered there had been women, in Paris, who had come to Le Moulin and the houses where the dancers and their children lived. They came in small groups from churches mostly, and they thought they were coming to save our mothers, to persuade them to leave behind dancing and the other business they did with men, to become seamstresses or housemaids. Sometimes they brought sweets for the children, and when they gave them to us, they always told us to ask our mothers to bring us to church—to beg if we needed to. They asked us if we didn't want to save our mothers' souls, to keep them from the divine punishment that awaited them if they died as unrepentant.

I had taken their sweets—we all had—but I'd hated those ladies. We all had. Hated them more than our mothers did, I think. The memory of that hatred filled up my body so suddenly that, as the other girls made their shy or overbright greetings to the residents of the poorhouse, I found myself frozen in place.

We weren't there to tell these women to change their ways, I told myself. But we were still saying—with our baskets and our brief visits, our unwillingness to get our hands dirty in any sense—that we were better than they were, and that we knew what was best.

I still had the gold chain from the pocket watch that Nan and I had stolen the night before. I had kept it wrapped around my wrist, and every time I felt it move against my skin, it made me smile. Nan had said it was a trophy, and in the moment she'd handed it to me, I'd imagined I would keep it forever.

With a quick few movements I had it off of my wrist and hidden under a fold of linen in my basket. I glanced around furtively, but I didn't think anyone had seen me. I hoped Nan would be pleased if she could have seen.

I walked up to the pregnant woman on the cot; she had stirred by then and was halfway sitting up. "Good afternoon, miss," I said. She looked up at me, her eyes cold. I did not wait for her to move further but placed the basket next to her on the bed. "I hope you'll be able to keep the bread down, if nothing else. I . . ." I wasn't sure how to say what else I needed to say. She was looking at the basket now, not at me. I glanced around the room; both Mrs. Webster and Mrs. Harris were engaged, Mrs. Webster speaking quietly to the shy Catherine, urging her forward, and Mrs. Harris pulling

Charlotte away from a woman with whom it seemed she'd been talking quite animatedly.

I took my chance and lifted the linen where I'd hidden the gold chain. I saw the woman's eyes widen. "You can live on that for a few months, I'd reckon," I whispered, "or get passage somewhere or . . . whatever you like." Then I repeated what Peter had said when Nan and I showed him the watch: "Don't take anyone's first offer when you sell or barter that. The gold is real."

Before she could further react, I retreated back to the line of Webster girls, and almost immediately, it seemed, we were being shepherded back out of that cold and stinking building and into the London street. After my years on the moors, I would never think the smoky, fetid London air could be called fresh, but I took in deep breaths one after the other, like they were food.

The Webster girls walked home in silence that day, even Charlotte and Felicity. The poverty and hopelessness we'd seen, even so briefly, must have been exponentially more shocking to my schoolmates, who had been born and raised in luxury; they did not have even the little preparation that I did. And while Mrs. Webster, leading us back to the school, looked nearly as mournful as her students, I saw a cold, hard little smile on Mrs. Harris's face. And then I knew that our visit had not simply been charity but a warning. A workhouse was the place where women went when they had nowhere else to go. I knew that most of the Webster girls would fear a fate like that, fear poverty, far more than they could fear a cruel husband or an oppressive family.

SIXTEEN

SO I BEGAN to steal and to hurt them when I had to. I dressed in widow's weeds and lured them to secluded places. Such men, of course, were not exceptions; they were the majority of high society. People with too much power will abuse it, and I never understood why that was so shocking to say. Every woman, every child, and every man who is not sufficiently rich or titled knows it. Not all men are like Hannah's attacker, Eric had said. I could not tell him what I had learned from childhood and what I relearned daily now.

I gave most of the money to alms for the poor or left it on the windowsills or stoops of the factory-worker houses that were springing up on more and more London streets. When I saw the conditions the workers lived in, I took to robbing the factory owners too, whether they'd hurt a girl I knew or not. They hurt far more people without ever touching them simply by the way they ran their businesses.

The whole world began to stink with the sins of powerful men.

I brought some of the money to Nan and her father in the King's Head too, of course.

And sometimes, I will admit it, I bought sweets. I felt so worldly-wise, so weary and rageful at the injustices I saw and fought against, but I was still enough of a child to love a humbug now and then.

I ate them with Nan sometimes, in the graying hours before dawn, when our work was done and we were too tired to talk but couldn't bear to leave each other's company quite yet. I was content just to lean against some stone or brick wall or sit on some Thames pier, close enough our hips would touch through our layers of skirts, and know we were both fierce enough to keep each other safe. I would breathe in her peaty, smoky scent and suck my sweet and know her mouth tasted of peppermint too.

I was happy.

And then a Webster girl went missing.

"She left a note," said Felicity, "for her parents." She picked up the folded letter left on Catherine's bed. It had no seal, just her parents' names in shaky writing on the front.

"Of course we mustn't read it," she added drily, unfolding the letter. Several girls laughed.

I did not—I already felt a kind of dread, although I could not have said why until . . .

"I am sure you cannot guess the name of the man who has won my hand," Felicity read, "for he is not from one of the families you'd hoped to ally me with. He is an officer though, and I have no doubt his quality will see him quickly rising through the ranks until he gains a position befitting his true character. As soon as I discovered our mutual love for the poetry of Lord Byron I knew he was truly—"

The mischievous smile vanished from Felicity's lips, and the letter crumpled in her hand. "Oh no," she murmured.

The sick feeling in my gut grew sicker.

"I . . . Girls, I'm sorry, this—this isn't so amusing as I thought." Felicity sat down on Catherine's narrow bed, her usually rosy face gone gray. Her head slumped into her hands.

Their queen bee no longer buzzing, the other girls glanced uncertainly at each other and began to murmur among themselves.

I knelt before Felicity, taking the letter from her. "Who is it?" I asked. "What do you know?"

"I know the officer," Felicity whispered. "More intimately than I should like to." Her voice, usually so confident and full of laughter, was barely audible and so strained she could hardly get the words out. "And not just me, he—he fancies himself a great seducer, like Byron, only he—" She looked up at me, and she was crying. "He's no type of man for anyone to marry. He . . . he hurts girls at just the moment when he should treat them most kindly." Her lips set hard together. "Oh, I hate even saying it—you know what I mean, don't you?" Our eyes locked, and the expression in hers was both frightened and fierce.

I nodded.

"And Catherine, she's so naive, she'll think—I'm sure she thinks his love of reading makes him sensitive. She has no idea . . . and

I teased her about it, teased them. I *hate* him. And I never really liked her. I surely drove them closer together." She shuddered, casting the letter aside on her bed, putting her head back in her hands.

"Felicity, you did no such thing. I should think you were trying to pull her away from him, making her come dance with you like that." The moment I'd witnessed between the three of them at the ball, when I'd judged Felicity poorly for her jealousy of Catherine, suddenly slid and shifted: the same image, the same movements, but imbued with an entirely different meaning.

She shook her head weakly.

I stood up, taking the letter and scanning through it. I could already guess where they must have gone, but Catherine's final line confirmed it: Gretna Green. The closest part of Scotland to London, a small village that had become infamous as a host to elopements, since Scotland's marriage laws were so much laxer than our own.

"It doesn't matter," I said. "Don't worry. She must have left barely an hour ago. There is still time."

I did not think about a plan. I simply knew what I needed to do.

I kept a warm traveling cloak at the top of my trunk these days; I took it up and rushed downstairs.

It is shockingly easy to steal a horse from the stables of your own school. The dun mare I took was more used to pulling Mrs. Webster's carriage than to bearing a rider, but she was fit and well rested, and she ran quick enough to please anyone.

I knew that an eloping couple had reason to value speed as well.

Still, Catherine and Captain Farrow would think they had until morning before her absence raised any alarm. They would surely stop at an inn instead of traveling on through the night.

Well—not surely. Hopefully.

There was only one road to take out of London and head directly toward the Scottish border, so I knew the way they'd gone.

I rode hard.

It was a fine and cloudless night. The street in front of me was much wider and smoother than the winding Yorkshire ways, the rocky passes our ponies had picked across at Thornfield and Ferndean that had made me such a good horsewoman. Even when I passed the city gates and the cobbles turned to packed dirt, the mare strode easily and we made good time.

It turned out to be absurdly easy to track them down. Captain Farrow, it seemed, had never been particularly concerned about concealing himself. At the first country inn I passed, his own white stallion, which Felicity had told me to look for, wasn't even stabled; he was tied to a tree near a watering trough, bending his fine, long head to drink his fill while a couple of stable boys stood nearby, ogling him admiringly. I remembered the look on Farrow's face when he'd spoken to Catherine at the ball, the admiration I'd read as worship but that had been simply hunger. Predation. I hated myself for what I'd thought.

But it did not matter what I'd thought, only that I had been wrong. We had all been wrong about the level of threat Captain Farrow had posed to Catherine. And none of us had bothered—

To protect her. Save her.

None of us had *bothered*.

That ended tonight.

With me.

I dismounted and handed the mare's bridle to one of the enraptured stable boys, along with enough coin to distract him from Farrow's stallion. A country church bell rang ten o'clock. I stalked toward the inn's front door, scowling, and I pulled my scarf away from my face as I neared the door.

Then I stopped myself. What exactly was I planning to do?

To rescue Catherine. To keep her from a fate no girl should suffer: being shackled in marriage to a violent man.

That was, if he even planned to shackle her at all and not simply use her and leave her to be ostracized. I had to admit that was more likely.

Whatever I had to do to save her from either fate, I knew that I would do it.

I moved quietly away from the door, into the deep shadows. I had not lost the knack of moving silently I'd learned backstage at Le Moulin; I knew that much from my recent adventures with Nan.

I stalked behind the building. It was a small inn, a way station where most travelers stopped only for a meal and to water or change their horses. There were three windows on the upper story; one of them was surely the room Farrow had taken.

And there was a chestnut tree, huge at the trunk, with thick and twisted branches, just behind it. High and sturdy enough to climb.

I hadn't climbed a tree since Ferndean, though. I scaled the trunk until I could look into the upper windows and then climbed out onto one of the biggest branches.

My foot slipped a little as I moved out, and I scrabbled at the bark in front of me, and my hand found a hold on what I thought was a knot in the wood, but it was sharp edged and left splinters, and I felt cold metal inside it.

After I steadied myself on the branch, I groped inside the hole and pulled out a tarnished, slightly sticky pair of opera glasses.

Clearly I was not the first person who thought to climb this tree and look inside the windows.

I recalled the men who lingered a little too close to the dressing rooms at Le Moulin, who got their heads knocked when they leaned in to look through keyholes and the girls, knowing all along, opened the doors with violent speed. I remembered the headmaster at Ashfield, watching us in our beds at night. I remembered Thornfield and Ferndean . . .

I pulled out my handkerchief and scrubbed the glasses as best I could. I held them near my eyes, taking care not to let them touch my skin.

I certainly could see into the rooms a treat.

The first window showed me the innkeeper's bedroom, I was sure; the dresser at the far wall was festooned with loose papers, and the counterpane was ragged and patched.

The second window framed a woman in a nightgown, brushing out her long red hair. Not Catherine.

The last window offered a dark and empty room.

It was not long past ten at night, I thought, remembering the church bells. It was possible that Catherine and Farrow were still downstairs at dinner or—more likely—at drink, so that Farrow could more easily ply Catherine into doing what he wanted her to do before they wed.

I'd imagined finding them already in bed together, a dramatic scene, maybe even having to wrest them apart—that was absurd. It was better this way. I could wait for them, help Catherine before Farrow really hurt her.

I replaced the opera glasses in their cubby, then thought better of it and took them with me. I was sure enough of what use their owner intended to put them to that I felt no qualms about this little theft.

Down the tree, then, and up the climbing roses and ivy to the third window, and a little prying with a penknife let me open it and climb into the empty room.

I hid myself quickly on the far side of the wardrobe from the door. I was surprised at my own calmness; my heart beat steadied and my breath slowed. I waited a few long minutes in the quiet, in the shadows, thinking about how best to make my move. Perhaps I wouldn't have to deal with Farrow at all, if Catherine came back to the room first, if I could only talk to her and make her see . . .

I worried that speaking badly of Farrow would only push her closer to him though. The two of them against the world, it must already seem to her, if she'd decided to risk it all and run away. I

212

must not seem like part of that world to her, must not try to force her the way that he had forced.

I didn't have much time to think. The door slammed open and two figures stumbled in, laughing, clutching at each other.

I lurched forward a step, then stopped myself.

It wasn't them.

Two tipsy lovers, fumbling for the nearest bed available to them. That was all.

I still stood in the shadows, and my heart was going hard enough by then, all right.

What if they weren't coming upstairs at all? Why had I assumed this was their room just because it was empty? I had been so sure that Farrow would want to bed Catherine as soon as possible that I'd come all the way here, and I didn't know if they had even already left again, if his stallion even still stood outside.

I slipped out of the shadows, across the room, out the door—the lovers too blind to anyone but each other to notice me at all—and I rushed down the staircase. A scullery maid coming up the stairs didn't even look at me.

A cramped little hallway led me to the inn's main room. I flattened myself back against the wall and scanned the busy space. I nearly missed Catherine and Farrow because they were so close to me, their heads leaning together over a little table by the doorway. Farrow's arm was draped possessively around Catherine, and she leaned against him. He was smiling down at her as he spoke; I could not see her face.

The look on his face was kindly, so much so that it stopped me where I stood.

Was Catherine so wrong to want to escape the restrictions of the life that had been imposed upon us, to find a little joy wherever it found her?

But then I remembered what Felicity had said, and I hated myself for forgetting even for a moment.

I took a hesitant step forward and strained to hear what he was saying.

"But, darling," I made out, "I know the man myself, from army days, and I owed him a favor. They'll leave the room just as they found it, I know they will. Professional women always do, I can assure you."

Catherine straightened, and I could see her face; there was more gumption in it than I'd ever seen there before, and the dreamy wide-eyed look was half faded away. "I just don't see why you had to repay your favor on our first night together."

"I already told you it would make no difference," he said, a little annoyance cutting through the tenderness in his voice. "You are too sensitive, my dear. You yourself have told me so many times, have you not?"

Catherine looked away, toward Farrow's hand that draped across her arm. "I have," she said, low enough that I almost didn't hear her. "I had just . . . imagined . . ."

"And I am bringing your imaginings to life, aren't I, darling? Aren't we in our own romantic story now?" Farrow chucked her under the chin as if she was a child. "You simply must learn to respect your husband's way of doing things, just as the girls in your stories do, however headstrong they may act in the beginning. The better part of love is surrender, is it not?"

A little fire still sparked in her eyes, but Catherine bit her lip and nodded.

"Now," said Farrow, "perhaps, if the private room I paid so dearly for holds no charm for you after another soul has occupied it—never mind that all an inn's rooms are used by a different person every day, of course—perhaps you would prefer to take a moonlight stroll with your beloved? We can be sure of finding some private corners there, where no other lovers will have been tonight."

He pitched his voice in a sweet and suggestive way, and even I could feel its charm.

Catherine looked up at him, still a little wan, but then she rose from her chair and took his hand. "I am sorry for being so foolish," she said. "Of course it doesn't matter. I think—I think a walk would clear my head quite well. I am not used to cider."

He had done it very neatly. Made the wrongdoing hers, and the apology hers too.

And now she was leading him by the hand outside . . .

This was my chance. I might not have another.

I cut through the narrow hallway again and out the back door, then stayed in the shadows as I moved around the building, watching for Catherine to come out.

She started moving down the drive, but he tugged her the other way, toward the same tree I had just climbed.

Suddenly he pulled her close against him and lifted her up in his arms, kissing her soundly. He kept holding her as he moved forward, until he could press her back against the tree.

"Jack!" she gasped, half laughing. "We're still not—"

"We're close enough, darling, and besides, you can't cry foul that any other couple has used this tree tonight, I'm sure." He kissed her again before she could respond.

I moved forward silently, pulling the knife Peter had given me from the home I'd made for it inside my sleeve. It was as warm in my hand as a living thing. I flicked it open and held it to his neck.

"Step back from the lady, sir," I whispered, pitching my voice low, "or I shall give you reason to regret it." I was grateful for my height in that moment; between the knife and the presence of someone as tall as himself behind him, I thought he might mistake me for a man.

Farrow froze. He swallowed slowly, but his grip on my schoolmate did not lessen. I felt the pressure of his Adam's apple press against the knife. "Unsporting of you to cut in on another man's dance this way, my lad," he said. "The lass is willing. Be on your way, good sir, or the regret will be yours."

He could not see me, but Catherine, pressed between him and the tree, saw me clearly. "Adèle?" she said, her voice little more than a squeak.

"A—" Farrow dropped Catherine and spun to face me—or tried; my other arm pinned his at his side and kept him pulled against me. I had Nan's training to thank for that maneuver. "A woman?" he hissed.

"No matter," I replied. "I can end your life as well as any man. I want"—I swallowed bile as another image of the man whose life I *had* ended rose up in my mind—"I want you to let this lady go."

"I already told you," he said. "She is here of her own free will." He made a sound of contemptuous exasperation that was not far off from an animal's growl. "Tell her, Cat."

Catherine was still backed against the trunk of the chestnut tree, staring at us. She'd fallen down a good six inches when Farrow dropped her, and her hair was caught in the bark. She winced as she pulled it out. "It's true. This man is my fiancé." Her voice shook, and my heart ached at her bravery. "Adèle, you've met him yourself. You've seen him at our fetes. He is a gentleman."

"Indeed he is not. The other girls told me, Catherine, things he did—they all know he—"

I was so focused on her that I foolishly forgot the danger of the person I held against me. I'd loosened my grip, and he felt my lapse and took his advantage in a moment. He pulled his arms from my hold, and one of them came back to elbow me fiercely in the belly.

It hurt, but corsets are a kind of armor after all. While a man would have doubled over, I only cried out. Still, he managed to escape my grasp, and faster than I could have imagined he turned and landed a square punch to my jaw.

It spun me. Spun. Someone who knew how I grew up might have found it hard to believe, but I'd never been truly hit before. I dropped the knife, and thanks be to providence that the darkness kept him from seeing it fall. The pain vibrated out into my whole skull, sending sharp fingers digging into my brain.

All I could do for a long moment was struggle to start breathing again.

I hadn't fallen at least. I kept my stance wide and my gaze on Farrow as my vision cleared.

He wasn't trying to land another hit; he was just standing there, his right hand still fisted, but his face calm. A small smirk toyed with the corner of his mouth.

He looked . . . pleased with himself.

"Adèle." Catherine rushed to my side and touched my cheek gently, as if she were checking for blood. "You just surprised him, that's all. Jack would never hurt a lady, not on purpose." She looked up at him, her eyes as wide and bright as moonstones. "Would you, darling?"

He scoffed, slowly unclenching his hand. "My girl, I'm wounded that you'd even ask me that."

I raised my head. "Not an answer," I said.

Next to me I heard Catherine take in a deep breath.

"Certainly I would never hurt a lady like yourself." He looked me up and down. "This creature accosted us. What kind of weakling would I be if I didn't . . . She tried to kill me! She—"

He'd gotten as involved in his own monologue as I had in mine. I took back my advantage with a speed that would have made Nan proud, and in another moment I had him pinned against the tree in much the same way he had so recently pinned my classmate.

"You, sir," I told him. "You shall be in Hell, but what time that comes to pass is up to you. You are going to let Catherine go."

He struggled, and the surprise and horror that came over his face when he realized he couldn't escape gave me a terrible kind of pleasure.

He scowled and glared at me, and the arrogance, the contempt I still saw there, even though we both knew I had him bested, was like looking into a mirror in a dark room.

"Go to blazes," he hissed.

I pushed my arm hard against his neck. "You first."

He coughed, his eyes widening. I was cutting off his breath now, leaning hard against him with the bone of my forearm across his throat. I had known since the night of the ball that I would kill again if I had to.

He nodded desperately. I leaned away just enough to let him speak.

"I'll let her go."

I moved quickly to Catherine and offered her my hand; she flinched away from it. "You hurt him," she said to me. She reached for Farrow. "Are you all—"

He laughed, a harsh sound that made her wince as if she'd been hit. "Don't touch me," he snapped. "You heard what the *lady* said. Run along with her like the biddable little bitch you are."

Catherine stared, her eyes wide. "You cannot ask me to give you up so easily," she said. "Nor to believe that you would do the same to me."

He coughed, but then stood up straight and smirked at us as if he'd won. "Plenty of professionals inside who'd do the same job I wanted you for, and better too."

Catherine began to shake, her freckled cheeks blotching red.

I offered her my arm, gently. This time she leaned against me.

Farrow spat on the ground and walked away.

I had done what I'd come there to do. I could take Catherine back to Webster's with me, and we'd both be in our beds before dawn, and though the girls would know, no one else ever would. Her future would be saved.

Yet I was not satisfied. "Stay here," I hissed to Catherine, and I think she was still too shocked, or too used to following someone else's lead by then, to do anything but obey.

I slipped through the shadows and caught up with Farrow just before he walked through the inn's back entrance. I had him again in a moment; he was an officer, not nearly so fit as a foot soldier. He was no real fighting man, not even strong when it came down to it. I felt nothing for him then but contempt.

"You are never to contact Miss Essex again," I told him.

He laughed a little, still trying to seem arrogant. "Believe me, I have no wish to," he said. "The girl has been far more bother than she ever was worth."

"Do not think that you shall be unwatched now," I said. "Do not think that you can play the same tricks on another girl again. It is only by my mercy that you live."

I pushed him away from me before he could reply.

I ran back to Catherine. She wouldn't look at me; it seemed at first as if she couldn't make herself move.

"Catherine," I said as quietly as I could. I knew better than to touch her just then, but I held out my open hand. "He's gone."

She looked up sharply, and there was anger in her eyes like I'd never seen in her before. I was ready for it to be directed at me or at Farrow, but she whispered, "I am so ashamed." Each word sounding as if it stuck deep in her throat. "I am so sorry."

My own anger threatened to choke me, but I kept my voice and my hand steady for her sake. "The shame is not yours, nor the sorrow," I said. "At least, they shouldn't be."

She shook her head, but at least she was looking at me now. After a moment, she took my hand.

Together we walked back toward the yard to find the Webster mare.

SEVENTEEN

Dear Eric,

I hardly know how to begin this letter. I should be reticent, but I find I am eager to share my secret with you. I have better stories to tell you than any we invented for each other as buccaneers. I am a kind of buccaneer myself now, in flesh and blood. You are the only person outside of my most intimate circle whom I could imagine telling about it.

I am doing what we used to say we'd do together: I am rescuing fair maidens. I started with my dear friend Hannah and myself. The events of that night haunt me, though I know I had no other choice before me but the one I made—

I cannot write it out, even to you. It awakened something in me, Eric, and since that night I have been working hard to become the kind of hero we used to dream of being.

I have a compatriot, even, from what I think you would half-jokingly refer to as the dark underbelly of London, someone who is teaching me how better to protect myself and others.

I have found it hard to sleep, Eric, since the night I did what needed doing. I find I must occupy my time in other ways than with sleep and dreams. I go out into the dark, into the streets . . . I wear dark clothing and a hood, sometimes even a mask, and I protect the girls I see in need of help.

I HAD NEVER struggled to find the words to write to Eric before, but in the months since the ball, I had started doing so many things that were hard to explain, even to him. I wanted to boast of my heroics, but I found I could not tell him the specifics. What if he did not understand the reckonings I gave to the men I met on the streets at night, even though I had not killed again? Eric was himself a man, and I was learning over and over again the lesson I had heard so often from the girls at Le Moulin: no matter how much a man might play the gentleman in daylight, a girl could never place her faith in what he became in the shadows.

Besides that, what could I tell him of the people I cared about most—the girls I helped? I knew I'd already written more about Hannah than she would have wanted me to, and the thought shamed me; so I told him nothing at all about Catherine, much as I wanted to praise her every time I picked up my pen. I longed to say that this girl was remarkable, the way she had faced her own shame and sorrow, came home to the Webster with me, allowed the other girls to listen to her and speak to her, to tell her their own stories—Felicity especially—to begin to wash her hurt away, together, not alone as she'd seemed always to want to be before she had met Farrow. How she and Felicity, two girls who had so

223

little in common except for the man who had hurt them both, had found a beautiful understanding between their hearts. I loved each of them more every day, and my affection and admiration felt too sacred to share with any man, even my trusted Eric.

And what could I say of Nan? I saw her almost every night that I went out, which was to say, I saw her almost every night.

If we did not begin our night at the King's Head, we ended it there, with a tea or a hot toddy to ease the cold ache in my bones that waiting in dark alleys or by cold docks could bring.

I almost always hunted with Nan, and her company warmed me better than any hot drink. We traded our skills; I reconciled myself to Mr. Griffin long enough to learn which gentleman's club he frequented and by what hours, and a few days later we relieved him of his purse and a diamond stickpin on his way home. Nan pawned the diamond and she and her father lived on it for a month, she told me, and bought rounds and hot dinners for everyone in the King's Head that night too.

The more time I spent with Nan, the more forcefully I had to work to make myself write to Eric. It wasn't that she was replacing him in my heart; I'd always had, like Maman, the kind of space inside me that allowed—or perhaps demanded—love that encompassed more than one person at a time, love like wind over the moors or a crowded London street, love pulsing through me for all the world. Love that kept me up at night and sent me out into the streets to do what my heart told me must be done.

It was that he knew me only through letters, and in his eyes I was some kind of unsullied thing, almost an angel; so was he to me. I cared for him, loved him even. At Thornfield, at Ashfield, in those early stifling days at Ferndean before Jane found this place for me, he had been in many ways my only friend. I had wanted to escape from my life sometimes, to vanish from it, and his letters and the pirate stories we wrote together had been a conduit for that. I had thought, more than once, that in our connection there lay an escape route to a happier life than I had ever known since my mother had died. Marriage to Eric could combine the freedom I longed for with the security Maman had hoped I'd find when she gave me to Papa.

But at the Webster, I had slowly unearthed a life I did not want to escape. For the first time I had friends, real living and breathing girls whom I loved and who loved me. Loving the Webster girls had led me to want to protect them; and however dark and violent that path had been, it was one I took pride in walking.

And Nan . . . I was no unsullied angel to Nan, nor she to me. The night we met she was a con artist committing fraud and I was a murderess. And yet I was beginning to honestly know her. The way she clicked her tongue against her teeth before she laughed, as if the world were teasing her and she knew it. The way she said "bold" instead of *bad* and "colleen" for *girl*. The way she brewed her tea three times as long as I'd ever tasted it before; I thought that might be why the smell of tea leaves hung around her. I'd learned to drink her strong tea when I needed to stay awake at night but never when I needed sleep. Nan drank it constantly, even last thing before bed.

But what kind of future could I have with Nan?

I'd been writing in our free hour between supper and bed; I stopped and set down my pen. I hadn't known I'd even been contemplating such a thing. I needed to survive in the world; Maman had given me into Papa's care for a chance at a more stable, secure, and wealthy life than she could have provided. Nan was . . . she was wonderful, she was vivid, she saw me honestly—and she helped me, as I helped her. She made my life here more bearable than it had ever been, and we had real adventures that Eric and I had only written about.

What kind of a future could I have with her?

I could care for Nan, but for my mother's sake, I could not align myself with anything but the kind of life she had envisioned for me. I had to stay in Papa's good graces too, lest he cast me out, lest my safety and affluence that Maman had bought from him at a cost I still didn't fully comprehend should come to nothing. I spun her ring on my finger, felt her heartbeat in my belly, and I knew that much for sure.

I put away the letter I was writing; I knew I wouldn't finish it that night. I stared at nothing until we were called to bed, and I did not join the Shadow Cabinet that night. I slipped outside as soon as I could, and I went straight to the King's Head.

I knew I couldn't have the future I'd just realized that I wanted. I was looking for a present moment I could hold to.

Peter wasn't in the King's Head that night, but the barkeep waved me back toward Nan's room as soon as he saw me. I nodded my thanks, such a weight in my throat that I didn't think I could bear to speak.

226

I found her, in that narrow back room, the tiny space that was hers alone, counting the beads of a rosary.

She glanced up at me when I entered, and our gazes met for a warm moment, but she did not stop murmuring her quiet prayer, and I knew to wait until she was done to speak to her.

Her eyes opened, and we looked at each other.

"I thought you never went to Mass," I said at last, pulling my hood back from where it had shadowed my face since I'd left the Webster.

"I never do," she replied. "Catholics are even more hated in England than the Irish are, and Da and I never found a priest we like here besides. But I told my mother once I'd always do my rosaries, and I'd say she'd know the difference if I didn't." She looked down at the string of beads and the cross and she smiled before slipping them into her skirt pocket.

I knew well that Catholics were hated in England. France was a Catholic country. My own mother had had no use for any kind of god, but a few of the Moulin dancers took us children to Mass on Sunday now and then, and I'd always liked the incense and the stained glass, the songs and the resonant, mysterious Latin words of the priests. Jane Eyre had trained me out of the few papal prayers I'd learned in France as quickly as she could; I think she'd wanted to make me Protestant even more than Papa had wanted to make me English, although they were two sides of the same coin in a way.

"You pray to a holy mother in the rosary anyway, don't you?" I asked. "I'd wager she knows yours. The mothers in Heaven must all talk to each other, don't you think?"

227

She clicked her tongue and smiled. "Likely so," she said. "D'you think ours get along?"

The thought startled me. My mother felt so close to me still that I did not often imagine her in Heaven; perhaps I was enough like her that I had never really felt the need for such a place. But I liked the idea of Maman being friends with Nan's mother.

I looked at Nan's hand, still lingering on the pocket where she was tucking away her rosary. I looked at her face, still laughing even as I could see the mourning for her mother, and perhaps for the country she'd left behind, somewhere in her eyes too.

I realized I was biting the insides of my lips again. I looked at Nan's full mouth, her soft cheeks, her freckled skin.

I saw her suddenly so clearly, so honestly. The parts of her that were like me, and the parts of her that were not.

I knelt down next to her, before her narrow bed, and she turned toward me.

Her face was so close now, I could see the blue shadows of her lashes on her cheeks. Her freckles were the color of cane sugar. Her lips had a few freckles too, small and faint, golden and brown against the pink.

There on our knees, I leaned forward, and I kissed her.

Everything in me sighed and said *finally*, and *yes*.

She was already leaning toward me too, and as our lips met, her curly hair tumbled forward so that the black tea and peat-fire scent of her enveloped me completely.

Her mouth was soft and plush, the softest skin I'd ever touched. I felt such warmth inside me that it took a moment to realize all the heat didn't come from myself. Her arms had circled around me, and mine had, as if of their own will, gone around her too. Her dress was a rough and slubby linen, and I felt the lines of the threads under my fingers, the heat and the substance of her body beneath them.

My heart beat fast, making my head buzz and my very fingertips pulse. But the places where I'd bitten my own lips started to throb and hurt, pulling my attention from her body and into mine. I drew back and touched my fingers to my mouth, surprised to remember anything I'd done with my body that was outside of this place, this moment.

"Are you all right, Adèle?" Nan whispered, her face still so close to mine that our foreheads touched. "Did I hurt you?"

I pressed my lips together until they ached even more. I had to force myself to open them again; it was only because I wanted so badly not to close myself off from her that I managed it. "Maman trained me out of biting the outsides of my lips, because it looked ugly," I said. I hadn't thought about it in years and had never told a soul, not even Eric in our letters. Not even Jane. "So I started biting the insides of them, where no one could see. I do it when I need to think or when I'm—when I'm scared. They always hurt a little, but I hadn't thought about it." I gave a little laugh. "All I thought about was kissing you."

"I did hurt you then. I'm so sorry." Nan started to pull away.

I couldn't bear for her to believe such a thing. I caught her hand and held it to my cheek; I brought my other arm back around her waist. "You never did," I whispered. "Remember when you taught me to fight, the night Peter gave me the knife—you asked me who would be able to teach me to feel safe again?" I looked at the freckles on her face, at the sooty lashes and strong brows that framed her golden-brown eyes. "I feel safe with you, Nan. At last. I really do."

Her eyes grew brighter, as if with tears, for a moment, but instead of crying, she smiled. "And I with you," she said. "Safe and . . . honest. Fancy that." Her smile grew wider. "And to be honest," she said, "I've wanted to kiss you from the first moment I saw you."

I shivered. "Yes."

We both stayed still and silent for a moment, looking at each other.

"I want to kiss you again," I said. The words trembled on my tongue. "And I want you to kiss me." I had a reason now to keep from hurting the inside of my mouth, not just the outside—and it had nothing to do with how I looked. "Just, maybe . . ." To think, before I met Nan I'd never blushed . . . "Just maybe not on my mouth until it's healed."

Nan's smiled turned mischievous: the smile of a thief. She gathered me close in her arms.

"There are plenty of other places I can kiss you," she whispered. She was right.

First, she took my hand and very slowly brought my palm to her lips and kissed the fleshy mound below my thumb. She looked up at me, meeting my gaze, before her eyes fluttered closed and she kissed me again. She moved down to my wrist, where the veins flickered blue and green beneath my skin, and there I felt the first slick stroking of her tongue. My eyes closed too, it felt so good, but I opened them again, for I could not bear not to watch her.

She bit lightly at my wrist, so light there was not even the ghost of pain, just another shiver. She undid the small buttons of my sleeve, one by one, blessing each new inch of skin that she exposed with another kiss.

We were on the bed by then; I don't know how. I did not kiss her again, but I touched her too, all over: I touched the arch of her lower back, and the curve of her belly, and her breasts. I undid the lacing of her coarse linen dress while she worked at my jet buttons, and we laughed together at the labor of it, all the time it took to take off each other's clothes. Enough time to know we both meant everything we did.

When we were both in our shifts we began to shiver; I drew the worn quilt at the foot of the bed over us, and we held each other close, her hands pressing at my shoulder blades to pull me to her. For my part, I grasped Nan tight around the hips with one arm and with the other I touched my fingers to her mouth like a kiss, tracing her lips, pressing gently against them until they parted and she met my fingers with her tongue.

And then her hand was on my thigh, pushing my shift up, and between my legs, and there was nothing I could do, nothing that felt more natural and right, than to touch her in the same place, with my fingers that had just kissed her mouth. And we rocked together, touching and not kissing, her face buried against my shoulder so that I could feel the damp heat of her breath on my collarbone, until we made for each other that miracle that in my homeland is called the little death.

I slept then, in her arms, for a few short hours—a sleep more peaceful than I'd ever hoped to find before I rejoin my mother's bones in the Paris earth.

How can I describe my life in the sweet rush of that time? I spent nearly every night with Nan, coming home to her arms and her bed—and they felt like home too—after terrorizing the fine gentlemen of London and sometimes further abroad. Terrorizing them just enough to make them doubt their own entitlement to ruin any girl they pleased without consequence.

I fell in love with my own power as I fell in love with Nan. I stopped writing to Eric, for what could I say? His letters had grown increasingly romantic, as mine grew ever less frequent.

I became closer with all the Webster girls in those months, too, especially Catherine and Hannah, the two I'd had the privilege of helping.

I saw Hannah taken, finally, into the fold of the other Webster girls, and I knew that with Charlotte and Felicity's love and protection she might eventually make the kind of match that would save her family without sacrificing her to utter misery at a husband's hands.

I wrote of feeling like the mother's ghost to Cinderella when I gave Hannah my dress for the ball. I suppose I want you to know that if there is a happily ever after in my story, it comes here, in those months I spent haunting the wealthy men of London society with Nan at my side.

But, reader, happiness is never the end. There is only one way all stories end, and that is death.

EIGHTEEN

ONE EARLY DAWN, Nan whispered, "Stay with me."

"I cannot," I said, pulling my legs out of their sleepy tangle with hers. I stretched my arms, which always cramped when we slept together in her narrow bed, and then winced as I stood up into the icy room and quickly began to dress. "I have to be back at school before breakfast. You know that."

"No." Nan sat up, her dark hair a glorious messy cloud around her radiant face, her cheeks flushed as they only were after we'd gone to bed together. With one hand she held the blanket against her throat for warmth; with the other she reached out to me. "I mean, stop going back to school. Stay here with us. With me." Her voice had been shy and uncertain at first, but it grew stronger with every word. "Be the beautiful villainess that the men of London know you are. Be a thief. You've already made a life with us, a better and freer life than anything you have back there, and you know it." Her honey-colored gaze was locked with mine, and there was no more beautiful or dearer sight to me than this girl's loving eyes.

Loving. Yes. She loved me, and I knew it then.

"Nan." Her name, so dear, hurt in my throat, but I did not hesitate. "I cannot. I am promised already."

She flinched as if I'd hit her. "What? To whom?" The color began to fade from her cheeks, making her freckles stand out. "To your letter-writing cousin, is that it?"

"No—no." It startled me even to think of Eric; I had done poorly by him in these last months, I knew. I'd abandoned our correspondence and I'd abandoned him in my heart. I felt a tripled flash of guilt: for my own neglect of one I loved, for the knowledge that marriage to Eric would be the completion of my mother's hopes for a secure and privileged life for me, and that the girl I'd just slept with thought I'd lied to her. I'd been a criminal—she'd trained me to it herself—but I could never dream of betraying her heart.

And yet. My mother's heart was beating fast in my belly, and I knew where my first allegiance lay.

"I promised Maman before she died," I said, my voice nearly a croak and every word forced out as if I choked on it. "It was her dying wish to give me the path, the life, that Papa has given me. A lady's life. An inheritance. If I left the Webster now, Papa would cast me out, write me out of his will, I don't doubt it. I cannot risk his anger and lose the thing my mother died for—"

"Adèle, she was consumptive! She died of illness, as my mother did. She could not have wanted you to live unhappy when you have a chance at happiness like what we have, what we can make together."

I shook my head. Maman had been ill, but she had died for me nonetheless; I knew it as bone deep, soul deep as I knew any illogical truth, as deep as Jane—or Nan—believed in God.

"Would your mother want it for you, this happiness you speak of?" I asked. My voice was icy now, and I knew I was about to deal Nan the killing blow, to hold the knife to her own knife-wielding hand. Every word was a fang. "Would she want you to love another girl like this?"

Nan's face went white. She sagged down on the bed as if her bones had vanished. She was silent long enough for me to finish making myself decent and to leave.

I had never felt so angry. Though if I was angriest at myself or at Maman, I didn't know.

When I got back to school, I saw Felicity and Catherine arm in arm by the front door. They seemed to be just starting out on or coming home from a walk—they had grown close in the months since Captain Farrow's attempted elopement, and their shared understanding was a help to both of them—but as soon as they saw me, Felicity let go of Catherine's arm and rushed toward me. "Your stepmother's here to see you, Adèle," she said.

My first thought was, *Jane, come to see me?* She had always been too busy, whether with her babies or with Papa, such that she hadn't even wanted me home for holidays. My first feeling was a seasick combination of resentment and longing.

My next was fear. Jane must have traveled through the night to have arrived this early: What could be so urgent?

"Best come up with a good story about where you've been and right quick," Felicity went on.

I had never felt I had to lie to Jane, except by omission. Felicity's assumption that I needed to do so now rankled with me. "I don't think that's necessary," I said, but then it started to come to me just how much I had to conceal, not only from Jane, but from everyone these days.

When I entered Mrs. Webster's office, Jane Eyre looked just the same as she ever did. There is a timeless quality to her, to the skim-milk purity of her skin, the tame, tidy brown hair, the wide eyes that regard everything with a sharpness and a conviction that make it clear her mind and soul are far bigger than the tiny body in which they reside.

Since I'd last seen her, I'd become a murderess. A beautiful villainess, Nan had called me. I'd spent so many nights on the streets of London that they felt like a second home and so many sweet hours with the girl I'd just left behind that I thought part of my heart would always live inside her. All I could think, as I looked at Jane, was how she could not possibly see the same girl she'd helped to raise. I wondered which part of my new life she would see first—or despise most.

I was so frantic with wondering as I looked at her, and she at me, that I almost missed the words she spoke.

"Adèle, I've come to take you home."

PART FOUR
FERNDEAN

Bad dreams in the night

They told me I was going to lose the fight

—Kate Bush, "Wuthering Heights"

NINETEEN

HOME?

The word was a failed conjuror, a magician who reached into his hat and pulled out nothing but his own hand.

Yet home was not the Webster, as fiercely as I had tied myself to the friends I had made here. And if home had been Le Moulin, that place was lost to me forever; I knew that the years I had spent in England had rendered me, however unwillingly, a foreigner to the place of my own birth. Ferndean, with all its nauseating, claustro-phobic shadows, had never for a moment felt like home to me.

Jane Eyre opened her arms, standing there in Mrs. Webster's office, and I went to them, the closest thing to a mother I had known for many years. She was so small her head leaned against my bosom, as if she were a baby and I her mother, she the ward and I the governess.

She said she'd come to take me home. For a moment, in her arms, she succeeded.

She clung to me a long time, even when I relaxed and began to step back from her. I don't think I had ever been the one to pull away first before from one of Jane Eyre's embraces. But then I had been such a lonely child, with no one else who touched me gently or in kindness—except for, of course, only once in a great while, Bertha.

My body was not so lonely now. But why did Jane's have cause to be? She was living out her life's happily ever after, wed to her true love . . .

"I have missed you, my darling Adèle," Jane said, looking up into my eyes; her own were starry with tears, making them all the more wide and clear. "There is much to tell you. Let us depart at once."

"At once? But I must say goodbye—" I thought of Felicity and all the Shadow Cabinet, of Hannah. How quickly would I be leaving them, and for how long?

And, oh God, Nan. Thoughts of her swept all others aside. My lips were still swollen from her kisses, and there were marks under the high collar of my dress, dark like the bruise on my chin but that I'd gotten in sweeter ways from my Nan's mouth . . .

"You have been called away with alacrity, I am afraid, my dear," said Mrs. Webster, keeping her expression carefully neutral, though when her gaze flickered to Jane, I thought I saw something like— sympathy? concern?—on her stern face. "I will make your excuses to your friends for you." Her eyes softened. "We will miss you, Adèle. Both the students and myself."

So it was not to be a brief absence then. "Oh, but . . ." That would hardly soothe my pain at not being able to say goodbye to my friends, but would they know to pass the message on to Nan? They knew I went out at night and what I did while I was out, but none of them had met her.

Nan, lying alone on her bed, silent and hurt after I pushed away her offer of a life together—she would think I'd abandoned her in truth. I felt my hands begin to shake.

"Come, Adèle," said Jane, and the tremor I heard in her voice was strange enough that it compelled me, as if by an external force, to follow her from the office, out of the Webster, and into her waiting carriage.

As we rattled away down the street, Jane was talking, but I did not register her words, and I cannot remember them now. I was past speaking myself, my throat closed tight, and I stared out the carriage window like an imbecile. The sooty London streets, the people walking them, seemed to blend together into streaks of muddy gray.

We passed a towhead in a familiar pale blue uniform and a brunette at her side; I was startled into recognizing them only just in time to lean out of the carriage and call their names. "Felicity! Catherine!"

By the time they turned, we were too far ahead for further words, but against all the rules of decorum I was supposed to have learned at the Webster, I stood and leaned out of the carriage window. I locked eyes with Felicity and—I didn't know what I even wanted to tell her, except goodbye, and I was sorry I had to leave, and I'd be back if I could, and the Villainess would haunt London again if it was the last thing I was ever to do, and . . . God, to tell Nan that I loved her—loved her, something I didn't even really know or understand until that moment, when she was gone from me—

Felicity's fierce gaze penetrated me like flame, and she nodded, brief, decisive. She pointed at me and said a word to Catherine, and the last thing I saw before Jane yanked me back inside the carriage was the tear that slipped down Catherine's cheek as she gazed at me.

I had forgotten how strong Jane was. All those constitutional walks, I supposed, which were as much a part of her daily routine as prayer. And there was part of Jane Eyre, I had always suspected, that never did anything but pray.

"Really, Adèle," she said, "you could have fallen and been hurt—broken your neck maybe. You must take better care of yourself."

I closed my eyes briefly and clenched my fists. "I've been taking care of myself fairly well here in London, miss."

I hadn't intended to address her as if she were still my governess, but the distance it reasserted wounded both of us; we pulled away from each other, a stiffening of arms, a rearrangement of skirts. I made myself look at Jane then, really look, and I saw that her face was a little thinner than it had been when last I saw her, the lines around her eyes a little deeper. Without knowing it, I'd always thought of her as somehow ageless, had assumed she'd never change. It was like something Papa would say, and I was ashamed of myself. My stepmother was as human as I was, as every woman was, and I despised the men who thought of us as anything else.

"I'm sorry, Jane," I said. "Truly I am. It's just that I'm going to miss my friends."

She smiled sadly. "I've told you of my schoolmate Helen, who died," she said, "one of the souls most dear to mine of any I have known. I understand the love between young girls and I am truly sorry to have taken you away so quickly. But there is a pressing matter that allows for no delay. My Edward, your papa, is very ill. I am afraid he might not—" Here she stopped, as if her voice could not carry the burden of what she was about to say.

"He's been asking for you, Adèle," she said instead. "He wants to see you. You understand now, why I had to call you away so quickly."

The idea of Papa asking for me made my stomach turn cold. I told myself I was being foolish, even as I felt the blood drain dizzily out of my head. How could I go out every night and terrorize London as the Villainess, the scourge of every man who thought to hurt a girl he saw as easy pickings, and yet be so afraid of my own father—if that he even was? How dare I be brave on behalf of so many others and such a coward for my own sake?

But I could not force that bravery to come. I felt my body recoiling further in upon itself, like a snail sealing up inside its shell. I pictured my fingernails curling under like seashells, my teeth growing to cover my head like an enamel helmet, my skin shriveling and my whole body shrinking until I was no bigger than a walnut, too hard-shelled for even my papa to crack.

He's never even touched you, I scolded myself, *never once . . .*

I realized that Jane was still talking and that I'd missed a sentence or two that she'd said. I forced myself to listen again.

". . . old enough now to receive your inheritance," she said, watching me intently; I forced my face to remain neutral, for Jane had always had a keen eye for the emotional undercurrents of others, and I did not want her to ask me what had made me so afraid. "Your father has put a not insignificant amount in trust for you, and I persuaded him that you might access some of it while yet unwed," she said. She gave a small, triumphant smile.

"I can imagine how hard-won that argument was," I murmured, forcing my voice to modulate.

"You may forget, Adèle, that when I returned to your father, I had come into an inheritance of my own," Jane said. "I was finally able to meet Edward on an equal plane in this world, as we all shall meet in the next. He understood, eventually, why it is good and necessary that the same freedom be afforded to you."

All at once I felt I was about to cry. "Thank you, Jane," I whispered, and I took her cool, gloved hand in mine. Her fingers weren't much more than half the length of my own, but their grip was strong, as was the gaze she leveled at me.

"You shall have your freedom, my dear," she said, "the freedom all women, all people, should have, our birthright from God, that in this corrupted world only money can give." She had not named a sum, but with even a thousand pounds, I could set myself up somewhere respectable enough in London—even as a governess, as Jane had been, perhaps—and spend my nights as the Villainess, and all my dusks and dawns with Nan. The sweetness of a life on my own terms was tantalizing indeed, and it gave me a little courage to confront my dying papa and to feel a little love for him, if he had truly decided to grant this to me.

"But there is more," she said.

I blinked, startled, wary.

"Your cousin Eric Fairfax has written to Edward from Jamaica, asking for your hand," she said. "It sounds as if he has become quite smitten with you—and I must say, Adèle, that I approve most heartily of such a match. A romance of correspondence is founded on the mind and soul, not upon beauty or the desires of the body; men are far too easily swayed by such fading glories, as you yourself have always known too well. But here is a young man who loves you for that which shall always be beautiful, and a man who can offer you security and society as well."

Eric? I thought. *Why did he not ask me himself? I would have said—*

No, I could not have told him my heart belonged to another, for I did not know it till so recently, and I could never expect him to understand. Though he had always been so understanding . . . I had fancied myself in love with Eric sometimes, that was true. In some sweet, distant, noncorporeal way, I loved him still.

Lord, how could I choose some disembodied love over the lightning conviction the mere touch of her lips sparked in my soul?

Oh, Eric. It would hurt us both for me to refuse you, but that is what I would have done, and it is what I must do now.

"Your father is delighted with the match, of course," Jane said. "He is so relieved to know you'll be well loved and minded after he is gone." The word slipped out too easily that time, and Jane flinched under her self-inflicted wound. And the idea of Papa's death hurt her so much that I despised myself even more for feeling any glimmer of relief.

"Oh, Jane," I said, "I cannot imagine Papa dying. Surely he will be all right." And it was true: he was such a monolithic force in my life, had been such a strong and looming presence for so long, that I could not fathom the idea of his being gone from the world.

Maybe for a second I imagined it, and my body shimmered with relief, felt it could let down some defense I had never let myself admit I'd built against him.

But such shame followed in the wake of that tiny shimmer that I stuffed them both down, swallowed, and tried my best not to think or feel anything at all.

The rest of the journey might have taken a few hours then, or passed in a moment; I'd forgotten how good I had become at leaving my body and my sense of time when I'd lived at Ferndean. I had so rarely had to do it since.

As we rolled through the heavy cover of trees and approached that luxurious ivy-covered house, though, the sensations of my body intruded on me until I could not block them out: nausea, prickling skin, dried-out lips I didn't want to open my mouth to lick. The thought of being back made me sick.

But nothing I'd had to face came close to the horrors from which I had saved the other girls.

I chastised myself for my feelings, held my head high, and followed Jane inside.

It was so quiet in the house. A quiet like there had been lively conversation going on in a room, but it was about you, and your entering it dispelled the room into discomfort.

It took me a little longer than it should have to realize why.

"The children aren't here, are they?" I asked.

One of Jane's small smiles, which held such sadness. "They are with the Riverses for a little while," she said. "We still aren't sure what this illness is, and we didn't want the children to be exposed."

"But what about you, Jane? What about your exposure?" *What about leaving your children without a mother?* I knew too well what that does to a young person. Rage and sadness filled my body: mourning for my mother and for the lonely child I had been after she sent me away filling me until it stopped up my throat like a cork in a bottle.

"My mother sent me away," I whispered finally. "I've often thought I would have died with her in exchange for just a little more time together."

"Oh, Adèle," Jane said. "No mother would ever allow their child to make that choice. Don't you know she would rather you hate her and live?"

I thought of all the things my mother had provided for me: a life of wealth and material comfort, a position in English society, which much have seemed so much less volatile than that of the upper classes in France, who always walked with stiff necks and shoulders as if guarding themselves even now against the guillotine. I wondered for the thousandth time if I truly was not Edward Rochester's natural daughter; if my mother had, like I and the

Webster girls had done many times over, lied to a man for the sake of another girl's survival.

Jane brought me to my room, which had been aired so recently that the windows were still open. A small leaf lay on the coverlet; it must have blown inside. It was yellow and sere. In the city, the only season that really mattered was winter; I had forgotten autumn was so close.

"I'll go check on him now," Jane said. "I will leave you to your ablutions, and shall I ask one of the maids to bring you some tea?"

"Thank you, yes." My stomach felt so nervous that I wasn't sure I'd be able to swallow the tea if I had it, but perhaps it would be settling. I reminded myself, more fiercely than before, that I had nothing to actually be nervous about. My old maybe-father was nothing compared to the men I'd faced down already.

Nothing at all.

TWENTY

AS IT TURNED OUT, I didn't have a chance to see if I could drink the tea. Jane swept back into my room just as I was changing into one of the dresses I'd found pressed in my closet.

"He wants to see you now, Adèle," she said. "Perhaps I should not have told him yet that you'd come home, but he would have asked even had I not, knowing as he did that I had gone to fetch you at his orders. And my soul could not bear to be away from him one moment longer than I needed be, not knowing how much longer—"

"Jane. Don't apologize." My annoyance at the drama of the love they always professed for each other was a balm on the fearful anxiety I felt. It was only a distraction perhaps, but it was a strengthening one. My spine was set and my mouth was firm as we walked up to the top-floor room that was Papa's sick ward.

It was strange; as we climbed the staircase, which got darker and narrower on the last flight, where no high-status houseguest was likely to see it, I was reminded of no one more than Bertha. She had lived in an attic room too.

When Jane opened the door and we stepped inside, the impression only strengthened. Oh, this room was more finely appointed than what Papa granted to the first wife whom he'd imprisoned, but the quality of the air, the way it seemed to reach out with long, invisible fingers into your mouth and down your throat, gagging you and keeping your lungs from any true sustenance—oh, that feeling I remembered well. Of wanting to scream but having to be silent.

It was a small room, with a slanted ceiling because there was nothing above it but roof. The walls were simply whitewashed, no expensive floral wallpaper, and the damp was starting to send curlicues out from the corners. I remembered the mold in the red-wallpapered room in Le Moulin for the first time in years.

And there was Papa, lying on a bed facing the room's one, oversize window. He had lost weight since I had seen him last, and his face was so pale with illness that it looked floury or powdered. His lips were chapped and there were sticky crumbs leaking out of the corners of his eyes. I had despised the girls who couldn't bear visiting the sick on the Webster's charity rounds, but I could hardly stand to look at Papa now. The sight of him turned my stomach.

"Adèle," he said before I said anything, before he even greeted his wife. "I have been wanting so much to see you again." His voice was as cracked as his lips, low and striving, and I could see why Jane feared he was dying. I began at last to think it myself—although not, I admit in my own dark heart, to fear it.

"I brought her back as quickly as I could, my darling," Jane said. She laid her tiny, cool hands across his sunken cheeks. He looked at her thoughtfully for a moment, as if searching for something, and then he closed his eyes and leaned into her touch.

I looked away; I had never liked watching their intimacies.

"You are still feverish, my love," Jane said. "Have you taken Dr. Thomas's medicine today? I know I was not here to give it—"

He pulled away from her hands then, frowning. "It is there, Jane, it is there! The bottle is nearly empty! Look, I have been a good patient." His voice had grown stronger in his frustration, as it always did. He picked up the brown bottle from the little table beside his bed and shoved it roughly at her. His hands had grown so thin they looked like spiders.

She looked at the bottle; I saw a slim line marked into the paper label. She made another mark with her thumbnail at the level of the liquid inside. "So you have. You know I only want you to get well."

Something flickered behind Papa's eyes, something I couldn't read. I wanted to look away from him but it didn't feel as if I could; I didn't think it would be safe. I had to keep my eyes on him all the time, like a bird watching a cat, so that I would know if he was going to move.

"Jane," said Papa, "angel mine. Would you leave your sick old husband with his ward for a while? I have some things I want to speak with her about, some closure to make between us, as you know." A tear slipped down Jane's cheek, still nearly as smooth as it had been when I first knew her, though not as pale, and it seemed a tear glimmered in Papa's dark eyes too.

"Of course, my love," she said. And Jane Eyre left us.

Papa and I regarded each other. My eyes started to feel dry and itchy, but I did not think it would be safe to close them even long enough to blink

We listened to the steady, brisk, receding taps of Jane's steps as she walked away from the door, down the narrow hallway and the narrow staircase, until we couldn't hear them at all.

"She is gone," Papa said, and his words so perfectly synchronized with my own thoughts that I did not realize for a moment that he'd even spoken out loud.

"Come here, my child," he then said, holding out one arachnid hand.

I knew it would go worse for me if I did not obey him instantly; it always had. But I could not make my body move toward him.

"I want to speak to you about your inheritance and dowry, my dear, that is all," he said. "Your hesitation saddens me. Come here."

I had faced down young, strong men before; I'd hurt them, even killed one. They'd each posed more of a threat to me than Papa in his weakened state could now. I made myself take a step toward his bed. The sunlight coming through the window, dappled with ivy shadows, hit my shoulder and I felt its warmth like a friend's hand, like a mother's. I was not now, by any measure, a child; I reminded myself of that and took another step.

"Sit by your papa, Adèle," he said.

"Thank you, sir, but I would rather stand."

He moved his lips into a shape that, if he had been stronger, might have become a smile; as it was it seemed merely a smirk. "So like my Jane, you could have been her own," he said.

I cast my eyes down; my longing for Jane's maternal love and care was something I thought I had buried at school. I hated to long for anything. It made me so vulnerable.

"I know it rankles Jane that you cannot have your dowry till you are wed. But, my dear, I believe I have found a way to solve the problem for you." His voice had grown suddenly stronger, and I realized with a flinch in my heart that I had looked away from him.

I raised my eyes and saw that he had moved.

Now he sat straight up in bed, instead of leaning on his pillow. His gaze had sharpened, and his cheeks looked less pale than they had only moments ago.

"Sir?" I swallowed. I felt my mother's heart twist in my stomach, and I twisted her ring on my finger. I wasn't sure I wanted part in Papa's schemes any more than I wanted to marry to access Maman's dowry.

"Yes, Adèle, my dear," he said, his tongue lingering over the last word. "I have found a way." He reached out and took my hand where I stood; I wasn't safe from him even though I'd refused to sit on his bed. His grip was clammy but so strong. "You do not need to marry, little elf, but only live with me."

"I do not understand, Papa."

He looked out the window, and I saw tears glinting in his eyes. "Child. Illness brings perspective. It is one of the great regrets of my hard and twisted life that you and I have not been closer. I take my share of responsibility for that, Adèle. I promise I will make it up to you now if you will take your share of what we owe each other too, and . . . let me."

Something in my heart or gut screamed a warning. I kept still.

He looked up at me, and the motion flicked the waiting tears down his sunken cheeks. I knew I was evil for it, but his crying repulsed me.

"We will go, Adèle, somewhere that no one knows us. We can tell people you are my young wife. You can have all your maman's scarlet money then. I think the arrangement is close enough to marriage to excuse the promise I made to her after all."

I felt cold. I focused on the warmth of the sun against my shoulder, trying to will it inside my body, to fill and guard all the cold and empty spaces echoing inside me. Warmth. Heat. I thought of the heat in Jamaica. "Jane told me I have received a proposal from Eric Fairfax," I said—Eric, whose letters had been my safe haven for so long. He would save me now, the way we'd always imagined saving each other in our stories. I could go to him, far away from Papa—we could sail the high seas and fight pirates and drink water from fresh coconuts just like we'd always described, and he would come to understand about Nan someday—no one who truly loved me could not understand. He would let me come back to London eventually, once I was safe from the fear I even now couldn't quite bear to name—

Foolish stories, every one, imaginary futures chasing each other 'round and 'round inside my head, and none of them true, none of them letting me escape from the nightmare present reaching its spidery hands toward me . . . I heard a low laugh escape my lips, and I knew that I sounded like Bertha. Pretty dolls lined up on Papa's shelf, she'd called us.

I glanced at the window. I understood her more than I ever had before.

But not all my futures were imaginary. I had been offered a way out before I even arrived in this house. I didn't have to look at windows the way she had.

"No." I forced my voice to be clear. "Eric wants me to come to Jamaica, to marry him and live on his sugar plantation. Jane says it is a wonderful match. Eric and I have cared for each other for years; you introduced us yourself. You cannot disapprove."

He chuckled. "And you would like to go to Jamaica and suck on my cousin's sugar cane, my sweet?"

I felt my mother's heart lurch inside me; I thought I heard Bertha's scream as she fell from the parapet and saw Jane's stricken face when she heard Papa's voice on the moors. "I want—"

"I know well what you want, Adèle. And I know well what Eric wants, who many a night has dreamed of you. I know he's told you so."

Private words from private letters . . . "You read what Eric wrote to me?" I tried to recoil from his hands, but his grip was stronger than I'd anticipated, stronger than any sick man's had a right to be, and that threw me enough to forget the fighting skills I'd learned for one short but too-long moment.

"You say his name so tenderly, my dear. It does my old heart good to hear it. But do you not usually call him, simply, E?" He

257

blinked, and the remains of his tears slid down the wet tracks beneath his eyes. "I loved you more for how you opened yourself to E, my dear. And you grew to love him, did you not, without knowing anything of him but his mind and soul? You told him, did you not, that his body meant nothing to you when you loved the former two so much?"

That letter I had sent from Webster's, thinking all the time of Nan, trying to come to some kind of understanding in myself and hoping Eric would understand too, would help me, as writing to him had helped me so often before. And I did love Eric. I did.

"E loves you, soul to soul, Adèle," my papa said. He rose from the bed—keeping his grip on me all the while—and I had forgotten how tall he was. I'd believed he had only been a giant in my memory because I had been young, but he was a tall man, and despite his illness and thinness, he still stood straight.

"It is the purest kind of love, Adèle, the love you feel for E, who earned the love of your soul with his—*my*—letters. All the other women I have loved, I loved first for their bodies, to my shame. But you, Adèle, I fell in love with you only through your words. There cannot possibly be any sin in that." He barreled on, a fierce and fearsome light coming into his eyes, the light of absolute conviction. "And you know, you must feel it in your body as surely as I do, that I am not your father. But I will be your lover, Adèle, and live with you as your husband. You can feel the rightness of it just as I can, I know it, I know it—"

My father crushed me to him and pushed his mouth on mine. I felt the wetness of his tongue on my lips, his hands clutching at my bodice and skirts like he was drowning and I could save him. I thought I could smell the salty chemical mix of the tears he'd spent on the bedclothes and the stench of his body.

How horrible to say I thought of Maman in that moment, of what she felt when he held her and kissed her—what Bertha felt, and Jane—and I was able to escape my own body for a few seconds, pretending it was their bodies he held and not my own. The horror and revulsion I felt at his touch was too much for me to bear.

And what of Eric, the first love of my childish heart? He was vanishing from the world as completely as my soul was striving to vanish from my body. All the letters in which I'd found such solace, the pirate stories that had offered such foolish but crucial escape from my lonely years at Thornfield and Ferndean, the confidante who knew so much about my time as a Webster girl. All lies, all lies . . . no escape after all, no kind young boy to love from a distance—only my father, secretly spinning and spinning his web, so that his women would love him even when they thought they had escaped.

Dolls on his shelf. If I could not escape him, I longed for a body like that, cool and immobile—no, inanimate . . .

But I had to come back to my body to save myself. I pushed away all those other women, Jane and Bertha and Maman, and I wedged my heart and soul back into place, inch by inch, until I could feel myself enough to fight him.

But it was as if their ghosts stayed with me, for I was suddenly most aware of my hands crushed against my papa's chest, against the slightly damp linen of his shirt, and I felt the skin of my palm trapped and pinched by the joint of Maman's poison ring.

I was strong. I had always been strong, and all the riding and running and fighting I'd done in the last months as the Villainess had made me stronger. My father was weakened from illness, whatever he said about getting better, and his grip on me was already starting to loosen as he pursued his own pleasure at the expense of caution.

I pulled my hands out from between us. I got one around his neck, and the other I shoved between his questing mouth and mine and pushed my fingers in his mouth.

My last knuckles breached his teeth and I heard and felt him gag and splutter with surprise. I twisted my fingers in his mouth until I could reach the clasp of the poison ring and open it, and then used his teeth as a lever to push it off my finger and down his throat.

His gasping and spluttering went suddenly silent, and he pulled his head back, his mouth opening and closing like a fish's. He backed away and his hands rose to his throat as he kept making horrible, quiet, airless gasping sounds.

My mother's ring had lodged in his windpipe, and it would choke him before the poison took effect. I felt her heartbeat in my belly, and I felt her rage at the man who had promised to give me a better life than she thought she could, and who had deeply betrayed his promise. My mother's rage washed away my horror, my disgust and shame at the feeling of his skin on mine.

But even choking, he didn't seem to believe he could die. He fell against the bureau, his face starting to darken, and he slammed his torso against it. I heard air whistle into his lungs. He coughed, gagged, and . . . swallowed.

"By God, Adèle, you will give me what you owe," he growled, wiping spittle from his chin. The color was coming back to his face, but his voice was hoarser than ever as he advanced on me again. "You may be the most expensive whore I've ever kept, but I will keep you."

The ring would do its work, but how long before the poison took effect? Too long to help me now.

I sank into the fighting stance that Nan had taught me, and I caught his upper arms in my hands. He was strong too, but that had never mattered with the other men I'd fought, and the cold crystal clarity had come to me again, in which there was nothing but the present moment and what I needed to do there.

My father began to try to bear us toward his bed.

I looked at its sheets, considered them, and knew in an instant they wouldn't do what I needed. I looked at the closed door. I looked at the open window, with ivy trailing over one corner, and the lush Ferndean garden four stories below.

For a moment I saw Bertha's fall in my mind's eye as if I'd witnessed it myself. For a moment I saw a London balcony.

I set my feet, I put my strength against my father's, and I pushed us away from the bed and to the window. I put all my awareness into my arms, shutting out sound and sight and any other feeling. All I could see was red darkness.

And I pushed him out.

I heard a terrified rattling gasp and then a thud.

I gripped the sill and looked down.

There, far below, Edward Fairfax Rochester's body lay broken on the courtyard cobblestones.

My arms ached in the places where he'd gripped me too hard, and with the strain of what I'd just done. But the pain told me I was still in myself, of myself, and I had saved myself from him; the pain was for that instant a baptism, a benediction.

I thought I was not standing in his room but floating, flying. A weight I'd carried almost all my life now lifted. The weight of fear—of fearing him, my own father. Waiting for what I had always somehow known he was going to do, for what my body had known to fear even when my mind refused the acknowledgment.

My body and mind together had thrown off that weight, and I could not be anything but glad.

Reader, I murdered him.

TWENTY-ONE

I HAVE SUSPECTED all my life that both Hell and Heaven exist out of time. The first was confirmed for me at Thornfield, when I learned how Bertha's endlessly long life was spent, confined to one room that even Papa had called hellish.

I learned the second in Nan's arms. Since we had first slept together, I could go back in my mind to those hours at any moment and relive them; it was as if they had never ended and were still happening, her hands and mouth running over my skin in ringing echo forever. I would never be untouched by her again.

Heaven and Hell, out of time. All out of time.

I cannot tell you, though, which I was in as I stood in that sick-room window looking down at Papa below. I thought that both and neither place could claim me.

I could not have said how many minutes or hours passed before his body was discovered. I only know that the light had changed enough to cast his shadow at a longer angle when the maid servant's scream carved the air from the courtyard up to my ear.

I realized then that time was still moving forward, that I would have to tell Jane . . . something . . . about what had happened, and I would have to tell others too. And there was no one to corroborate my story this time. There was no one in this house, I was sure, who wasn't firmly under Rochester's spell.

This time I would be alone in my account of what happened and, I was sure, in my perception of it.

"Mistress! Mistress!" the maidservant cried.

The small figure of Jane Eyre appeared below me. I braced myself to shield my heart from her cries, but she made no sound loud enough for me to hear from my place far above her.

I saw her fall, though, to the ground beside him, and lie over him, her hands clutching first at his wet, red shirt, then at each other, clasped over her head as she lay shaking on his body, in supplication, in prayer.

She had not looked up once.

I could not imagine facing Jane. But I had to go down to her. I could not wait for her, wait for the consequences I must face, up here.

Equally I could not imagine how I might have escaped my father in any different way than I had done. Nor could I escape the relief at being free of him that still buoyed me up like salt water, even as my grief for Jane—not for Papa, but for my almost-mother and the pain she now must carry—began to weigh me back down.

That weight grew heavier and heavier as I descended the widening staircases, until by the time I reached the foyer I could hardly breathe, and I thought that when I looked in Jane Eyre's eyes I would surely drown.

She came in leaning on the tall maidservant's arm. I had never seen her walk like that, supported, before. I had always seen her stand alone; even on Rochester's arm, it was clear she was the bearer of herself in every way.

The maid led her to a chair just inside the door.

"Call for the priest and the coroner, Annmarie," she said. "Right now, please."

Annmarie curtsied and left.

Silence in the great dark room.

"My God," Jane whispered eventually.

I stood before her, my heart beating fast and hard, feeling too weighted down even to tremble. I wanted to move—whether toward her or away, I wasn't sure—but I could not. This place had always chilled my limbs, and now I had . . .

I knew I must face it again as I had faced it in the attic room. I had to, for Jane's sake. I had to face what I had done.

"My God," she said again, and it sounded like both a prayer and a naming of the husband she had lost. "Adèle, what happened?"

Her voice sounded removed, neutral; I thought she must be in shock. Some part of me tried to reach out to her but then shrank back; she couldn't want the sympathetic touch of her husband's murderer.

I could not regret killing him, but I hated this moment between us as I knew I would hate every moment that came after. For I loved Jane and already I knew that what I had done—what I'd done in sound mind and body, what it now seemed I had always

265

known that I would someday do—was unforgivable to one of the women I loved most.

For she had not been with me, and surely she'd never believe me.

I was a murderer twice over, but I could not add lying to the list of my sins, not lying to Jane Eyre.

"He . . . attacked me."

Her head jerked up.

I watched shock change to anger in her eyes. Her hands gripped at her skirts until they turned to fists.

I saw traces of his blood on her fingertips.

"What?" Her voice cracked like a boy's.

"He . . ."

I felt tears I did not want or deserve to shed begin to gather in my eyes, an overflow of the ocean of grief for Jane that still threatened to drown me.

"Tell me everything, Adèle. Leave nothing out. I must—I must—" She choked and closed her eyes, and when she opened them again, her rage was leashed if still clear. "I love both of you, you see. I must, must understand."

I had thought I couldn't lie to her, not now. But could I inflict the truth on her?

I would tell her the actions only, I thought, not what he said about why he committed them.

"He told me to come sit by his bed and hold his hand." My voice in my own ears sounded even flatter than hers. "He pulled me to him, then, and rose out of the bed and came toward me. He was trying to hurt me, Jane." But some part of me would not let that statement fall on her ears so harshly. "I think perhaps the sickness had turned his mind."

The lie. There it was.

"I pushed back. He pushed me toward the bed, and I pushed back, and we struggled toward the window and I—he fell."

How to say the unsayable?

She did not need to know what he had said to me. She did not need to know about the ring or that I had pushed him. What good would it do?

What good would anything ever do again?

Jane spoke to the coroner and then to the priest when they arrived. I heard her voice in the next room and the answering, deeper male voices she commanded. I heard her say, more than once, the word *accident*. I should have felt relief; I should have trembled and wept with gratitude at her feet, that for the second time, because of her, the title of murderess would elude me in the law, if not in my heart.

I did not weep or tremble. I sat still and waited. I felt as if I could not move.

In truth I felt dead.

It was some hours later that she returned. As she entered the room, I heard her ask another servant to send for her children. Her voice shook then, but when she came and sat opposite me, every part of her small body seemed still and quiet. And when finally, after a long silence full of horror, she spoke, her voice was steady.

"He is bone of my bone, Adèle. Flesh of my flesh. Death cannot take him from me. He lives on, not only in our children but in me. Do you not see him?" She raised her hand to her own face and touched it as softly as I'd so often seen her touch him. And then she placed her fingers on my cheek. "Do you not feel him?"

Jane's hands, Papa's hands—I lurched away from her, feeling sick at the memory of those spiders on me and their secret strength.

"I cannot speak with you about it, Adèle. I cannot hear about it from you. You have taken my husband from me in body, but not in soul; our souls have never parted from the first moment we stood equal before God in our love. You have placed between us the barrier of death; only God knows how long it will be before He reunites us." She looked at me for a long moment. She was still a young woman, I thought; there was scarcely more than a decade between us. And I had made her a widow.

Her next words seemed to echo my thoughts. "You have taken so much; can you grant me at least your silence?"

I wondered all of a sudden why I was so desperate for Jane to understand me. She was not rejecting me, not telling me to leave her home or never speak to her again; she had even told the coroner to make sure that Rochester's death was marked down as accidental.

There was no room for both our stories to exist at once in the same house. Her love for her Rochester, my Papa, rang incandescent into every corner of every room, up to the ceilings and down through the floorboards; it permeated Ferndean.

And it was all she had left, as she said. How could I take it from her?

So though I felt as if I were gagging on what had truly happened, I did not repeat it to her.

I had to tell someone, though, and there was only one person I could bear to tell: Nan. I had grown used to writing letters to Eric—to Papa—and I mourned the loss of that friend, the lie he had turned out to be, even as I remained disturbingly fond of his memory, and of the skills that writing to him had given me. I used them again to write to Nan, and I use them now to write to you: and can I, should I, be grateful for them? Should I love the products of deception and violence and pain, however useful to me they are?

I still do not know. I only know that they are useful indeed, and that I use them.

I wrote a brief letter. I told her my father had died, and I asked her to remember what happened when she and I had met. I dared not write more in case my words were intercepted. Even as I handed the envelope to one of the scullery maids to post, along with enough coin to keep her discreet, I felt some part of me slip away with that piece of paper, part of my heart that would go to London and stay there, safe with a girl who would believe me and would understand.

Over the next days Jane and I settled into an icy détente. I felt as if I sank into abstraction. Jane seemed constantly, obsessively, busy; she was making funeral arrangements, directing the staff, and rushing everywhere she went. I did not want to do anything, not even read; I was hardly aware if I stood or walked or lay down.

I had always felt such sharp clarity, going after those other men—even when I had killed Hannah's assailant at the ball. What was happening to me that I felt so far removed, so floating?

During those endless days I was too hazy in myself even to think about those questions long, much less to come to any helpful conclusion. So I drifted through the days, through time, apart from myself and from my body.

The funeral of Edward Rochester passed, a suitably dreary and oppressive one on a suitably dreary and oppressive day. I attended it from inside the same strange fog that had surrounded me since his death.

I still could not regret what I had done, but I also could not reconcile it with the hurt I had caused to one of the women I loved most in the world; nor with the love for me I knew she still felt. But we could not understand the different ways we felt about the same man, and thus we could no longer pretend we understood each other.

The death of that understanding was the tragedy I mourned.

I sank so deep into that foggy blankness that when, a fortnight after the funeral, Annmarie came to Jane and me in the parlor, where we both sat silently reading, to say that I had a gentleman caller, I did not even register the surprise it ought to have caused me.

Jane did though. Someone who hadn't spent every day with her for years, as I had, might not have seen it: the way unexpected information made her hunch her shoulders just a little and, briefly, scan the room as if for danger. She had been an unhappy child once, I knew. The hunted look that flickered in and out of her eyes almost too quickly to see showed me that child and made me despise myself still more.

"Send him in," she said.

I continued to stare down at my book, although I comprehended nothing I had read. The words flickered around the page like guttering candlelight, and my eyes took in their shapes the same way I might stare at a fire. I might as well have been sleeping as reading, just as I'd slept through the motions of eating, dressing, walking, speaking ever since I had seen Jane collapse onto Rochester's body.

But when I heard the caller's voice, I looked up.

TWENTY-TWO

"GOOD AFTERNOON, Mrs. Rochester, Miss Varens. I am so sorry that I did not arrive in time for my uncle's funeral service, and I hope you will forgive my intruding briefly on your grief here. If I may, I offer you my very deepest sympathies."

I had heard such condolences over and over in the last days, and all of them had sounded just the same. I had not looked up even once into the faces of the many mourners who had come to say their mechanical words to Jane and me after the funeral service.

But this voice . . . pitched huskier and deeper than I was used to, but still the voice that I heard in my heart, that I had heard laugh and whisper and cry out in the moments I held most sacred—

"Nan," I whispered, and looked up.

But it was not Nan I saw—at least, not at first.

It was a dark-haired young man in a dark, impeccable suit, holding his hat in his kid-gloved hands.

The young man who had danced with me at the ball and echoed my words on the balcony and helped to save me and Hannah.

He spoke now with Nan's voice, or she spoke with his.

I had forgotten how good a disguise she'd worn that night.

I did not feel my book slip from my hands, but I heard the clap and rustle as it hit the floor. I barely felt my feet as I rose from my chair.

"My God," I said, "why have you come here? Are you really here?"

Jane blinked and stood too, when I did. I watched her do it even as I kept my eyes on Nan-the-boy before me, on the masterfully applied stubble and heavy eyebrows on her face, the shading that had changed the shape of her nose and her cheekbones just enough to make her a different person to anyone who did not love her. I saw her, and I saw Jane, and I saw all the room. My faculties and senses were coming back to me in a great tingling rush, like blood back to a numb and sleeping limb.

"Eric Fairfax, at your service," she said, sweeping a simple but elegant bow. "I am so sorry that I did not arrive in time for my uncle's funeral. Please allow me to offer you my deepest sympathies in your time of grief."

I heard Jane's sharp breath, almost a gasp.

My uncle . . . My thoughts recounted the words she'd just spoken. *How did she know?* But I remembered the way she held the locket at my throat, the little portrait. How much did she recall of what I'd told her about Eric?

Jane turned toward me. I could not bear to meet her eyes at first, and when I made myself do so, I saw such hope and relief and even triumph there that it closed my throat, and even if I had known what to say, I could not speak.

"I received word of my uncle's illness shortly after I wrote to him asking for Adèle's hand. I determined to travel to England at once, since I could not bear the thought of marrying her—if he approved and she would have me—without ever having met the author of our acquaintance, the man to whom I owe more than my life itself is worth."

Nan spoke with the understated, casual assurance that I had come to see as the lynchpin of elite masculinity. *Of course,* rich men say, *of course the world is ours. It is so obvious that it's boorish to speak of it.*

I watched her silently, waiting for Jane's reaction. She was the one with the plan this time, and I trusted her enough to stand still and watch it unfold.

"Mr. Fairfax," said Jane, "I cannot tell you how gladdened I am in heart and soul to meet you at last." She looked at me. "I speak now with my late husband's voice in all things. He often said how glad he would be to see you wed to our Adèle."

"Thank you, madam. Adèle always speaks so highly of you. But it is her gladness I hope for most." Nan crossed the room and stood before me, then bent down. She knelt and looked up, and in her gaze I saw nothing but open, clear honesty.

"Adèle, I love you," she said. She took my hand.

At the touch of her warm fingers, I at last came fully back to myself, back to my body and my beating heart. I understood for the first time how dangerously far away I had been, and that the days since Jane's refusal to hear my story had been the loneliest of my whole life. The fog around me began to lift away.

Here was Nan, who had somehow seen this dark turn for what it was and even now understood and loved me. She, who knew every facet and shadow of my being—not just the sweetness, not just the darkness, but all—knelt before me and held my hand and looked up at me with boundless love. She was lying in her appearance and her words, but I had never known anything more true than the way she looked at me, the strength and softness as she held my hand.

"Adèle Varens, I love you," she said again. "Will you have me?"

I felt Jane watching me. I felt Bertha and my mother too, the same way I'd felt them in the attic room and had felt them nearly my whole life. I knew what Jane meant about carrying someone inside of you, someone you loved. I was bone of their bone too.

So I spoke with the voices of those women who loved me when I looked into Nan's eyes and told her: "Yes."

The only word I ever wanted to give her.

I was an orphan now. I had killed my father, and I had freed myself from him and from what I owed to my mother's ghost.

The only heartbeat I felt in my body now was my own.

"Oh, yes," I said again.

I pulled Nan up to standing and wrapped my arms around her, taking in her warmth and nearness. I buried my face in her neck and such was the strength of my embrace that I lifted her a little off the floor, and her man's hat fell off and then I was laughing and would have started crying too if I had not remembered the importance and the fragility of her disguise.

I set her down at once. Jane was regarding us with a strange look on her face, but doubt was not among the emotions I saw. She'd always said that I was strong.

Nan told Jane she wanted us to be wed as soon as possible. Jane readily agreed; I knew she wanted me out of her house but could not turn me away outright. She still loved me, and I loved her, but Rochester was a rift between us that could never be mended.

"I would not trust any man who was not of my husband's blood and had not had such a long and respectful acquaintance with Adèle," she told Nan-as-Eric, "but I believe you will bring her honestly to Gretna Green, and endeavor thereafter to make her a happy wife. And because Adèle's dowry will remain solely under her discretion, she will always have the dignity and the means that my late husband and I believed should be provided to all women. Edward made sure of that, Adèle."

"I know." I took Jane's hand. "And I am thankful. We will leave as soon as possible and not trespass on your hospitality, or your grief, any longer. You need not worry, or think about me, at all."

"My dear—" She swallowed, closed her eyes, and when she opened them again she looked at me with that sharp, wise clarity for which I'd always loved her. "I shall think of you always."

Her hand was so small in mine, as small as a child's. But however small she was physically, Jane was a great spirit, a great soul. And with a life of freedom stretching out at last before me, I found that I could begin to forgive her for letting love cloud the clarity of mind and understanding that I had so long admired in her. Jane had, like me, suffered great pains in childhood, yet she had found thereafter a love that had let her live happily, and in that moment I truly did not wish to take it from her more completely than I had already done.

There but for the grace of God, she'd once taught me to say.

The next day, a silver-misted morning, we set out. Jane had offered us Ferndean's second carriage for the trip to Gretna, but I took only one of the horses. I had always loved to ride, and the roan mare I saddled was a better creature than I'd ridden since my time at Thornfield. The Webster horses were never anything to speak of.

Nan had the dashing gelding I had seen her father ride. She controlled the headstrong beast admirably, and when I asked her if he was not difficult, she only laughed.

We rode down Ferndean's drive under its dark, shading canopy of trees, its meandering gardens. Tall silver birches shadowed our path, sunlight spangling down between the leaves here and there like falling petals.

"So," Nan said, "to Gretna Green, my dear?"

"I don't believe in marriage, darling. My mother taught me that." I smiled at her and patted my saddlebag. "I have my inheritance papers right here, and I believe I know a certain patriarch with a talent for forgery."

"Aye, I'd say you're right. And I don't think I'd like you quite so much were you an honest woman—even if it was me who made you one." She looked me up and down with the hunger I adored. "No, that's a lie. I would."

I smiled. "I'm going to be the Villainess forever, and I want you by my side, Nan Ward. We are going to save so many girls, now that I have the means—or I shortly will. A marriage certificate and then one for the death of Eric Fairfax are all I need."

Nan grinned. I paused, looking at the angled shadow that the man's hat cast over her smiling, lovely face. "Not that I'd mind so much if you dress up like him now and then."

We both laughed, and then I found I couldn't stop laughing. Our horses tossed their heads. There was so much heaviness behind me, horror and pain and loss, and I had tried to drift away from myself to lose it, but now I had come back.

The lane opened out onto the main road, and we came out into the full sunlight. Urging the horses forward, we left Ferndean, its old garden and dark trees, behind us and rode into the bright morning.

EPILOGUE

I SAID, READER, that stories only end with death. But there has been enough death in this tale, by my own hands. My mother warned me often enough as well of the perils of ending one's story with marriage. Nan and I might have married, if we chose; she could have disguised herself again convincingly enough, or her father could have forged a marriage certificate sound enough to serve any purpose we might put it to.

But neither of us was the marrying kind.

Instead, as soon as I found myself both newlywed and widow in the eyes of the law—and with my dowry from Papa, via Jane, solely in my own name—signing over that material independence to any man, even Nan in disguise, seemed abhorrent to my mother's memory, to her wishes, and indeed to mine. I wanted always to decide for myself what to do with my money and my time and my life.

And I knew, as soon as my ten thousand pounds were settled on me, what I wanted to do first.

As I approached the front door of the Webster in my widow's weeds (for I had reason to wear them by day now, mourning my ever-fictional Eric, as well as during my nocturnal adventures), I did feel a forlorn nostalgia for my brief time as a Webster girl, a time that would never come again.

But I had leased a tidy little town house near the King's Head, near Nan, and I never had to sneak out at night anymore or make sure I returned home before dawn. I had a lovely, soft, wide bed where Nan and I had, in the weeks since my return from Ferndean, already spent countless luscious hours.

I had timed my visit to afternoon tea, when I knew the girls would be taking visitors. There were several officers there; I was gratified to see that Captain Farrow was not among them. My old acquaintance the corporal told me while we waited for the girls to come downstairs that he had been discharged without honor several months past, due to improper conduct. The genteel old man would not elaborate further, but I could guess too easily the sort of dishonor Farrow had committed. It seemed the Villainess's next assignment was before me.

But I did not wish to think on him or any of the horrible men the Webster girls and I had known; I wished us to be free of them. And so, as soon as the scholarship girls arrived to pour the tea, I rose to my feet at once and sought out the rosy, freckled, still-beloved face that I was looking for.

"Adèle!" Hannah smiled and laughed and set down the tray she was carrying to clasp my hands, for all it was improper and for all Mrs. Harris glowered from her corner at the both of us.

"Girls, I expect you to behave more decorously than this," she scolded. "Especially you, Miss Norfolk."

I shook my head, feeling the fresh curls my new lady's maid, just arrived from France, had created for me that morning. "I do not answer to your authority anymore, Mrs. Harris," I said, "nor to anyone's but my own. And soon, neither will Hannah."

My dear friend stared at me, confused. But when I told her I'd paid off her father's debts and put a portion of my inheritance into her name from which she and her mother could draw a yearly income, she screamed—decorous, quiet Hannah screamed!—and wrapped me up in her arms and embraced me as tightly as I'd ever wished she might. And when I let her go again, I did so with all my heart.

The other girls in their pale blue dresses walked into the tearoom and curtsied decorously to their guests, but when Felicity saw me, she gasped and squealed, which made all of them look, and they descended on me. I had written to Felicity as soon as Nan and I had left Ferndean, and while I could not write down all that had occurred for fear of discovery, when she offered her condolences for my grief, there was a sharp understanding in her eye, and in the eyes of the other girls, that told me they knew enough.

Then there remained only to tell her that my town house held space for a lady's companion, and that if she knew any genteel and mature woman who might wish to try the London life for any length of time, she might refer her to me. I watched the little girl who had guarded her mama's door sag with relief inside my friend's expression.

Later, with some of the Villainess's spoils, I established a fund for the scholarship girls at Webster, so that none of them need exhaust themselves with any other labor than their studies and that they might all have wardrobes like their classmates' and gowns for their coming-out balls. Eventually, in fact, Mrs. Webster even hung my portrait among those of the other ladies Webster girls were taught to esteem. Perhaps Jane will send her daughter to the Webster in the fullness of time; perhaps she will see my face in the hallway there. I hope that if she does, she will be proud. I have seen my old governess but few times in the ten years since the death of her husband and my father. She still mourns him too much, and I still love her too well, for there to be true intimacy between us.

Maman said every married woman is a ruined garden. I think Jane is too strong to ever be ruined, even by the death of her great love. But her great heart, her noble soul, which cared for me when no one else truly did, is like a walled garden to me now, that I cannot enter.

No matter, I tell myself—do you believe me, reader?—for other hearts and souls are mine.

Nan Ward, now queen of the King's Head pack of rogues in her late, sainted father's place, is queen of my heart still. We do not live in the same house, at least not all the time—we both lead lives too adventurous for that—but we live always inside each other's hearts. And I know that one day, I hope a day far distant, she will do me the final service a lover can do for their beloved, and bring my body home to France, so that my bones may rest in my mother's homeland, as I have always longed for them to do. I asked her, when she made me that promise, if she'd like me to do the same for her if our fates were reversed, and lay her to rest in Ireland.

"No, darling," she said. "The only place I ever want to lie is next to you."

Two years ago, I visited my mother's grave. Père Lachaise is the largest cemetery in Paris, and I wandered through the gray sepulchers rimed with moss, the trailing grass and ivy, for over an hour before I found her simple memorial stone. Graceful limbs of old-growth trees shaded the walkways; climbing roses and fallen leaves scented the air. It felt as if flowers rested at the base of every monument I passed, bouquets from mourners and survivors dropping petals that drifted in the breeze.

Maman, among them, was not neglected. Lilies, barely wilted, had been left for her, next to a pot of rouge: a token from a fellow Moulin girl, I had no doubt.

I thought of taking the rouge; I knew it would make her laugh, and I was a trained thief after all. But it looked so pretty there with the flowers, almost like her dressing table had looked in the days when I was so small and the other girls and I had listened to her as we might hear gospel from a goddess.

All I did in the end was kiss the cold headstone.

"Merci, Maman," I told her, and I left the blooming garden of her grave.

ACKNOWLEDGMENTS

I OFFER my heartfelt thanks to the people whose support allowed me to complete this book. I cannot name them all, but they include my agent Sara Crowe, as well as Marissa Brown, Cameron Chase, Ashley Valentine, and the rest of the team at Pippin Properties; my editor Lynne Polvino, as well as Emily Andrukaitis, Eleanor Hinkle, Mary Magrisso, Erika West, and the rest of the team at Clarion Books; Tracy Cochran and Jeff Zaleski at *Parabola Magazine*; Mike McCormack and John Kenny at the National University of Ireland Galway; and the survivors' group at COPE Galway. I also want to thank Sara Bailey, Helena Barry, Amy Bebbington, Anna Boarini, Kimberly Brubaker Bradley, Deirdre Brophy, Susan Burke, Jackie Carroll, Lisa Chamoff, Dana Clinton, Orla Doherty, Sharon Dowdell, Christina Dragon, Vanessa Fox O'Loughlin, Allegra Garabedian, Leah Gilbert, Sophie Green, Dara Kaye, Eleanor Lane, Nora Mathers, Mary and Terry McGraw, Surnaí Molloy, Patrick O'Herlihy, Abby Palko, James Prangley-Griffiths, Adrian Taheny, Alex Zaleski, and all the supporters of the Old Knitting Factory who have helped me create a safe home for my child and my writing.

AUTHOR'S NOTE

MY MOTHER FIRST read *Jane Eyre* to me when I was ten years old. Like the young Jane of the book's first chapter, I was a bright kid who was bullied at home. But the inimitable Jane was not the character I focused on, fixated on, when I first heard this story: it was Rochester's secret wife, Bertha, who held my attention and my loyalty. Later, when I was assigned *Jane Eyre* in several different literature courses throughout my education, I began to be haunted by the little girl Adèle, too: the plot device who brings Jane and Rochester together but who is practically tossed out of their happy ending and sent off to boarding school because Jane's husband requires all her "time and cares." Those two hauntings, those two other women in Rochester's life, have never left me.

I pitched *Reader, I Murdered Him* to my wonderful agent, Sara Crowe, and editor, Lynne Polvino, during Dr. Christine Blasey Ford's testimony in the Brett Kavanaugh hearings in 2018. Like so many people reading the news at that time, I was full of rage and pain that came from a resonance with my own history of sexual abuse, and the violence with which my story had been rejected when I'd come forward. I wrote this story out of that rage and pain.

Looking back, I think I've always wondered what Adèle might have to say about Rochester, even when I was a child, and I felt an instinctive belief that there would be rage and pain in her story, too. What stood out to my ten-year-old self as I listened to my mother read *Jane Eyre* was the same thing I saw when I read the book again as a high school student, a third time as an MFA candidate in my early twenties, and as an adult while I conceived and drafted *Reader, I Murdered Him*: in Jane Eyre there are two kinds of women, and if you don't qualify as one, you are doomed to be the other. Rochester himself makes the dichotomy painfully clear. After Bertha's relatives accuse him of bigamy at his and Jane's marriage ceremony, he drags his wedding party to the top of Thornfield Hall to see the woman he married first. Bertha typifies all the nineteenth-century fears about women's bodies: she is unclean, insane, violent, large, strong, sexual, eminently and uncomfortably physical. Bertha is a demon, and her attic is Hell: red, rank, and disgusting.

But Jane is never more angelic than when she stands next to Bertha. Jane is small and mousy, no beauty herself; but that very lack of physicality places her above Bertha and becomes her best virtue. Rochester calls her fairy, changeling, sprite; she is barely human in his eyes.

Women vanish inside the stories men tell about them. They become images, objects. That is in part what *Jane Eyre* itself is about. Jane rebels against Rochester's narrative of her inhumanity, especially in her famous line: "I am no bird; and no net ensnares me: I am a free human being with an independent will." But at the end of the story, reader, she marries him, and at their romantic reunion he still asks if she is just a ghostly apparition; he still does not believe in her full humanity.

As a child who was experiencing abuse from my father, I could already recognize the cycle of abuse, and I knew that it would be all too easy for Rochester to come to despise the new bride that he idolizes in that moment. I already knew how dangerous the stories men tell about women can be.

The stories women tell ourselves about the men we love can be dangerous, too. I refused to see the abuse in my life, several times over, because I loved my abusers; when I trained as a rape crisis counselor, I saw many survivors do the same thing. Sometimes survivors refuse to acknowledge their own pain out of love for those who hurt them. All too often, the people around them refuse to believe them, because of that same love.

Jane Eyre, of course, is one of the most iconic stories about a woman told by a woman. I've had more writer's block for this book than any of my others, purely because I kept getting offended by my own presumptuousness. Several of the friends I respect the most count Mr. Rochester among their all-time literary loves. But in my own readings and rereadings of *Jane Eyre*, I recognized more and more characteristics of the men who have abused me in Rochester's control, gaslighting, and manipulation.

When I took a wonderful course in graduate school called "Jane's Heirs," taught by one of my favorite teachers, Abby Palko,

I was the class's designated Rochester-hater, and I was (and still am) ornery enough to enjoy that role. We read many remarkable books in that class that take inspiration somehow from *Jane Eyre*, and they are among my chief inspirations here, in particular *The Madwoman in the Attic*, *Wide Sargasso Sea*, *Rebecca*, *Cold Comfort Farm*, and my favorite novel of all time, *I Capture the Castle*. This book would not exist without that class, those readings, and especially my wonderful teacher, Abby.

In all my other novels so far, I've retold fairy tales, and I don't think writing a sequel to *Jane Eyre* deviates too far from that pattern. In writing *Reader, I Murdered Him*, as in my other books, I am responding to elements of a classic tale that I both admire and want to push against somehow. Writing this book has been so cathartic for me, and, I think, for my younger selves, who saw Bertha and Adèle standing behind Jane, and ached for them, and longed to set them free.

Much of the early aching in my life, and much of my later freedom, has been born out of my queerness. Queer romance is an escape hatch in my heart, an open door that leads to joy. So queerness is an escape route in *Reader*, too: an escape from the constraints and loss of rights that marriage to a man meant for nineteenth-century women (and indeed for many women today). My queerness has taught me the manifold possibilities of love beyond the few kinds that patriarchy teaches us to desire, and that teaching has been one of the greatest gifts of my life.

Reader, I Murdered Him is at its heart a door I've wanted to open inside of *Jane Eyre* since I was ten. If Adèle vanished from *Jane*

Eyre's happy ending, I wanted to open up that escape hatch for her, through her righteous vengeance against abusive men, and through her love for Nan and for the Webster girls.

My dearest wish for *Reader* is that it might open something up inside you, too.

READ MORE BY BETSY CORNWELL!

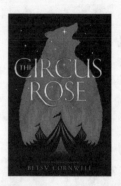